Spoon Knife 6:
Rest Stop

Edited by

B. Martin Allen and J.S. Allen

Weird Books for Weird People

Previous volumes in the Spoon Knife series

The Spoon Knife Anthology: Thoughts on Compliance, Defiance, and Resistance
    Edited by N.I. Nicholson and Michael Scott Monje, Jr.

Spoon Knife 2: Test Chamber
    Edited by Dani Alexis Ryskamp and Sam Harvey

Spoon Knife 3: Incursions
    Edited by Nick Walker and Andrew M. Reichart

Spoon Knife 4: A Neurodivergent Guide to Spacetime
    Edited by B. Allen and Dora M. Raymaker with N.I. Nicholson

Spoon Knife 5: Liminal
    Edited by Andrew M. Reichart, Dora M. Raymaker, and Nick Walker

Contents

Foreword

For as long as I can remember, I have been obsessed with how people make decisions. As an admitted over-thinker, I wonder where are the other over-thinkers? Are they over-thinking in the same way I over-think, and if not, does their style of over-thinking provide a better analysis of the facts than my style of overthinking? What makes me the kind of person with forty-three open browser tabs comparing charger cables priced $20 or less so that I can find the perfect charger cable before someone in the household needs a new charger cable? I want to know the decision tree that led Naxos to secede from the Delian League. I also want to know how you picked those toppings on your pizza.

But what really fascinates me is how people make decisions in circumstances where there are no good options, when the choice is between peril and compromise, heartbreak or danger. How do people behave when picking the least worst option? That fascination was the impetus for *Spoon Knife 6: Rest Stop.*

Why Rest Stop? A product of mid twentieth century car culture and the U.S. interstate highway system, rest stops symbolically embodied the myth of the American Dream. In reality, a rest stop can be clean and welcoming. Or it might be filthy and frightening. Because you never know until you enter, the rest stop is a respite of last resort.

Ahead lie twenty-five pieces offering a respite of last resort. Stories and poems for when the GPS is broken and the roadmap flies out the window. Hope you enjoy the ride.

B. Martin Allen

March 2022

Bill Bolin

Rest Stop Miniature

We pulled into the rest stop parking lot. A Scarlatti arpeggio was interrupted by buzzing semi-silence as the Volvo's engine cut off. I had chosen the darkest parking space near the exit, away from the cars and semis bunched around the cement-enclosed public bathrooms and vending machines locked behind rusting metals cages, away from the glare of the large overhead floodlights on their leaning poles, away from the insects madly swarming in the stark light.

The we was me and the small woman sleeping in backseat. Sand. Sandra Lynne Copley. As we were no longer in motion she would be presently waking. But for now, I was able to see her sleep. She was small, very pale with wispy blond hair cut short, short enough to spike slightly in the back where it gave way to the lyric of her neck. She wore a torn, black t-shirt, drastically faded jeans with tattered knees, pink kneecaps peeked through.

When she woke, she would stretch and ask about food. I had made note of a place next to the rest stop. Pit Barbecue and Catfish Barn. And it was an actual barn, painted a violent red with a blinking neon sign instructing all to "Come On In." Sand would be enthralled.

But before food or any portion of what one could call conversation, she would drink deep from the large flask that was always handy. Cognac or brandy from the smell. I couldn't know for certain as this was one of the many things that she would not share with me. Like the pills in the crumpled paper bag she stashed under the passenger's seat, like the contents of her large leather-bound notebooks, like almost all personal information.

At least she shared the strong mints that she kept in a tiny tin shoved deep in the pocket of her faded jeans. Those mints would come in handy as Sand was sure to have an order of onion rings with her truck stop barbecue. She loved roadside chow, the more rural and greasier the better. She liked to chat up the waitresses and fry-cooks. She left generous tips. We usually came away with a large slice of pie or Tupperware tub of banana pudding on the house.

But before food Sand would pull her beaten Nikon camera from the large gym bag that acted as her suitcase, portfolio, and handbag. She would wander about the rest stop photographing empty picnic tables and overflowing trash cans. Somewhere in hilly Tennessee she had shown me some prints of her work. They were a stark black & white combination of Edward Hopper and Diane Arbus. They were sad and funny and masterful. Sand offered no explanations or commentary on her work apart from "these three go together" or "this will look better in a frame." The whole of our conversation on her work lasted no more than twenty minutes as there were cheeseburgers to dispatch.

Early in our trip there had been a tentative, liquor-flavored, close-lipped kiss accompanied by a graceless grope. All that came of that was that Sand would occasionally sit close to me on a park bench or touch my arm during one of her quiet conversations. As rare as those moments were, they felt intimate, tender even.

Before she woke, I tidied the passenger's area which was messy with soda cans and empty plastic water bottles. The cassettes of Baroque harpsichord music would be returned to the plastic travel case with the broken latch. I paused to review the line of sticky notes that Sand had placed along the dashboard. "Just ideas that come to me" was all that was offered by way of explanation. Once when I thoughtlessly rolled down a window, one of these notes was swept out. "Well, there goes another thought," she said with a slight, sad smile. This did prompt a brief speculation on what might happen should some traveler encounter the note. "They might take it for a message from the universe," I suggested. "I guess in a way it would be," she replied. We shared a laugh.

There were few laughs, but many smiles. And no arguments at all. Sand didn't seem to have many travel preferences. She chose the music: Bach or her beloved Scarlatti. The cassette would go in and music would fill the Volvo with color from another time. For a while Sand's fingers would perform a ballet on her exposed knee. A shy smile would play about her eyes. But before long, she would fetch a pill or three from her paper bag, take a pull from her shiny flask and climb into the back seat.

Soon Sand would wake. She was sure to notice the bats swooping in to dine on moths circling the floodlights. To her this would be greeted like a flight of doves at dawn. And the silly sadness would stretch on and on into the parking lot of another day.

Ambassador

2160, or so. Time is a tricky bugger.

There were so many names for it. The Everlasting One. The Inconstant Constant. The Lazy Observer. One of the many challenges in communicating with this alien was that it took decades for it to tell us its name. I will be using Manifestation which is short for Local Manifestation of an Eternally Fluctuating Phenomenon. It called humans Insult.

Its existence had been theorized by an eccentric mathematician named Maybeth Hinkle whose stated field of inquiry was something called Abstract Nonsense. It was a complicated, looping proof to a supposedly unsolvable numbers puzzle. The data/theory had languished in an obscure academic information cloud for decades until it was uncovered by a brilliant theoretical physicist, Clayton Renborne, who somehow managed to convince wealthy backers to fund the construction of a detection device. The detection device was repurposed to serve as a communicator/translator/interface by the Manifestation.

The Manifestation was a constantly self-organizing latticework of highly charged particles that both existed and didn't exist all at once. Forever. It spanned the universe. It is understandable that it had great difficulty speaking with humans as we had almost nothing in common.

The Manifestation initially perceived corporeal life and humans in particular to be some form of Thought Weapon.

Our very existence was an abomination, a sin against their concept of nature, which is how we came to be referred to as Insult. It should be noted that this appellation was not reserved for humans alone, but for all cellular life, sentient and otherwise. The Manifestation was not the first alien life that humans had encountered, but it was, by far, the most unlike us in every regard. We shared knowledge of the Manifestation with the many wily species that exploited us, but those chittering hive beings and clever goo-things seemed to have little interest in what they considered to be an impractical, speculative, religious delusion. If they couldn't make something out of it, explode it, fuck it, or eat it, they gave it no thought.

But we wanted to talk to it. Early on, when it was learning our languages, it attempted to speak to us using music. Sound attenuators attached to the complex of translators would spew snippets of Mozart or a nocturne by Chopin. Or we would hear things that sounded like human music, but no known composer could be identified. As it turned out, the Manifestation was attempting something akin to courtesy. When it mastered the spoken word, the cussing began. Our conversations would usually begin the same each time we engaged: There would be hours, days even, of foul and pungent name-calling. As the Manifestation learned more about us, these tirades became lengthier, more specific and rather ornate.

When the Manifestation learned laughter, we were treated to a month of very disturbing cackles and sneering snickers. As it turns out, this was its commentary on our mathematics. When we told it about sexual reproduction there was a prolonged hissing followed by a strange playback of Beethoven's 9th Symphony with all the tympani and brass elements replaced by robust farts. We misinterpreted this as humor.

It was nearly one hundred years after our initial contact with the Manifestation that a cruel form of humor was to be perceived. Since a large portion of communication with it involved mathematics so complex as to completely re-define the concept for humanity, it took our most brilliant minds years to conclude that some of what the Manifestation had taught us was its version of a rather convoluted knock-knock joke.

One of the few human byproducts that seemed to interest the Manifestation was music. It was appalled to find that musical compositions were conceived by individuals. It found this outrageous and profoundly offensive. When it was explained that it would not be possible to communicate in any direct fashion with Brahms or Branca, the Manifestation invested years in expressing disgust. Corporeal decay and cellular demise was a conceptual abomination to it.

All of which lead to my personal involvement with the Manifestation. I'm C. Abbott Fenster and I make music. I compose; I invent instruments specifically for use in playing my compositions and I meticulously document my work. My work was not popular nor widely appreciated outside academic circles. I was not in demand and my works were rarely performed. I was, however, of some slight interest to the Manifestation. It had mentioned my name in one if its communications. It also played a piece of music that sounded very much like something I might construct. This was of interest to the scientists in charge of communicating with it.

It should be noted that the Manifestation had mentioned, referenced, and even requested the presence of millions of individuals over the years since it grasped the concept of individuals. Our scientists initially submitted image files and vid feeds. This proved to be confusing to the Manifestation as it seemed to confuse live feeds with archived records. It took long years for it to accept that although the works of dead creators could be appreciated in recordings and performances, the composers, and creators themselves were frequently unavailable due to death.

The scientists proposed that the Manifestation become familiar with living creative types. The first person chosen from the very long list (that still included a number of people no longer among the living) was the well-known "one-woman choir" Zilla Jane Strathmore-Jones. Zilla was to be humanity's first ambassador to the Local Manifestation. An encounter environment was constructed to the Manifestation's specifications in the orbit of Neptune. The Embassy, as it came to be known, was roughly ovoid with a waiting room not unlike a business conference room, but equipped with a foam cot, a water closet, a vending machine, and huge Marshall amplifiers that would be used by the Manifestation for speaking to the chosen subject prior to direct interaction. Direct interaction would occur in a transparent enclosed vacuum chamber roughly the size of Manhattan. Everything that happened in the waiting room would be recorded, while what happened in the encounter chamber proper was between the ambassador and the Manifestation.

The recordings from that first meeting have been studied in great detail. The Manifestation spent the better part of a week verbally abusing poor Zilla in a variety of voices, languages and volumes. There were loud bursts of barely coherent music. The Marshall stacks seems to spit and hum. She managed to get a few polite words in during brief pauses. Zilla attempted to inquire about the Manifestation's musical and artistic preferences. It seemed to take days to respond. "Zilla Jane Strathmore-Jones' yelling is a long dusty ocean of pain," it bellowed. It played Zilla's music back to her at stadium intensity. The Manifestation also played music that was very similar to Zilla's own compositions. She later reported that this music was identical to something that she was composing but had not at that time performed. The Manifestation was then silent for several hours. Eventually, in the eerie, soft voice of a child, the Manifestation instructed Zilla to put on her environment suit and proceed to the encounter chamber.

Zilla interacted directly with the Local Manifestation for 4 hours. When she returned to the waiting room, she was visibly shaken. She was bleeding slightly from mouth and eyes. The Manifestion played Bach sonatas to her and read Adrienne Rich to her in that same child's voice while Zilla drank coffee from the vending machine. She cleaned herself as best she could and waited for her long ride home.

In the debriefings, Zilla, who had been a very outspoken and demonstrative performer prior to meeting with the Manifestation, said very little. She said that it went into her, and she suspected that it still might be there. She said that the experience was "like a year of pain and pleasure" and "just too much." She retired from public life and secluded herself on her property on the coast of Oklahoma.

After Zilla there were seventeen more such interactions with artists, writers, physicists, and one profoundly confused young chef. All of their encounters were similar: days of vile abuse and loud music, a child's soft voice and then intense pleasure/pain. All reported a timeless quality to the experience. All of them bled. There seemed to be no permanent physical injury. As to the impact on their mental health, the scientists could only speculate. All subjects, Ambassadors as they were to be called, withdrew from social life. Those that had families were cared for by them, those with no close relations were provided with professional caretakers and nurses. Each of them declined psychiatric treatment and no such treatment was imposed upon them as it was determined that they were not a risk to themselves or society. They all continued working, but in complete seclusion.

As preparation for my own interaction, I was allowed to review all the waiting room recordings as well as the debriefing interviews with the Ambassadors that had proceeded me. I found little there to reassure me. In the flood of loud abuse and cacophony that made up the recordings, there was little repetition and no pattern that either I or the scientists could detect. With the exception of the chef, each ambassador had played to them some version or interpretation of their own work. The deeply disturbing child voice always preceded the instruction to enter the encounter chamber. The voice always said "you disgust me" again and again, like some childish chant. Then it said, "I will eat you." Then the doors to the chamber would open.

I found this disconcerting.

On the trip to the Embassy, the scientists provided me with drugs: depressants, painkillers, and muscle relaxers. I had never been one for any chemicals more powerful than a strong cup of coffee, so this was new to me. I was given a cleansing enema, which was also new to me. When I entered the waiting room, I was wobbly, drowsy and my ass was sore. And despite the drugs, I was frightened.

The loud music and confrontational abuse began as soon as the scientists departed. Some snippets of music were recognizable: Bach, Chopin, Patti Smith, Branca and long passages of my own microtonal percussive work. Were the verbal abuse to be edited out and the volume reset, the resulting playlist would have been interesting. I attempted conversation in the infrequent lulls. The abuse simply continued, sometimes in my own highly amplified voice. This went on for days while I drank coffee and ate vending machine energy bars. I suppose that the drugs that scientists used were time-released as I was woozy throughout my time at the Embassy.

And then came a silence that seemed to scream. I prayed the only prayer of my long life. Then a little girl's lisping voice said, "You are wretched, you are an insult to existence, you disgust me." There followed a storming pause and then, "I will eat you." I put on the bulky encounter suit and the door to the encounter chamber opened.

As it turns out, the door led to a very long, narrow hall. It went on for countless kilometers. Near the end of the corridor I saw dim, flickering lights. Stars. The huge encounter chamber was transparent. I floated weightless. After some time, the space about me began to glow. Light danced about me. A quiet voice said, "Now." The voice was everywhere: within me, all around me.

Then all of my feelings, all of my nerves were set ablaze with both searing pain and absolute pleasure all at once. All memory at once. All love, all bitterness, all at once. Convulsive beauty. Flowering heat and stark cold. Everywhere the Manifestation sang, "Now." I was lost in screaming non-time. Everything went white.

I returned to myself as the door to the waiting room slid open. The first movement of Branca's 6th Symphony began. The volume was brutal. Somehow, I found myself on the floor. I tasted blood.

When the scientists collected me, I was given more drugs. Painkillers and muscle relaxers as before. I didn't seem right to myself. My peripheral vision seemed somehow jerky. My gait was wonky. My grip was weak. It seemed to take days before I was able to speak in clear sentences.

There were months of tests and hushed debriefings. Blood, urine and even spinal fluid was collected. I was probed, body and mind. I thought I might go mad from the questions, questions for which I frequently had no answer. After some time, I was informed that I had forgotten some details of my personal life. I could not recall some small things: dates, minor events, and common household objects. A spatula baffled me.

It was equally disorienting that I somehow now knew things that I had no way of knowing. I knew of astronomical occurrences that had not been made public. Certain aspects of complex mathematics seemed obvious. I could read dead languages.

With rehabilitation and exercise, I grew steadier on my feet. I was able to hold utensils and use tools. I could type again. As expected, there were notable aftereffects: pronounced and untreatable insomnia, tingling sensations in my extremities, frequent nosebleeds, vision deficits. When I closed my eyes, I would sometimes sense phantom limbs where no limbs would or should be. My own internal voice didn't sound familiar. I felt I was being watched.

Like all the other Ambassadors, I withdrew from society. And like the others, I refused psychiatric care. I returned to composing. My work changed in subtle ways. Whereas my previous pieces where strictly microtonal and played exclusively on homemade instruments, my new work incorporated more traditional tonalities and used some woodwind and brass elements. I wrote a tango for banjo and penny whistles.

The scientists continued to probe, test, and observe, but much less frequently and with diminished intensity. What had begun as weekly focused interrogations under irritating fluorescent lights gave way to monthly physicals and short-form questionnaires. I welcomed the gradual return of the bland quotidian of life as an obscure composer of seldom-heard and rarely performed difficult music.

At the relatively young age of 120, I retired from composing and set out to travel. I had made peace with the after-effects of my harrowing encounter with the Manifestation. Although I had lived in solitude for decades, I found that I wanted company. I sought out other Ambassadors. I didn't know why, I simply wanted others like me at my side. I was startled to learn that I was late to pursue this impulse. Of the dozens of Ambassadors, only Zilla remained. The others had already begun to set out years before. Although Zilla was nearly 200 and relatively frail, she welcomed my offer to travel to lesser-known places and to see new things.

We traveled far from those worlds that had been settled by humans and the aliens that exploited us. Once we bathed in muddy drugs with a distributed being called Nest of Snakes. We visited a green gas giant planet whose cloudy atmosphere was an ancient, nearly extinct race with a name that took weeks to say. We politely declined offers of sex from goggly-eyed quadrupeds whose collective name was something like White Dwarf Screw Buddies. Our state-of-the-art translator devices were often of little use as many of the aliens we met had no common points of reference on which to form a basis of communication. News of these encounters we sent back to our scientists for follow-up, while Zilla and I moved on. Some aliens when informed of our background in the arts requested performances. They seemed disappointed when all that we offered were files of our past work. We had no intention of singing for our supper. We were able to book passage through livable space with a race of highly intelligent nocturnal waterfowl called the Xeeoona Blue Legs by selling copies of our old performance files, mathematical solutions (a handy lasting side effect of our encounter with the Manifestation), fingernail clippings and nose hair.

The Xeeoona Blue Legs took a fancy to us, Zilla in particular. We were invited to be visiting teachers/ambassadors on one of their earth-like colony worlds. They were one of the few species that we had come across that expressed any interest in our encounters with the Manifestation. Most aliens politely and abruptly changed the subject when the matter came up. It was viewed by other species to be an eccentric delusion, and by some to be outright dangerous insanity. Humans were still not well regarded in those days. The memories of our encounters with the Manifestation were still painful to us after all those long years. The Xeeoona Blue Legs frilled and sputtered when we declined to discuss the matter.

Despite our refusal to share information regarding our encounters, we were allowed to reside with the Xeeoona Blue Legs. They performed a well-attended concert of Zilla's music. The Xeeoona Blue Legs were talented vocalists and they managed to do justice to her complex, multi-layered choral pieces. As it was among humans, my own work was less celebrated. I was a mere added diurnal curiosity.

We had been among the Xeeoona Blue Legs for over a decade when Zilla was diagnosed with a terminal degenerative disease. Zilla made arrangements with the Xeeoona Blue Legs to have herself be treated as they treated their own honored dead. The Xeeoona Blue Legs fed their recently deceased to their newly hatched offspring in a joyous sundown ritual called Babies Take Their First Bite and Everyone Dances. It sounded much more poetic in the Xeeoona Blue Legs language of clicks and hisses. Zilla welcomed the thought of being the first human to be honored this way. I was mildly appalled but kept my objections to myself. A person's funeral is their own affair, and it needn't be sullied by my narrow-minded reservations.

The Babies Take Their First Bite and Everyone Dances ritual was crowded. There were hundreds of Xeeoona Blue Legs, their feathers painted in bioluminescent pinks and greens. There were a variety of other alien species in attendance as well: clanging mechas, cogent gases in impressive containment suits designed to resemble waterfowl, chittering hive beings that seemed to get into everyone's hair, and a contingent representing Nest of Snakes who had tiny humming servos following them to wipe up the slime they left in their wake. As it turns out, Nest of Snakes had been invited to contribute one of their recently expired members. Since the species was a distributed being, I was made to understand that this was rather like contributing an eyelash. The Xeeoona Blue Legs, however, seemed to appreciate the gesture.

The celebrations carried on for several days. Everyone did, indeed, dance. I confess that I was moved when the Xeeoona Blue Legs played one of Zilla's well-known pieces. Their performance was steely perfection. As the affair was ending, Nest of Snakes requested a private audience for the following afternoon. I was mildly intrigued.

I met with Nest of Snakes in a long, dimly lit hall with low ceilings that had been made available to them by the Xeeoona Blue Legs. At one end of the hall was a pool which I assume was filled with the muddy drug that had so entertained Zilla and myself decades ago. A lumpy slither of the distributed being and their attendant servos entered behind me followed by a slender girl that I estimated to be between 10 to 12 years of age.

"Ambassador Fenster, we wish to avoid conflict with your people," said Nest of Snakes.

"Although I can't claim to represent all humans, I'm certain that we would also wish to avoid conflict," I stammered, following with, "perhaps you could clarify."

Nest of Snakes ceased slithering for a long moment and said, "This child that we brought with us is a clone of Ambassador Zilla Jane Strathmore-Jones. We apologize if her construction goes against the norms of your species. We had hoped that by making this child we might someday reproduce the communication that you humans established with the Local Manifestation. We sought profit. We must concede that we may have committed a grave error, an error that could pose a significant risk to Nest of Snakes. We now wish to give her to you so that she might be with those of her own kind. We are willing to negotiate reparations."

The little girl approached me slowly. When she stood directly before me, she focused her small, pale eyes on mine and said in a soft lisp, "You disgust me."

Bill Bolin is a wandering photographer living in Fort Worth, Texas. You may have seen him with his dog on the side of the highway and said to yourself, why is that man taking a picture of the ground? The son of a military family, his youth was spent all over the world before settling eventually in small town Louisiana. After earning a degree in fine arts and literature at LA Tech, Bolin frittered away his adulthood in mid-level corporate management, composing music in his free time and serving for 20 years as a telephone counselor for the Suicide and Crisis Center of Dallas. COVID-19 forced him into an early retirement that has been invested in learning the art of photography and looking down.

J.T. Eisenhauer Richardson

Pace

There is that locked door again
with the glowing red exit sign.

Soles scuff the surface
of a well-worn path
past empty tables
past occupied phones
past notebooks in drawers
past phantasms on the wall
past your best intentions
past nostrils singed by disinfectant
past seeing the lady through a crack
past their heads barely poking above the desk
past showers with short timers
past fragrance concealing the stank of mold
past that assumption you made a moment ago
past closed doors mumbling questions
past tense is present tense
past the lady standing on her bed
past the locked door again with the glowing red exit sign
past stacks of unauthorized biographies
past the shadow of the man that joins me
past him saying he wants to be deep inside me

past vanishing at points in the distance
past the drawing he made for his girlfriend
past complimenting his artistry
past dirt in corners that mops won't reach
past the woman who dropped like a rag
past how slow they were to their feet
past the puddle her cup left on the floor
past wasted last breaths
past hackneyed white walls
past needing a fresh coat of paint
past the next time you say crazy
past the next time I end up in this place
past the word I

If Only

A few feet away from my faux wicker chair,
I notice the peculiar walk of a wasp.
I don't run or silently slip off like a stealth coward.
No ambush is planned, sandal in hand,
to squash his body and leave it to dry
in this raging heat to be washed away by a driving rain.
Anesthetized by my infatuation,
I am captivated by watching
how he paces, so preoccupied.
His joints move like volitional threads
that he stretches and wraps around each wing
as if cleaning himself with spit on furry mitts.
I so want to cuddle with him,
to gently scoop him into my palm
and stroke each one of those tissue-thin wings,
if only he wasn't a wasp.

If Only
(alternate)

I note the peculiar walk of a wasp,
an arm's reach from my plastic wicker chair.
I don't slip away like a stealthy coward.
no ambush is planned, my sandal in hand
to squash his body and leave it to dry
in this raging heat to be washed away
by driving rains. I am captivated
watching how he paces, so preoccupied.
His joints and legs move like volitional threads
that he stretches and wraps around each wing
as if cleaning with spit on furry mitts.
I want to gently scoop him into my palm,
to stroke each one of those tissue thin wings

Masquerade (alternate)

I note the peculiar walk of a wasp,

An arm's reach from my plastic wicker chair.

I don't slip away like a stealthy coward.

No ambush, no plan, my sandal in hand

To squash his body and leave it to dry

In this raging heat before it's washed away

By driving rains. I am captivated,

Watching how he paces, so preoccupied.

I am a Lost Boy from Neverland.

As fireflies die in jars, come sting my chest

Beneath this floral shirt. Without nectar

A flayed fabric garden falls on pavers,

Worker ants are stunned under its falling weight.

I'm naked. Don't ask, *What is your real name?*

J.T. (JT) Eisenhauer Richardson is an associate professor at The Ohio State University where JT teaches and is taught by students in courses related to the arts, education, creative writing in research practices, and disability studies. JT engages with ideas at the intersection of genre-queering research and writing practices and neurodivergent and Mad experience. JT's artwork, writing, and thinking often lives in fragmentations, loose connections, and unanticipated juxtapositions. JT's creative output includes a range of media and practices including collage, textile, installation art, scholarly articles and book chapters, and poems and prose published in literary journals. JT received one Pushcart nomination.

Mark A. Nobles

Everybody Stops by the Blue Plate Diner

Most of the time the Blue Plate Diner sits on the north side of the Bankhead Highway between Van Horn and Tornillo, closer to Tornillo but only by a skosh. Hard to say exactly where on that stretch of the old National Auto Trail system the Blue Plate sits because it is only there to those who see it.

The diner is a little worse for wear. A simple cinder block rectangle with a tar and gravel roof built void of architectural imagination. The only advertisement is a freestanding neon sign with the name of the establishment lit up in red for some long-forgotten reason. The 'u' in Blue and 'i' in Diner strobe in syncopated 2/4 time. The 't' in Plate is completely burned out.

The front door has a bell with no clapper. When the door opens and closes, the bell waddles to and fro, silently announcing customers. It's like having a mime for a night-watchman. The parking lot is pea gravel and spacious unless you drive an eighteen-wheeler; if that is the case, you have to park on the Bankhead shoulder and walk the thirty yards to the Blue Plate. The only exterior lighting besides the neon comes from the moon.

The interior of the Blue Plate Diner has blue Naugahyde booths and chairs, white Formica tabletops and countertops all sitting on blue and white checkerboard asphalt floor tiles. The booths have wall mounted juke boxes offering three songs for a dime. If you don't like country or smooth jazz, keep your dime in your pocket.

There are two waitresses, one cook, and one busboy employed at the Blue Plate Diner. Jo works the tables and booths. Jo wears a powder blue waitress uniform with a white apron. She wears a name tag with no name. Dress code says employees must wear a name tag but doesn't mention anything about whose name or even if a name has to be printed on it. Jo never carries an order pad but keeps a needle-sharp Berol Black Warrior pencil tucked behind her right ear. More for protection than a writing utensil.

Henrietta works the counter. Don't call Henrietta Henry unless you want to be charged extra for refills on coffee or iced tea. Henrietta wears a white waitress uniform with a powder blue apron. She carries a white and green order pad and a black click pen that says, 'Property of the U.S. Government.' Her name tag says Henrietta T. No one knows what the T stands for.

Pietro is the busboy and dishwasher. He always looks tired because he always is tired, and he always looks unkempt because he has the dirtiest job at the Blue Plate Diner. Pietro wears a white tee shirt, white pants, and white shoes with insole supports because of his fallen arches. Pietro's clothes are stained from ketchup, gravy (more the white gravy than the brown gravy, because the Blue Plate sells more chicken fried steak than pot roast). His clothes are always wet, especially around the midsection and crotch area because of water splashed from the sink. Pietro wears a name tag that says Peter because the Blue Plate already had a name tag that read Peter, and no one wanted to make a new one. It doesn't matter because the name tag hangs down where it can't be read, as Pietro's tee shirts are two sizes too big.

Beet Augie works the grill and frier. There's nothing Beet Augie doesn't know how to cook because Beet Augie has cooked everything. He says he learned the trade in the Merchant Marines. Both of Beet Augie's forearms are scarred from grease splatter and needle marks. He had a heroin problem as a teenager. That's what got him sent to the Merchant Marines. Beet Augie wears a white garrison chef's hat, white tee shirt, starched white pants, white socks, and rubber sole white shoes. He doesn't wear a name tag because he never goes on the floor or deals with customers but mostly he doesn't wear a name tag because no one wants to make him. Beet Augie chain smokes Camel shorts and no one complains.

The Bankhead is heavily traveled in both directions, but more people drive west than east, that's why the Blue Plate sits on the north side of the highway. The traffic traversing the Bankhead is what some would call a cross section of Americana. Long haulers, traveling salesmen, families on vacation or moving from one place to another, as well as the lost, weary, and transient souls looking for the light. There's rich, there's poor, single, those who wish they were single, couples with children, couples with secrets, people running from their past and people running to the abyss (although no one running to the abyss knows they are running to the abyss).

The Blue Plate Diner is always crowded but there's always a table, booth or seat at the counter when someone new steps in. Even though the Blue Plate is busy the atmosphere is subdued, as if everyone's aura is cradled when they step through the door. Jo and Henrietta bust their buns taking orders, refilling coffee, and carrying food in a constant blur of motion. Pietro pushes his bus cart steady and deliberate. Diners chat and drop their dimes in the juke boxes to play Lefty, Tex, or Jarreau, or Sanborn. Waltz Across Texas or Bumpin' on Sunset play, or don't play.

There is no crackle to the bustle of the Blue Plate Diner.

When Vernon Teagarden dozed off and drifted his Nash Metro into oncoming traffic and narrowly missed becoming roadkill from an oncoming F250, he decided it was time to pull over. Vernon had been driving eighteen hours straight, save two pullovers for gas. He'd also pulled to the shoulder twice to relieve himself, but Vernon didn't count those as stops because he left the engine idling.

But after Vernon nodded off and almost caused an accident that would have splattered his little Metro into a grease spot, he decided it was time for a pitstop. He was hungry anyway and when he saw the red neon of the Blue Plate Diner, Vernon slowed and pulled into the parking lot. The gravel barely crunched under the slight heft of the green and white Metro.

Before getting out of the car Vernon waited for the reel to play out in his head. Vernon possessed an extraordinary memory. He had absolute recall of everything in his life exactly as it happened back to the age of 11. His almost total recall even stretched back to infancy although most recollections before turning 11 were spotty and disjointed. He remembered a stuffed tiger he had as a baby. He could see it as if he were in his crib back in his parent's old house on Jessamine Street. He could not remember any thoughts from when he was an infant, only emotions. He loved the hell out of that tiger. He hated strained peas but loved when his mother did the 'here comes the choo choo' thing when feeding him.

Problem was he had little control over his memories. They popped into his head at random. Vernon was a two tour Vietnam vet and the memories from the war played over and over through his mind like Led Zeppelin songs on classic rock radio stations.

Vernon and his platoon had returned to basecamp after an especially bloody and protracted firefight that had started in dense jungle and ended in a small village. His platoon had chased three to five VC through the jungle, exchanging fire along the way. The VC drew the GIs into a small village where everyone, men, women, and children turned and attacked. It was horrific. Most of the village was boobytrapped. If it moved, Vernon fired at it. The platoon lost six men.

When the firefight ended and Vernon and what was left of his platoon returned to basecamp, Vernon sat outside his tent. Exhausted and still in shock. Months ago, Vernon's mind had stopped processing the horrors of war but continued to catalogue and store. Vernon unstrapped and removed his helmet and held it in his lap. Looking down he saw the helmet covered in blood splatter and bits of skin and hair. One particular congealed blob of human bit—about the size of a gum ball, and consisting of flesh, black hair, and a splinter of bone—stuck miraculously near the crown.

Lieutenant Chicory, not affectionately nicknamed Lieutenant Chickenshit because he gleefully ordered men to their deaths but always managed to avoid dangerous sorties himself, walked by and casually flicked the bit of flesh from Vernon's helmet. "Clean yourself up Teagarden, you smell like you shit your pants." Vernon turned and watched Lieutenant Chickenshit walk away. He had shit his pants but most soldiers in combat had shit or pissed or both at one time or another.

Vernon's memory was so vivid that, like Billy Pilgrim, he felt he had come unstuck in time. The moment Vernon relived the most was being outside his tent, blood splattered, and sitting in his own feces watching Lieutenant Chickenshit walk away. The first five or six hundred times he relived the memory Vernon vomited upon himself.

So, he sat outside the Blue Plate Diner in his green and white Nash Metropolitan until he returned from Vietnam.

"You look like you got a lot on your mind, sugar."

Vernon jumped when Jo spoke to him. He had not realized he had entered the diner and taken a seat at the counter. "I always do, I suppose."

"Do you need a few more minutes with the menu?"

Vernon gawked at the menu in his hands. "I suppose I do."

"Do you suppose you want some coffee?"

"That would be nice."

Lickety split, Jo was back with coffee in a cup on a saucer in her right hand and a cream server in her left. "Here you go, sugar."

"Thank you. I don't need the cream."

"As you like it." Jo put the coffee in front of Vernon and stood across the counter, her right hand on her hip. "What'll you have?"

Vernon looked back at the menu. He had been too confused to really take it in. "I don't know."

"If you don't mind me saying, you look like you could use some Dutch babies."

"Now you mention it, that does sound good."

"Trust me, Beet Augie's Dutch babies are the best in Texas and all three contiguous states," she leaned in and lowered her voice. Instinctively, Vernon leaned in as well. "Between you and me, it's the only thing he cooks really well." She cut her eyes back to the kitchen to make sure Beet couldn't hear. "Everything else he cooks is par, at best, and his omelets," she leaned in further, "are runny as a toddler's nose in winter."

"Good to know."

"Dutch babies it is." Jo nodded and began to walk away.

"One more thing, please."

"Sure, sugar."

"I changed my mind about the coffee. I'll pay for it, of course, but could I get a glass of buttermilk instead?"

"You're the boss." Jo picked up the cup and saucer and whisked away.

Vernon looked around the Blue Plate. It was over half full, but no one was talking much and if they were talking, they were talking to a waitress. It was unusually quiet for so many people. No muted, murmuring conversations, no clanking of utensils scraping plates. The busboy pushed his cart precariously high stacked with glasses, cups, and plates. The dishes wobbled but did not rattle. The front left wheel of the cart wiggled and squeaked but aside from the squeaking everything seemed muffled. As if the air in the diner wrapped all sound in cotton.

Jo appeared in front of Vernon. "Am I right or am I right. Those are the best Dutch babies you ever knocked your gums around."

Vernon looked down and saw he had been eating his Dutch babies, at best only a few bites. "Yes, I think they are delicious."

Jo bent down eye level with Vernon and leaned her elbow on the counter. "Listen, Vern, can I call you Vern?"

"I didn't tell you my name."

"I seen you cutting your eyes around the diner. It's an unusual place."

Vernon felt uncomfortable but tried to show no confusion.

"We have a special clientele at the Blue Plate Diner."

"Seem like ordinary folk."

"Is anybody ordinary folk, Vern?" Jo paused. Vernon remained silent. "Why did you come into the diner, Vern?"

Vernon thought. "I don't remember... I was tired and hungry, I suppose."

"You do a lot of supposing, Vern."

Vernon shook his head in the affirmative. "I suppose I'm not sure of anything."

"Folks come into the Blue Plate Diner because they're weary. They slouch in dragging their big wearies because nobody brings small wearies into the Blue Plate Diner. They take a table or a stool, order just what they want, except omelets, I discourage the omelets but Henrietta will serve them, they sit for a while, have a cup of coffee..."

"Or a glass of buttermilk."

"Or a glass of buttermilk." Jo slapped the counter with the palm of her hand. "Now you're catching on, Vern. Or orange juice, or sweet tea, whatever they're thirsty for." Jo leaned in again, almost nose to nose with Vernon. "And before you know it, their big wearies are gone. Tell me, Vern. Do you feel weary?"

Vernon furrowed his brow. "I don't think so." He pondered and smiled. "No, I'm not weary at all."

"There you go." Jo stood back up and smoothed out her apron. "There you go," she said with a smile.

"But I don't remember feeling weary to begin with."

"Did you hear the one about the guy blowing a loud, single note over and over again on his flugelhorn on a busy street corner in New York City?"

"I don't think so."

"Over and over again, just one note, when finally, a cop comes up to him and says, 'Hey man, what on earth are you doing?' 'I'm keeping away all the elephants,' says the man. The cop says, 'this is New York City, there aren't any elephants around here.' And the man says, 'you're welcome.'" Jo grinned proud as a peacock and walked away.

Mark A. Nobles is a sixth-generation Texan. Born on Fort Worth's infamous Jacksboro Highway, Mark proudly claims blood and kinship with Thunder Road's gamblers, outlaws, and wastrels. He is a Pushcart nominee and his work has appeared in numerous publications and anthologies. He is the author of Fort Worth's Rock & Roll Roots and has produced and/or directed three feature documentaries and several short, experimental films. Mark lives in Fort Worth but hopes to die in the desert. He loves his two dogs, two daughters, and Texas, but not necessarily in that order.

Dean Gloster

Death's Adopted Daughter

The Ferryman's long bone hands gripped the pole as he pushed the flat-bottomed boat through the fog that smelled of ashes toward the girl splashing in the marsh beyond the river's edge. The Ferryman's sigh was ponderous. Because he existed partly outside time, he knew from the sigh that this human would be trouble. She wore overalls, a long-sleeved orange shirt, and yellow galoshes.

She wasn't even dead, which was modestly unusual.

The current was strong but didn't move the boat, just complained in murmurs against the teak hull. The girl glanced up. She didn't look alarmed at his tall, cowled figure. "This was my favorite outfit to play in when I was little."

The Ferryman sighed again, but it was a small one. He could make out her features clearly now, but human ages were hard to guess, especially when they were still breathing somewhere. "You still are little."

"Yeah, here, in this kind of a dream. In the real world, I'm older. Well, still kind of young. Ish."

He brought the boat expertly to the river's edge, and it hissed onto the sand at the bank, settling with a bump.

"You're tall, though." She stepped back. She was less than half his size.

"Large boned." He shrugged, and as he stretched, his sleeve drew back showing the white of a skeletal hand, wrist, and long bone forearm.

Her laugh was an explosion of joy in the quiet, and she gave him a smile. "I'm fifteen, but that's probably, like, two months in skeleton years." Her mouth curled down into a more serious expression. "I'm in a coma, back in the real world. Brain tumors." She looked around with curiosity, then peered into his eyes, which she would see as empty hollows in a skeletal face, framed by the hood. "You seem to be doing okay without yours, though. Brain, that is."

"This—" He managed, in a bony hand wave, to take in himself, the fog, the grass-covered riverbank and stately flow of the Lethe behind him. "Is just appearance. A...representation. How I manifest."

"I'm Hanna," she announced. "And you...?"

His bow was somewhere between courtly and playful. "A semi-autonomous construct. I help people across. From life. Some of you humans have difficulty with...transitions."

"No kidding. I've been in a coma for days. I might have even more trouble than most." Her forehead crinkled with a tiny fold of curiosity. "So you're Death?"

"I can wear that name." He nodded. "Or the Ferryman. To the Other Side."

The fog was thick, but irregular, offering an occasional glimpse of dark water far out, but mostly shrouding everything beyond the two of them.

"What's on the other side? I can barely see the water."

That, Death had been asked uncountable times. "I don't get out on the Other Side. Just you Passengers. A path goes upward through the fog, toward...light."

"To something? Or nothing?"

"Perhaps," he said at last, "something. I don't know. And you won't exactly be you anymore."

"That sucks. I'm the world's greatest expert at being me."

"It's not in the world."

"Which might or might not suck, depending. I have cancer in the world. And bedsores that ooze." She stretched the word ooze out, adding several ooh syllables. "Seriously yuck. What do you think? Will it suck?"

"I'm not an expert on what would suck. I don't even inhale."

She laughed again, the sound bright and leaping over the quiet murmur of water and muffling fog. "Guess not. Anyone else around? Who's more of an afterlife Wikipedia?"

"Just me. This is not a place of cross talk. Among Passengers."

"How about good deeds? Any I could do? Some last-minute cramming just before the test, in case it's a heaven-or-hell deal over there?"

"I like to think my function is a good deed. Aiding people. With transition."

"Cool," she said. "I can help then, but you might still have to do the pole-pushing part."

Death shook his skull. "You get into my boat. We go to the Other Side. You get out there. None return."

"Oh." There was only the quiet rippling flow of moving water.

Death was okay with the sound of water and silence.

"My, what big teeth you have," Hanna said after a while. "You don't bite, do you?"

"No. Nothing here can hurt you."

"Really? Good-byes hurt."

"Ah." Death said. "Then I was mistaken. This is the place of good-byes."

"That sucks."

Death tilted his head, as if looking at something familiar in a different way. "Perhaps. But it is beyond...other kinds of pain."

"Probably better than the morphine, then," the girl said. "Unless it also makes you goofy. And constipated."

"This is a place beyond biology in general. In my experience, it also does not make people...goofy. They are mostly solemn."

"I don't do solemn. But the no constipation—I'm totally good with that." The light, from across the river and through the fog was the gray-and-almost pink of twilight or just before dawn. In it, Hanna looked pensive. "Do you have word retrieval problems? I just say," she rushed on, "because you sometimes pause. When my tumors got big, I got word retrieval problems." She looked out into the fog. "It was like reaching into a bag for a hammer, and all I could find was a screwdriver—you know? But I could fake it pretty good. Just picked up the word near the one I wanted or said, 'that thing for hitting nails.'"

Death shrugged. "For me, there are many languages. And many people's memories. To sort through."

"People leave you their memories?"

He nodded. "It makes it easier to let them go, if the memories go somewhere. Not just...gone." Those they held most strongly, beyond regrets. "Family. Home. Love." He extended his hand to her and held it out, as if to shake.

"Makes sense," Hanna said. "So, if I shake your hand, you won't pull me into the boat, or anything?"

"No." Death shook his skull. "I am here when you are... ready." *And also to make you ready.*

"Cool. Interesting to meet you, Death." She stepped forward and reached out. "Pleased seems like the wrong word. No offense."

He shook hands with her formally, with a slight bow that she mirrored. His large bony fingers wrapped around her smaller hand. "None taken." He continued to grip her hand. He had an urge to pull her into his boat. Strange, because she wasn't yet dead. It was as if talking to her was somehow dangerous.

"So you can talk without inhaling, and think without—" She peered up at his eye sockets. "Any brain."

"Things work differently here." He shrugged but kept clutching her hand. Each movement in it was a quivering tiny dance. And it was warm, with a warmth beyond heat. The way orange and yellows were warm in the memories of dead landscape painters.

"That's *miraculous.*" Her smile was mischievous. "So maybe you could help arrange a miracle recovery for me?" She waved the thumb of her free hand over her shoulder at the bank, just a shape though the fog. "That's what we're hoping and praying for, back in the real world."

This was more familiar territory. Death relaxed but did not let go of her odd, live, pulse-fluttering hand. "Not my department. I'm just transportation."

She tilted her head, as if hearing something distant. "Oh. Hey—mom's coming into my room. Back in the world. Can I, uh, see you later?" She tugged within his hold.

"Certainly." He released her, finally, unwrapping her flesh hand with his finger bones almost regretfully. "Inevitably."

"Okay," she gave him a parting smile and quick wave. "Wait up." She clambered up the bank, becoming indistinct in the fog, then disappearing, bright yellow boots and all.

"Of course." Death leaned on his pole, although it wasn't necessary to hold his flat-bottomed boat against the current, which seemed not to affect the boat at all. "I await everyone."

A timeless time later, Hanna wandered back through the fog and plopped herself down on the bank, below a willow glistening and dripping with condensation. "Hey, Death!" She waved, as if excited to see him. Now she was wearing a short-sleeved tee-shirt with a picture of a frog on it, and jeans, with running shoes. Her brown hair was pulled back into a ponytail.

"Greetings." He returned her wave, his more restrained. "Would you like a ride to the Other Side?"

"Not yet," she shook her head, swinging the ponytail. "But I was wondering—when the time comes, can I just swim? I used to be on swim team. I bet I could make it across, especially if I don't have to worry about breathing, when I get near the other side. Plus, I probably float great. 'Cause back home I'm in a persistent vegetative state. You know—like trees." She stood, put her arms above her head, and balanced on one leg.

"I don't think...you can swim across."

"But you don't know?"

Death considered as they looked out at the dark ripples. "No one has done it before. I take them in a boat. The boat changes. But it is...a boat."

"So it could be fun. It could be special. You could turn your boat into a submarine and stay below me. If I got tired, you could surface. You ever do a submarine?"

He thought back. There had been wars. So many young men had died, clumped in groups. Some had wanted to cross together in a submarine, just as they had died in one together, and it had been fitting. "Yes. I've 'done' submarines. But the river is Lethe—forgetfulness itself. You'd forget. How to swim."

"Ooh." She took a half step back from the water's dark edge. "Right." After a moment she brightened. "Then I'll make 'No Swimming' signs. To make sure nobody makes that mistake. Can you bring me a hammer?"

"My functions do not include," Death said, "hardware supplies."

"No problemo. If I can make this outfit with my mind, I can come up with a board and tools. I'll look around in the grass. I'll show you later. You know what would be cool? If you came back in a pirate ship. You could even put your face on the flag."

Death bowed. "As you wish."

Death glided through the fog at the wheel of a pirate ship and approached the bank again. The ship was a shrunken, vaguely Disneyland version of a Spanish galleon. There were, of course, no cannons. None interfere with Death on the river Lethe, and Death knew too much of the harvest of cannon to use them for decoration. At the stern, a black flag stirred, with his face on it above a pair of his crossed forearm bones.

Hanna climbed along a thick branch of the willow tree, and then sat, one leg dangling on each side of it near where it joined the trunk. "Ahoy, Death!"

"Ahoy, Hanna." He was on the quarter deck. Lethe was plenty deep there, right to the edge. He spun the wheel, heading up into the light wind until the sails luffed, a rattle of flapping canvas. The headwind killed the ship's momentum, and it floated side-on to the bank, where it came to rest with a thump.

Hanna applauded.

Death bowed. It had been nicely done. "Would you like to come aboard?"

"No thanks. Not yet. But way cool boat, and nice steering. I thought you could come ashore for a picnic, to check out my signs."

"I do not ordinarily disembark."

"I'm not ordinary," she said. "I give you a shore leave. C'mon. It'll help my 'transition'."

If that were true, it would, perhaps, be fitting. Death climbed onto the quarterdeck railing, where he balanced for a moment, uncertain. It was as if there were something frightening on land below. *None interfere with Death*, he reminded himself. He dropped silently to the bank. Hanna scrambled down from her tree.

She grinned. "I have a surprise."

"Role reversal. So often it is Death...that is the surprise."

"I made us a picnic. We can talk. It'll help us both with word retrieval—practice, practice, practice. Or, as we people with word retrieval problems say, whatchamacallit, whatsit, and that thing what's repeating stuff."

He gave a small shake of his skull. "Practice? This place is... an end to striving."

"Fuff," she exhaled. "Just because you're Death, doesn't mean you have to be *resigned*. Also, I have awesome sandwiches."

"The dead—don't usually eat."

"*That's* how you keep your slim figure," Hanna said. She tugged on his metacarpals with her warm flesh ones, and he followed her up the bank. Her footfalls were a light *pad pad pad* on the grass, while he moved silently. At a flat spot on an overlooking bluff, she had laid out a blue and white tablecloth as a ground cover, with a picnic basket. White bread sandwiches with trimmed crusts sat on red plates.

"These sandwiches—peanut butter and honey with banana slices," Hanna said, a little breathless, like she was describing an extraordinary feast. Gold and brown oozed out from between the white slices above a scattering of crumbs. "Mom used to make them for me when I was little. Beats the hell out of eating through a tube up your nose."

"I believe you," Death said. "And I don't even have a nose."

"Wait." The girl frowned. "You don't have a tongue. For tasting."

"I accept memories," Death said. "Think of the flavor. The sensation." He lifted the sandwich to his teeth and let her sense wash through him—of the sweetness, the sticky lumpiness of banana, the thicker sticky of the peanut butter, all filled a mother's warm love. Death was struck silent for a moment. "You remember...vividly."

"Hmmph," Hanna said, but she looked pleased. "You're just not used to senses from people still alive. Now let me show you my signs. Close your eyes."

That wasn't exactly possible, but he drew the dark sleeve of his cloak across his face and cast his awareness elsewhere.

"Ta da!"

He dropped his sleeve and brought his awareness back.

She had three wooden signs on stakes, planted at wobbly angles in the grass. The first said, in purple paint on a white background "No Swimming. By Order of *Death*!" The second said in red "Forget Swimming (or Forget Everything!)" The third was blank.

"We could work on this one together. Not many sign painters get to collaborate with Death, right?" She wrinkled her eyebrows. "Unless all painters collaborate with Death—the mortality thing?"

"I'm not really creative," Death said. "I usually handle destruction."

"Your pirate ship was great. And it'll be fun."

She tilted her head, as if hearing something from far away. "Oh. Sorry. Could you excuse me? Mom walked into my hospital room again. She likes that I know she's there. My pulse goes up." Hanna glanced down at her running shoes. "She talks to me. And sings. I'm blind now, back there. But she puts strawberries in front of my nose so I can smell them. And flowers."

He caught a waft of her memory—or maybe even a live sensation—the smell of cut apple and sweet perfume of lilac, so intense it was almost dizzying. "Don't let me hold you up," Death said. "We can meet here later."

"That'd be great." Hanna looked relieved. She stepped into the fog, away from the river becoming indistinct and then disappeared. Death remained, sitting cross-legged on the tablecloth that was a picnic blanket. In the half-light, because of the angle, where her footsteps had pressed the damp grass flat, it looked lighter.

After a time, neither short nor long, Hanna returned. "Sorry about that."

"Don't be," Death shrugged. "Life goes on. Temporarily. Would you like to embark?"

"Not yet. First, you have to help with my signs."

He did. His lettering was more precise, but she was better at coming up with what to write. They spent the timeless late afternoon making a dozen signs in the meadow, using

Death's canvas mainsail as a drop cloth under a sprawl of paint cans bearing drips of bright yellows, reds, and blues.

"Would you now join me on my boat?" Death asked, after they stopped.

"Not yet. Will you come back later?"

"Of course."

"See you then, Death. Have a good day at work."

 He left her eating her sandwich. She seemed to be enjoying it hugely.

"You should adopt me," Hanna explained, in a matter-of-fact way, on his next visit. "Not to replace my real parents. Just for the afterlife and pre-death part." She stood on a flat meadow covered with sawgrass, at the down-current edge, where it turned marshy and the reeds bobbed.

"Adopt?" Death hopped lightly out of his boat onto the land. He'd gone back to his former flat-bottomed punt of dark wood.

"It would be totally cool." She waved both hands for emphasis. "I could stomp around here and tell the plants I'm Death's adopted daughter, and they'd get all worried that I might pull them out of the ground. But then I'd make friends with them. And I'd tell them I'd put in a good word for them, when their time came."

"It doesn't work like that."

"Well, sure. But what do plants know?" Into the pause, she added. "So—adoption?"

"By what Authority?"

"I had an election while you were away," Hanna said. "I'm bank president now. Of this whole bank of the river. I'm, like, in charge. Except there's nothing to be in charge of, except plants and adoptions. Which I've just authorized."

If Death had not been holding his long pole, he would have folded his bony arms in front of him. The two of them stood for a long timeless time, the girl in her confident pose, her arms on her hips, looking up at him, Death leaning on his staff, looking down.

"It will be good for you," the girl said. "Family's important to people. It'll give you empathy. The best hospice nurses, the ones who help you let go—they have that. It'd help with my 'transition.'"

Death sighed again, the restless sound of desert wind through the gap under a door. "I cannot adopt you."

"Then I'm adopting you," Hanna said. "As my afterlife Godfather. To advise on spiritual matters and the afterlife."

"I am not qualified. To provide spiritual advice."

"I'll be the judge of that. I just appointed myself judge, too, not just bank president."

"Perhaps we should have another presidential election, now that I'm here."

"Sorry. The polls closed. Plus, you need a birth certificate to vote, and I'm pretty sure you don't have one."

At her eyebrow raise, he shrugged an admission that she was right.

"But." She smiled. "I could appoint you bank vice-president, so you can take over my job, when I die."

"When you get your death certificate."

"Exactly."

"Very well. Would you like a ride in my boat...Madame President?" He bowed deeply and gestured toward it, as if inviting aboard a head of state. "Now that we've resolved succession issues."

"Jeez, Death. You've been vice president for, like, ten seconds, and already pushing for a promotion. Too soon. Get some experience."

"Two million years is not enough?"

"*Relevant* experience. You already said you don't get out much on the bank." Hanna lifted her chin. "Also, I've got some things to sort out here at the bank, now that I'm in charge."

It's possible, as he sailed away, that Death gave a tiny, amused shake of his head.

He came back later, poling through the dark water. On the bank, Hanna was barefoot, wearing what looked like a prom dress, all shiny blue silk. It rippled as she moved.

After her wave to him, Hanna launched into a jig on the embankment. "Check it out. Riverdance!"

"Very...exuberant," Death said, after a bit. It was quite unlike how he was usually greeted.

After dancing for several minutes, Hanna flopped down on the blue and white picnic tablecloth, her cheeks flushed, chest rising and falling with deep breaths. Beside her on the sawgrass were matching pumps, with heels.

"Dressed for...a journey?" Death asked.

She shook her head but smiled.

He brought his boat smoothly to the shore and waited.

"So," Hanna finally said after she'd caught her breath. "I know you'll have trouble believing this, but I've never had a boyfriend."

Death didn't know what to say.

"I mean," Hanna went on, "I've had crushes. And maybe some boys had crushes on me, before I went all Franken-baldy. But never a real boyfriend." She cleared her throat. "So. Maybe you could introduce me? There must be absolute piles of cancer kids on this edge of the river, getting ready to cross. Or, somewhere in the weeds, a cute snowboarder with head injuries, also in a coma. I bet some boy would love to have a girlfriend, before crossing over."

"I am not," he considered the words. "A dating service."

"Branch out. Bet you've been doing the death thing practically forever."

"Yes. But time isn't the same here."

"My point exactly." She clapped her hands together. "*Time for a career change!*" She held her hands out, palms up, as if presenting him something, and paused dramatically. "So— cute boy. Possible?"

If Death had been wearing eyelids, he would have closed them for a moment. "I don't carry Passengers up and down this bank. Just across to the Other Side. And carry none back."

"Well, see—I'm special."

He regarded her. "I'm sure you are. But I cannot bring you a boyfriend."

"Hmmph," she said. "And you claim *not* to be an expert on things that suck."

Death laughed. It was impossible to deal with humans for long without a sense of humor. "Implausible. Yet true. As long as you're dressed up, would you like a ride?"

"No thanks." She folded her arms across her chest and glanced at her high heels. "If you're not going to bring me even a boyfriend-candidate, I'm definitely getting more comfortable shoes, before a long boat ride. Wait here. I'll change. I also have a plan B."

After she disappeared into the fog, carrying her shoes, Death looked up and down the bank. He addressed the fog and the reeds by the shore. "A plan B?"

She reappeared out of the fog, wearing jeans, running shoes, and a tee-shirt reading *Death Coach* across her chest. "I've decided on my good deed."

"Indeed?" If Death had eyebrows, he would have raised one.

"I'm going to improve your process. As a consultant."

Death knew every language, including thousands now dead. Yet words failed him.

"See, of the two of us, I'm the only one who's been alive, right? And I'm going through the process. So I'm the expert. With ideas."

He gestured with a long, bony hand, palm up, to continue.

"First, appearance." She waved a hand up at him. "This

whole huge skeleton thing, black hooded cloak. Especially for kids, that could be scary. Not exactly welcoming."

"What do you...suggest?"

"A makeover. Live eye for the Death guy." Hanna regarded him with an appraising expression that somehow conveyed affection. "You've got the color right. Definitely a winter. But update the look. With the traditional black cloak, a tee-shirt. With a picture on the front. Which could change, depending on who you're picking up."

"A tee-shirt."

"Yeah. Like if I was a huge fan of a band, you could have the band's picture on the front of it, and we could talk music the whole way across and about concerts I'd been to. Or famous dead people's pictures. For scientists, have Einstein's face on your tee-shirt. They'd go, 'wow, Death gave a ride to Einstein. Wonder what *they* talked about,' and climb right into your boat."

"A tee-shirt. With a band is...inappropriate."

"Well, think about it. Also, on the subject of looks—you shouldn't be so tall. To some people, you're imposing."

"As I should be. Otherwise, some passengers—who are already dead—argue. About coming. They are accustomed to... negotiating exceptions. When there are none."

"Hmmph," Hanna said.

"In the end," he made a joke. "Turns out—size does matter."

"And you say *tee-shirts* are inappropriate?" Hanna rolled her eyes. "Fine. But make an exception. For little kids. You don't have to be, like, ten feet tall to get a five-year-old to cooperate."

"That," Death conceded, "is a good idea."

"My other ideas are even better."

"Than a 'makeover'?"

"Yes. And don't drip sarcasm on my tee-shirt, just because I suggested you wear one. Which, by the way, would have to be extra-extra-large. The crop-top bare-belly look doesn't work, with just bones."

"Noted."

"The first other idea is about the memories you collect. You should share them."

He looked at her, waiting.

"When people first get into your boat, share with them a memory from someone who went before. So they'd know their memory would also get shared later. Not be forgotten.

"Also," she added. "The memory could be something that the person getting into your boat otherwise missed out on, in life. Like, if they'd never been in love, they could feel it from the memory of someone who had been. In love. People would like that. And we want to be remembered. Trust me. I'm an expert on being a person. Been one my whole life."

"Yes." Death said after a long pause. "That could be helpful." He bowed.

"Of course. My brain is tumor city in the real world, but over here, it works fine."

"Indeed."

"My last idea is about dealing with kids. Little kids. Much younger than me. It would help if you had a puppy or something for the kids to play with, on their way across. Don't you have a three-headed dog?"

"No dog."

"That's a shame. Kittens?"

Death shook his skull.

"Well, don't have a kitten, then, Death. It's okay—I've got your bony back."

"You've got...my bony back?"

"It's an expression."

"Yes," Death said. "It certainly is."

She reached down into the grass and drew out a worn stuffed toy bear with dark eyes, tan fur and a broad stitched smile. "Carry this," she said. "Looks like cotton. But he's *comfort.*"

It was, Death understood immediately, Hanna's teddy bear, from childhood. "But. Don't you want to keep *your* bear? For...comfort?"

"Hello? Death—I'm fifteen." She gave him a look. "I don't care how young that is in skeleton years. I've *way* outgrown a teddy bear."

Death was not certain of that, but existing partly outside time, he wasn't good with ages.

"Besides," Hanna went on. "I bet lots of kids need him way more."

"There are. Many children." Always too many, to be brought over.

"So. This little guy." She held up the stuffed toy bear, which flopped in her hands. "Ted E. Bear. The E stands for Either something or nothing, like what's on the Other Side. But it can also stand for Everything, so he can be a stuffed dog or cat, or a blanket, or a toy fire truck. Whatever. Anything a kid—or even a grownup—wants. Or needs. Like my shirt. I change it with my mind here. Just change Ted E. Bear into whatever someone needs. Like *their* teddy bear. From when they were a kid."

She handed him the toy bear, and as he touched it, her memories flooded in. Holding the bear as she drifted to sleep. Carrying it. The fabric softener smell and warm feeling of the stuffed bear just out of the dryer. The feel of clutching it in a fierce hug. The sense of not being alone. The amazing...comfort, when there was no other comfort, for a child with cancer.

He set Ted E. Bear reverently in the front of his boat. The bear leaned slightly toward the bank, off center, his arms wide, as if inviting a hug. It made the boat look cozy, less severe. It was still, somehow, fitting.

Death visited many more times. It may be that Death stopped asking if Hanna was ready for a boat ride.

Eventually, on one visit, Hanna was lying on her back identifying animal shapes for Death, in the thicker wisps of fog that drifted by. Death sat next to her, his long legs of bone tucked under him. His boat rested against the bank, with Ted E. Bear propped on the prow.

"Your bear is a great success," he said. "As a comfort object. And sharing memories helps. Passengers know they are not forgotten." A thought occurred to him. "Do you want someone's memory of what it's like to have...had a boyfriend?"

"Nah." She managed to combine looking over at him with an eye roll. "Probably inappropriate. Also, I thought about it, and decided my imagination is probably better than most people's memories."

"In your case," Death said. "Probably true."

"You should definitely do the tee-shirt thing, though." She propped herself up on her elbow. She never gave up on that. "Just imagine how cool it would be for a guy into death metal to see you wearing a shirt from his favorite band. 'On the one hand, I'm dead. On the other, my taste in music is *endorsed*. Check it out: Signed Pestilence tee-shirt. From *Death*!'"

"There's enough pestilence," Death said, "without another shirt."

"Or 'My Other Boat Is a Submarine.' Or go surreal: 'My Other Shirt Is Also a Metaphor.' Or mess with the new arrivals. Your shirt could say 'Ask about the Special' and when people say, 'What's special?' you could say, 'everyone is special.'"

"Some more than others."

"Of course," she said. "Like me, for example."

"Yes."

"On that note," Hanna sat all the way up. "I'm worried about you, D. Because of your job."

"Do not be. I never face unemployment."

"But you have the loneliest job in the universe."

That was ridiculous. "I meet new people. Every day."

"Then never see them again. And when you get them to the Other Side, you're all, 'It was nice talking with you. Good luck as you move toward the light,' but they've just left behind their memories. *Including* their memory of you. So they're all, 'Uh, do I know you?' Just when you get to know them, you lose them. Forever."

It was as though something broke wetly in Death. "Ah," he said, and the sound was like the moaning of wind through a cavern, empty and enormous.

"So." Hanna cleared her throat. "That's the other reason to keep Ted E. Bear. Because you need comforting too. Also, to remind you of me.

"And," she went on. "Even if you don't do the tee-shirt thing for Passengers—which you totally should—you could wear one for yourself, under the black cloak that no one else could see. It could say 'I'll Be Okay'. To remind you, you have a really hard job, but you do it well. And you'll be okay."

"I'll be okay," he repeated.

Hanna stood up then, and arched her back in a volleyball stretch, with her hands above her head, as if getting ready for a long journey.

"Oh, no," Death said, but so quietly, it's possible he didn't hear it himself.

Hanna finished her stretch and looked over, her eyebrows raised.

"I...see," Death said. And he did, because he unfolded his legs and rose to his feet and picked up his long pole from where it lay in the grass. With almost infinite slowness, he boarded his boat, which did not even rock as he stepped into it.

"Actually," she said, looking down at the grass. "I've been kind of ready for a while. But Mom and Dad weren't."

"That's often the case with—" He paused. Hanna, he knew,

didn't think of herself as a child. "—young people."

"Would you say hi for me? To Mom and Dad and my brother? When their times come? Tell them I got across okay. That I was fine with this whole thing?"

"Yes," he said solemnly.

"And you'll know them?" She looked worried.

He nodded.

"I mean, there's like eight billion people on earth. And they'll probably be really old when they show up. I hope."

"I'll know them," Death said. "They're in your memory. You're in theirs."

"You won't forget?" she asked.

"Never."

"Okay then." She straightened, as if a weight had left her shoulders. "Told you I'd get you to branch out—message service and toy lending, not just transportation and boat design."

His boat seemed too small, in its dark teak, set off by the light-brown bear. Seemed somehow not enough. "What kind of boat," Death asked. "Would you like?"

"I love your boat just the way it is. Always have. It's perfect."

"Thank you." Death bowed his head. He did not want to ask the question.

"Yes," Hanna said anyway. "I'm ready to go."

He reached out to help her, but she just bowed and gave him another handshake, like their first. "It's been wonderful getting to know you, Death. You've been a great friend." She released his hand and climbed into the boat by herself. "Now," Hanna said. "About my trip across."

Death waited for her instructions.

"We're going to sing, together, the whole way," she said.

He nodded. He had difficulty speaking. It was not a word retrieval problem.

"And we're going to take our sweet time. Long enough to sing every song I know. From years of campfire singing."

"Or until you forget." There was vast sadness in his voice, which broke. "The words."

"Nah." She moved to the front of the boat, making it sway. "Longer. When I forget, we'll just hum. There's beauty beyond word retrieval, D."

"Indeed."

She seated herself, near the prow, the stuffed bear at her feet, but she didn't pick it up. Instead, she faced the far bank, invisible in the fog. She leaned forward as if into a headwind. He pushed, slowly, almost regretfully, and a gap of dark water opened behind the boat.

"Michael row, the boat ashore..." Hanna began, her voice sweet, a little breathy, but not sad. Death joined, in a rich baritone an octave below. "Hallelujah." They sang until they were out of sight of shore, and far beyond, moving through the fog toward the light.

Dean Gloster is a full-time writer in Berkeley, California. His debut YA novel, *Dessert First,* is out now from Simon Pulse. When not downhill ski racing, practicing Aikido, or teaching writing, Dean is usually posting jokes and opposing authoritarianism on Twitter: @deangloster

Robert Wilf

Constellation

I once told you I lived
on the moons of Mars.
Deimos and Phobos
hold me back from
the infinite void.

But there is life between
Mars and Venus.
A shifting fragile life,
fluid like the ocean.

Sometimes it drifts close
to the shores of one,
sometimes to the other.
never quite still.

I told you once
there are no stars to guide us,
only jet plane constellations
reflected in dark waters.

The star-ships are mapped
to look like man-made myths,
shifting in dizzying chaos
they claim are perfect circles.

Now I leave the red sands
In a jet plane,
adding my own light
to the void.

Robert "Shadow" Wilf is a graduate of the class of 2020 and is still salty about it. They have been surviving Quarantine by playing Dungeons & Dragons online, serving as an Americorp Member at City Year Philadelphia, and lying to themself about getting that book published. They have been published previously in Spoon Knife Anthology 4, for their work about an alien ghost trying to escape her past. Follow them on *frozen-odin.com* and insta @frostfox208

Verity Reynolds

Halftermath

The bunk she'd been assigned on the bottom deck of the rickety cargo ship was barely wider than her shoulders, the engine was cycling directly beneath her head, and the air was a comfortable seven degrees Celsius. Koa Nantais should have been having the best sleep of her life.

She wasn't.

She was staring at the sloped edge of the bulkhead a half-meter from her face, its edges scarcely visible in the darkness. Thinking of nothing in particular. For a rare moment in her life, Koa had very little to consider: the ship wouldn't reach Antigone for several days, nobody on her team had so much as a hangnail, and for once, the ambassador was sound asleep.

Koa approved. The ambassador needed all the sleep she could get.

Even her inbox was empty. For the first time in months, Koa had actually managed to answer all of her mail.

But boredom had lost its novelty.

She rolled out of her bunk, sat up carefully to avoid hitting her head on the bulkhead struts, and groped for her boots. Hendor would still be awake. Hendor never slept.

Devori rarely slept outside their hibernation cycles, apart from the occasional catnap. But Koa had never known Bemlish Hendor to sleep at all, not since she'd met him during her internship on the *Pais*, nearly thirty years before. Hendor was weedy-looking for a Devori, but it was the sleeping that had convinced Koa something more than common deep-space malnutrition was involved. Genetic alteration, probably. Hendor would try anything once.

"Kula," he said as she stepped onto the cargo ship's tiny bridge. "Look at this."

Koa allowed herself a small smile—he's been calling her *beautiful* for thirty years, too—and leaned over the back of the pilot's seat, examining the sensor readout as he pointed.

She glanced up, out the forward windows, then back at the tiny screen. No visual—but a distinctive sensor blip.

"Is that an asteroid?" she asked.

He pointed to the screen again. "That half is." His fingers twitched, punching up a second readout. "That half is not."

Koa was a doctor, not a pilot, but even she could see what he meant. The second "half" of the asteroid was a jumble of RGC, aluminum, tetrasilicide, borosilicate glass, and the sort of radiation readings that only happened at a...

"Crash site," she said.

Hendor waved a hand: amusement. "Poor bastard."

Koa reached over his shoulder and tapped the sensor controls. A moment's scan confirmed her suspicions. "That's a *recent* crash site." Only a leaking reactor core could produce that spectrograph.

Hendor looked, too. "No more than half an hour, I'd guess."

Koa's spine prickled in the way her vocation had taught her never to ignore. "How long would it take us to get there?"

"Ten minutes. Eight if I punched it." Hendor showed no signs of punching it. "No point, though. It's not worth salvaging. Wouldn't send a team out there anyway, not till that reactor leak pisses itself out."

"Hendor, the pilot might still be alive."

"In that rad storm? No way." But Koa could tell by the way his hands curled that she'd made him uncomfortable. "Anything alive in there now soon won't be."

"Change course," Koa said. "And punch it."

This time, Hendor shifted in his seat to look at her. "Assuming you're right, how do you intend to get in? Look at those readings. You'll bake like akti."

"I have to try."

Hendor sighed and activated the engine controls. "Waste of a pretty face, kula."

Koa, already halfway off the bridge, only half heard him. Eight minutes. She had to get into an environmental suit in eight minutes.

Hendor had gotten her as close to the crash site as he could, but the cargo ship dwarfed the asteroid, and a 200-meter gap was the best the Devori captain could manage.

From the hull of the ship, the magnetic boots of her environmental suit anchoring her in place, she had a somewhat clearer view of the site. It was a vessel of some kind: small, but large enough to have nearly doubled the asteroid's size.

Any ship Koa had ever known would have seen a space

rock that large from several hundred light-years away. What had gone wrong?

She tapped the comm switch on her helmet. "Hendor. Do you read me?"

"Clear as dawn, kula," Hendor's voice replied in her ear. "No trouble on this end. Transferring controls."

The suit's heads-up display shone to life as he spoke. Koa kept her eyes trained on the asteroid, using her peripheral vision to identify the necessary readouts: navigation, oxygen and temperature controls, and the mission clock, which she'd set from the computer's best guess as to the time of the crash. The Golden Hour was an hour only for humans; most interstellar-traveling species were hardier. Still, every minute mattered.

She left the comm channel open. Just in case.

Koa glanced to the lower left corner of the display. She had to do it twice before the nav controls bounced to the center of the screen in response. The eye tracking in these old suits was notoriously finicky.

"Disengaging magnetic controls," she said into the open comm channel, "and engaging navset-1."

"Yaene anevpa," Hendor said. Koa smiled. The most commonly known Niralanes phrase in the galaxy expressed the least Niralan of sentiments: *good luck.*

As her feet lifted, weightless, from the hull of the freighter, Koa felt a familiar warmth spread through her limbs. The Earth Standard word was *joy*, and it accompanied every zero-gravity experience for her. Only the intervention of her mother, at the last minute and in person, had kept Koa on her path to medical school instead of hard-forking onto a path as a zero-g mechanic, based on nothing more than her love of spacewalking.

Well. The engineering major she'd been dating at the time hadn't dimmed the appeal, either.

The distance to her target slid by on one side of Koa's peripheral vision while the seconds ticked past on the other. For the ninety-three seconds it took her to cross the space between the freighter and the asteroid, Koa was totally at peace.

She let the suit's sensors negotiate the landing nonetheless. Koa would take chances with her own life, but not another's.

Her boots brushed the hull of the wrecked ship, then gripped it with a snap of the metallic seals that Koa felt rather than heard. But the connection registered only dimly, lost behind the bright red glare of the helmet display and the screaming alarm in her ears.

"Kula," Hendor's voice said, half-buried in static and the noise of the suit's radiation alarm. "It's worse than we thought. Your suit won't hold out for-"

"Five minutes," she said over the comm, silencing her helmet with a sharp tap. Apparently, the helmet thought her reply was directed at it, for it reset the mission clock as well.

Koa ignored the clock. She examined the opening in the wreckage for a moment then moved toward it, slowly, sliding her feet along the hull.

The wrecked craft was scarcely larger than a life-support pod. Two Niralans might have fit in it, albeit uncomfortably; two humans would have killed one another for lack of personal space, and two Viidans wouldn't have fit at all. Koa recognized neither its configuration nor the raised grooves running along one side of the hull. Ornamentation, or language?

The pod's transparent forward section had shattered. Koa wedged herself into this, causing a fresh wave of protest from the suit's rad alarm, which she silenced again. Three minutes. She'd administer her own rad protocols back on the freighter.

She pulled her medical scanner from the suit's large external pocket and turned it on.

The scanner made no more sense than her visual impressions did. The mess of biomatter in the cockpit was... silicon-based? Vaguely humanoid, with something resembling limbs twined through what might have been steering controls. But utterly loose, rubbery, even gelatinous in places. Whether this was typical or the result of trauma, Koa couldn't determine and had no time to find out. Nor did she have time to ponder whether the pilot's outer covering was supposed to be half glass.

The one thing the pilot did not seem to have was a vital sign.

Koa flipped through the scanner's screens, one by one. No pulse. Nothing resembling respiration or circulation. No movement at all, in fact. No electrical activity.

The pilot posed a xenobiology question, not a medical one. Dead, alive, or in some uncategorized third state: whatever the problem was, it was not one Koa could fix.

She checked the mission clock again and preferred discretion to liquefaction.

Koa dropped her scanner into her pocket and turned back toward the hole through which she had entered.

The catch in her leg stopped her dead a full second before an entirely new noise filled her ears and the display flashed two ominous words in blue: TOLERANCE CRITICAL.

Koa froze. Her heart seemed to stop as well.

The onboard sensors had reacted too late; if she'd needed the alarm to tell her that the suit had snagged something and was about to tear, she'd already be dead.

Sensing the direction of the tug on her leg, she shifted her weight toward it slightly and bumped metal. A moment's exploration with one hand told her the suit's pocket had caught and twisted on a jagged corner protruding from one of the pod's walls.

Koa ran her fingers along this corner as far as she could reach. No, it *was* the wall.

Four and a half minutes, by the mission clock. Thirty seconds to get out of this mess.

Koa silenced the tolerance alarm and touched the bend in the metal again, exploring the place in which the edge of the pocket had looped itself around the metal edge. The gap was wider than she'd realized. Wide enough to slip her fingers into.

Koa slid two fingers into the gap and pulled.

The shriek of separating metal was inaudible in space but she felt it, a sharp vibration that set her teeth on edge. But the panel gave way. Another good pull would separate it from the ship—if Koa could get enough leverage without tearing her suit.

Her fingers brushed something behind the panel. She fished it out.

It was a book, paper printed in Earth Standard and bound with glue, a bit battered but readable nonetheless. Its cover boasted a riot of colors that Koa liked at once.

She dropped it into the suit's pocket. Bracing herself, taking what she hoped would not be her last breath, Koa grasped the panel again and yanked.

The panel popped free before she expected it, sending Koa sprawling backward into what remained of the unknown pilot. But she noticed only the bright red numerals of the mission clock. Five minutes. Time to leave, or die.

She set the suit's nav controls to autopilot and disengaged her boots.

"Hendor," she said into the comm the moment she cleared the asteroid.

"Kula," Hendor's voice replied in her ear. If a Devori could sound relieved, he did.

"Tell Alarah I'll need her help."

A cot and cabinet in one corner of the freighter's galley served as its medical bay. Koa was lying on the former when Hendor appeared, carrying the book.

"You might have been killed, kula," he said.

"I know."

He waggled the book at her. "I hope this was worth it. Especially as you nearly lost it."

"How's that?"

"The pocket was torn nearly off your suit. No trace of your medical scanner. But one of the thermogel packs ruptured; glued this thing to your leg. It took me five minutes to scrub the gel off." He laid the book on her bedside table. "Lucky mishap."

"I suppose so."

"You get some rest. We'll be orbiting Antigone before you know it."

As he left, Koa picked up the book, turning it over in her hands, and smiled. Luck.

Koa still didn't believe in luck by the time she turned the last page. But she did believe in possibilities.

"Hendor," she said, returning to the bridge.

The pilot looked up.

"Did you say you were headed further out than Antigone?"

"Yes, to IS Station 32," Hendor said. "Why do you ask?"

Koa handed him the book. "I need you to deliver this to someone."

He eyed her warily. "This someone is...."

"Dar Nantais," Koa said. "Head of IT on the station. You'll know her when you see her."

Hendor took the book. "Nantais. Your sister?"

"Not quite."

The ambassador didn't even open her eyes as Koa rolled back into her bunk. "Where have you been?"

"Saving the world," Koa replied.

She hadn't slept better in years.

S. Verity Reynolds is a freelance writer and sometime author. She is currently enjoying a new android body.

Lorraine Schein

Failed Finkbeiner

Despite discovering the Theory of Everything,
he was a role model for other men—
a husband who found time to nurture his children,
feeding them hot, nourishing breakfasts,
packing their lunches
and driving them to school.

He'd bake brownies for his colleagues
and always remembered their birthdays.

His beard was kept tidy and trimmed
and he looked handsome in his lab coat
without being distractingly sexy.

Despite having a full teaching load
in addition to his research,
he made a great beef stroganoff and Jello salad,
followed his wife from job to job,
and took eight years off from work to raise a family.

A pert brunette
with an easy smile,
he looked great in jeans
and much younger than his age.

And when he became a she,
was always seen in high heels
matched her bag to her lipstick
and was as proud of her doll collection
as her motorcycle collection.

AUTHOR'S NOTE: *The Finkbeiner test is a checklist to help journalists avoid gender bias in writing articles about women scientists. It requires the article not mention: The fact that the subject is a woman, her husband's job, her childcare arrangements, her personal looks, her state of being single, how she has time to attend to domestic duties despite her job, and other criteria. The "Reversed Finkbeiner" test is an exercise in writing an article about a male scientist that would fail the Finkbeiner test if it were about a woman.*

Lorraine Schein is a New York writer. Her work has appeared in VICE *Terraform*, *Strange Horizons*, *Pen & Brush*, *NewMyths*, and *Little Blue Marble*, and in the anthology *Tragedy Queens: Stories Inspired by Lana del Rey & Sylvia Plath*. *The Futurist's Mistress*, her poetry book, is available from Mayapple Press: *www.mayapplepress.com*

Benjamin McPherson Ficklin

Poet/Cheerleader

Satomi knows her visits to Satoshi's bookstore are compulsive, but they seem harmless, perhaps even healthy—plus it's not like the shop is out of her way. Every school day begins the same: shower, natto and raw eggs with tea, pack onigiri and a banana for lunch, leave the apartment with an hour for the short walk to Kyoto University, where she is in her third year studying business. Plenty of time for the bookstore. She walks down the wooden stairs of her building, past the tea house, past the shrine, past the convenience store, past the antique shop where the orange cat sleeps in the window (good morning kitty), and here's Satoshi's bookstore. A bookstore as small as her apartment. So, believing herself fully aware of the compulsion, she checks her watch (9:07) and slides the door far enough left to admit her and her backpack. Satoshi, as usual, looks like he's been awake all night. The old man sits at his cluttered desk with a cigarette in his mouth and a beer in his hand. He nods at Satomi, she bows, and he turns back to the TV, which is playing American baseball. She, as always, begins by inhaling deeply, appreciating the smell. The next step is greeting *The Invention of Morel*. She pulls the store's only copy from the foreign fiction shelf, a book that's sat there for years. She opens to the first page. The ground lurches; the ground rises, lifting every-

thing, dropping everything—dust explodes off the shelves—
the ashtray and books on Satoshi's desk clatter to the floor—
Satomi shrieks and slips, falling backward—Satoshi gasps;
the floor, the pavement, Kyoto's foundation, a 500-km-deep
hunk of Earth spasms, shakes arrhythmically until, after the
first ten or so seconds of lurching, the thick central book-
shelf leans forward over the crumpled Satomi. It descends
toward the floor, her upturned face. And she realizes there's
a selfishness in her horror, not that she fears the moment
when her life becomes a death, but it's the condition of *this*
death that she despairs, and not because of Satoshi's bookstore (this is a sanctuary). Satomi shrieks as the books begin
to slip free of the plummeting bookcase because her parents
will remember her as a cheerleader. There's the photo on the
wall of their Kushima home of her in a skirt and midriff-re-
vealing top and knee-high boots with her fist held high, smiling widely, and the photo of her whole team standing together after they came in 2nd in the 26th All-Japan High School
Tournament. She fears that after she dies, her parents will
only remember how she was lifted to the pinnacle of the pyr-
amids, how she leapt high enough to double backflip into the
arms of her teammates, how she was thrown into a 720° spin
to land gracefully on a teammate's shoulders—always smiling. They, her parents, will tell how she was co-captain two
years in a row. This is the daughter they cherished. These are
the stories in which she'll endure. At this angle, she realizes,
the top shelf will impact the bridge of her nose. She tries to
lift her arms, but they are pinned by the straps of her backpack. Still shrieking, she projects herself into the only fac-

simile of her mind that's been published: a poem titled "This poem is your home." It was published by *A Bent Tree*, an online journal started the previous year. The poem begins with three suns, one half-set, one descending toward the oceanic horizon, and one dawning: three separate days occurring simultaneously, recurring simultaneously: the beloved, the lover, and Satomi with you; three mountains, one growing as the planet cools, one growing from the first mountain's crater, and the third almost beyond the planet's curve, barely tall enough to spy the other eruptions; three cell phones, one searching the internet, one calling the first phone, and one a black hole, a device consuming anything inputted, devouring knowledge and directions and clever memes; three inboxes, one exchanging news with friends across the world: Nigerian friends, Canadian friends, Haitian friends, Bulgarian friends, one emailing the former email again and again and again with no response, and one filling: 11 unchecked emails, 78 unchecked emails, 119 unchecked emails, 812 unchecked emails, 1913 unchecked emails, 1728 unchecked emails, 5353 unchecked emails; three people, one Argentine woman sitting outside a cafe watching the clouds and sipping café con leche, one Chilean man sitting at an adjacent table fiddling with his phone but straining his thoughts toward the daydreaming woman, and one Japanese girl inside the cafe, wearing big round sunglasses, sipping yerba mate (with you beside her) and taking notes on the man watching the woman; three cherry blossoms forming in the Winter, one blooming to die—exploding pink against a naked sky, one blooming to accompany death, and one tightening to save strength for a Spring that never comes; three rappers, one chart-topping, genre-redefining, performing as a hologram in a concert occurring simultaneously worldwide, one collaborating with the former in a song that holds the number one spot in American charts for a week, and one performing in the mirror (only for you) of their downstairs bathroom. And, no, Satomi isn't sure what it's about. The poem *might* be a pledge to a book she fell in love with as a thirteen-year-old, a book she found in her high school library, a book that (for reasons she's never understood) beats synchronized with her soulful arrhythmia. The poem *might* hold your hand or cup your face or stare you in the eyes, a poem that might give you a bridge to nowhere, but a solid bridge to stand on. A poem not to hide from, dear reader, it's a poem for you. There's nothing to get. Be a postal worker, be a drunk, be a steelworker, be a boxer, be a ballerina, be the insomniac Satoshi who aspired to own a bookshop that would host the great thinkers of his age, and here's the poem for you. I tried at least, she thinks. Not everyone will be Borges. The shelf continues falling. The Earth shudders. There is a comment someone posted beneath her poem. It reads, *I love this so much. It reminds me of Shuji Terayama.* Her poem has seven likes. She cranes her neck to try and avoid the heavy shelf. There're worse ways to die, she thinks, though I should have shown my parents the poem. But perhaps this personhood isn't the end of me, and as this shelf falls, maybe a correlative tectonic plate rises off the coast of South America, somewhere in the Pacific, and as my last breath fails to fill my lungs, my rocky peak will emerge from the waves. I may come to host tropical flowers, coconut trees, endangered tigers. The earthquake stops. Satoshi calls out to Satomi. A hand shoots up from the pile of books beneath the shelf. It waves in the percolating dust. "I'm okay! I'm okay! I'm okay!"

Benjamin McPherson Ficklin will never surrender—Benjamin McPherson Ficklin will always love you. They are the author of the chapbook *A Cynical View of Dystopian America*. Their work has been published in *Lomography, wildness, Ursus Americanus Press, Cheap Pop, STORGY, Clackamas Literary Review, Tahoma Literary Review, Autre, Oregon Voice Magazine,* and recognized in *Best Small Fiction 2019* and *Best American Essays 2020*.

Roo Vandegrift

It Feels Good to be Friendly

A long, dark, empty freeway somewhere in Idaho confronts me, and Virginia feels about as far away as Timbuktu. Mountains all around, but I'm driving on a ramrod straight two-lane highway down the flattest valley I've ever seen. This 'more direct' route is starting to feel like a bad idea—should have stayed on the 30—but the chance to cut off a hundred miles or so seemed too good to pass up. Why did I decide to *drive* home this summer? And (perhaps more importantly) why did I leave it until the last possible day to start the trip back to grad school?

The stars were shining brightly a couple of hours before, but now they're occluded by gathering, thickening clouds. There was a shooting star as the clouds came in, slower than I would've thought possible, and green as a cat's eye. All I can see now is the stream of yellowish light thrown in front of me by the headlights, which catch drops of rain like insects pinned to cardboard, holding them for a single instant, immobilized, frozen, dead. It's hypnotizing, watching the rain stick in the headlights, then disappear; listening to the wipers thump, thump, thump.

I catch myself drifting, nodding off just a bit. Tires on the rumble strip bring me back to full alertness; the rain is get-ting harder, crashing against the windshield faster than the wipers can clear. But the road is still straight, empty, easy, and I'm still behind schedule, so I turn up the radio, pushing Bob Dylan into the rain ("*...I'm not sleepy and there is no place I'm going to...*").

A flash of lightning and near-immediate crash of thunder bring me back to the road and dispel any illusions that the rain is getting lighter. I was nodding off again. Dylan's still singing, but it sounds like a different song. Fear of dying on a rain-soaked highway in the middle of nowhere keeps my eyes open, but just barely. Maybe I should pull over, wait for the storm to pass; I can't really see anything through the lashing rain.

Suddenly, after God-knows how long, a gravel pull-off rears into my lights a few feet ahead, and I jam the breaks, pulling over, afraid of overshooting in the rain and the dark. There's a crunch, and I'm jolted hard against the seatbelt; the headlights are momentarily blindingly bright against *something*, and I think, "Oh God, I'm going to crash!" —and then the car is still, and the headlights illuminate nothing but rain. I sigh and lay back; I don't even remember turning off the car.

When I open my eyes again, it's to squint against the glare of early morning sun. The dashboard clock reads 07:02, and I have to pee so badly I wonder if I've somehow absorbed some of the thousands of gallons of rain that were pouring onto the car last night, by some sort of mystic osmosis. Silly.

I climb out, stumbling a bit, stiff from sleeping in the driver's seat and bleary-eyed from not enough sleep. My head feels like my hair was trying to work its way into my brain through the back of my skull while I slept. I piss what feels like a gallon into the ditch, the color letting me know I've drunk way too much coffee in the last few days, and not nearly enough water: sort of like aged whiskey. I lose myself for a moment in the pleasure of relieved stress, looking up into the crystal blue sky. Strangely, this seems to relieve the squeezed feeling on my brain, and as I zip up, I feel almost good. Ready to get back on the road again, at any rate.

I look around, really for the first time, and realize that the terrain is really different from the last thing I remember driving through. It doesn't feel right, and I'm having trouble placing why. The mountains are lower, and closer; I am tempted to say that they are *brooding*, but really, they're just dark, an effect of the low sun. Behind the car is better; the peaks catch the rays of the sun, showing blue-green up rounded flanks, line after line of large hills or small mountains disappearing into the distance, with the road I'm parked on twisting up the valley between them, two lanes of pot-holes fading into the morning mist. I remember the road as straight, but maybe it was just the rain, making me drive so slowly it seemed straight.

Obscurely troubled, I get back into my old blue Subaru and pull out onto the asphalt. The road curves gently back and forth, almost hypnotically, slowly climbing out of the valley. It's a full fifteen minutes before I'm bothered enough (or maybe awake enough) to pull my iPhone out of my pocket to check the GPS. Where the hell am I? This can't be the same road I was trying to short-cut through last night—I must have missed a turn-off in the rain and was now climbing into the foothills of the Rockies, or something. But it feels wronger than that, somehow. And my phone is dead: searching for service all night. Great.

I pull over again, this time just onto the shoulder, and yank open the glovebox, spilling maps all over the floor of the passenger's seat. For a second I'm angry, white-hot furious, with nothing and nobody. *Fucking* Idaho. I take a deep breath, and decide that maybe I should eat something, stop worrying about being late for the first day of class, and just figure out how to get back to the 30, or the 84, or whichever highway will be impossible to get lost on.

After a cardboardesque Cliff Bar and a slug of yesterday's coffee, I collect all the spilt maps into my lap, then sort through them looking for Idaho, the lingering pounding of my headache adding an obscure urgency to the search. The last one in the stack, of course. Fucking Idaho. I throw the rest of the maps onto the passenger seat and unfold Idaho, finding US30/I84, where it turns south towards Utah. Somewhere around there, the GPS on my phone had suggested the less traveled, but potentially more direct, route into Utah and past Salt Lake. But I don't see anything that looks right here; I turn the map over a couple of times, looking for a blow-up of the area I think I'm in, and don't find one.

I look at the key and see that this is one of the roadmaps my mother gave me before I started school: dated 1986. I shake my head, trying to clear some of the cobwebs and kinks from last night, feeling like I'm in some sort of fugue. Feels like I've been driving for weeks, and it's only the second day.

I pull back onto the road, heading east, squinting into the sun. At least that's the right direction, even if it's the wrong way. Nearly an hour goes by without anything but logging roads and trees. This part of the road is a green tunnel, with trees blocking views of the mountains on both sides. I'm contemplating the way the morning sunlight slices through the gaps to blind me every time I round a curve when I realize what's been bothering me since I woke up.

These trees have leaves.

They're oaks, maples, that sort of thing. In Idaho? Shouldn't this be a dry pine forest? It doesn't feel right. And I don't remember having driven through any forest like this on the way west in the spring. Though a summer can change a landscape drastically, I know that. But—leaves! I wonder why I didn't think about it before, because now I can't stop thinking about it. Fucking *leaves*. And then the smallness, the closeness, of the landscape hits me again: what happened to the broad valleys and ridiculously tall mountains? I think I should be able to at least catch glimpses of some of the big peaks around, as I drive.

As my unease is peaking, I come around a bend to see one side of a mountain totally denuded, with parked equipment waiting patiently for their operators to come back. Huge earth moving vehicles that I don't even know the names for sit beside a mountain that looks like it's slowly being eaten away. Or quickly being eaten away, I think as the full scale of the operation comes into view. It's like they're removing the top of the mountain, to get at something precious hidden within. Then the trees come back to blot it all out, save the little square of my rearview mirror.

I'm still looking mostly in my rearview when the gas station appears around the next bend in the road, so I almost miss it. I screech in, pulling into one of the pumps because I have no idea where the next place I can fill up will be. I sit for a minute, feeling strange, lost, confused, before remembering that I need to get out and pump my own gas here. I'd hoped to ask the attendant for directions back to the interstate. I guess I can ask inside when I pay.

As I fumble with the gas cap, I read the price and am amazed how cheap the gas is: It's nearly fifty cents down from the last time I stopped, somewhere near Boise. I fill up, feeling better and worse at the same time about paying so much less for gas, then walk inside to pay. By the door there's a display of roadmaps. Ah ha! I can update mine, and maybe not have to ask for directions from the extraordinarily large man eating, with much gusto, a sausage and egg biscuit behind the counter. I spin the display, looking for the most detailed one they have, and then simply looking for an Idaho map. West Virginia, West Virginia, Virginia, Maryland, a couple more West Virginias, one for Kentucky, and one at the bottom for Ohio. I stare, feeling more lost than I've felt since I woke up. I must have been looking more concerned than I thought I was (not that I wasn't concerned), because the fat man puts down his breakfast and yells, "Hey buddy, you okay?" at me.

I look up, and make a conscious effort to straighten up and breathe. "Yeah, I'm fine. I was just looking at your maps, trying to figure out which one I need. But maybe I should just ask you for directions. How do I get back to the interstate from here?"

He gives me a funny look.

"I'm sorry, I've basically been driving all night. I was trying to take a short-cut, and got a bit turned around in that storm..." He's still looking at me like something he pulled off the bottom of his shoe, so I ask again, "How do I get back to the freeway from here?"

"Y'ain't from 'round 'ere, 're ya?"

"No sir, like I said, I've been on the road all day, trying to get back to school in Richmond, Virginia."

"Richmond! M' niece live out thata way."

I wait, expecting this to lead to directions.

Just as I'm deciding to open my mouth to ask again, he goes on, "You musta taken a mighty strange short-cut thar, fell'r. But, best way out thataway'll be take Claypool Road," and I must have looked confused again, because he adds, "that's this one 'ere yer on. Take 'er up to State Route 20 then hang a hard right and that'll take ya down to I64 but ya cain't get on thar you gotta head left at Elton; follar the road nex' ta th' in'erstate up a good piece and you'll be able to get on when you see a trail'r park. Ya got all that?"

I nod.

"Well, g'luck fell'r!" And he goes back to his greasy looking breakfast, and I go back to my car. Just as I'm opening the door, I hear him yelling, and I turn around, realizing that I never paid. I walk back and pay, ignoring his idle conversation, only hearing his accent.

How the *hell* did I get to West Virginia?

Only after I've been negotiating switchbacks up and over the next ridge do I start to wonder what day it is. I'm in West Virginia, as much as it hurts my head to contemplate, there's no denying it. The trees, the road, the gas station attendant. It doesn't make any sense; how did I get here? I must have driven. What other explanation is there?

What other explanation can there be?

My mind skips back to the pouring rain, the seatbelt cutting into my shoulder; the headlights too bright as I pulled off the road. I shudder, suddenly cold despite the streaming sunlight coming through the windshield. Maybe I'll remember all that driving if I try hard enough, if I rest, if I relax, if I stop thinking about how impossible it all is. If I could only *relax*. Relax.

God, this is ridiculous. And that gets me back to what day it is. My phone's dead, the car's old dashboard clock doesn't say. I was driving across Idaho on Tuesday night, and this, right now, *feels* like Wednesday. But it can't really be. Somehow, knowing the day will make me feel less crazy, one way or the other. If I've been, I don't know, *transported*, I'll know it. Or if I've forgotten the last couple of days, I'll know it. I should feel better either way, right? But I'm uneasy deep inside, in the pit of my stomach, afraid of either answer.

An hour later, and I'm still on Claypool Road, and wishing I'd asked that attendant for more detailed directions. Did I miss a turn? How far can it really be to Route 20? Maybe I should've gone back to sleep after I pissed this morning. Maybe I would've woken up in Idaho.

I take a deep breath, straighten my back, and turn on the radio. I scan stations for a minute, trying to find something that'll soothe my jangling nerves, or help my unease about hopping across the damned continent and not knowing how I did it. It's all country music (big surprise, I guess), but I settle on a station playing something mellow enough that I think it'll help (Johnny Cash singing: "*...stumblin' and fallin' somebody's callin' you're lost on the desert...*"). I relax a bit, driving slowly, feeling like the turns in the road are coming in time with the music, one then another, left and right, driving through a green tunnel of trees, sun shining through the leaves, making a stroboscope on the walls of my poor old Subaru.

After another half hour of this, I'm considering turning around and driving back to the gas station for better directions. Fucking West Virginia. Nothing but winding roads and trees and country music. I turn off the radio, trying to decide if it's really a good idea to turn around. Just as I've decided *yes, I'm gunna do it*, I come around a bend and see an intersection at the bottom of the hill, and a sign telling me "JCT 20, 1/4 MI." I close my eyes, just for a second, and breathe in deeply, saying a thank you in my head to God-knows-what. It's the closest I've come to prayer in years.

There are two buildings facing each other across the intersection: another old gas station with an outdated TEXACO sign, and a run-down looking clapboard building, a diner by the looks of it. I pull into the diner's parking lot next to a couple of muddy pick-ups and a beat-up old jeep, thinking it'd be a good place to ask for more detailed directions. When I get out of the car, I'm hit in the face by the smell of frying bacon, and I realize I'm starving.

Inside, it's dark and full of cigarette smoke. Everyone, even the woman behind the counter, is smoking. I shake my head, trying not to think about lung cancer, and sit down on a narrow barstool at the front of the little place. There are five stools at the bar, and two little tin-topped tables with vinyl chairs that are a dirty pastel pink/brown now, but clearly started life out as fire-engine red. Both tables are occupied by mud-spattered men with dirt under their nails and grizzled beards. They're eating piles of scrambled eggs and drinking Bud Light, talking in quiet voices in accents so thick I couldn't eavesdrop if I wanted to. There's one other fellow sitting at the bar, and he looks like he's been there since the night before. He's nursing a Bud Light too, and has a breakfast plate (scrambled eggs, bacon, hash browns) in front of him that looks entirely untouched and stone cold. His eyes are closed, and I can't tell if he's asleep.

"How y'doin', sweetie?"

Startled, I look up at the waitress. She's older than I thought when I came in, maybe in her mid-forties, with too much makeup on. She holds her cigarette between the fingers of her left hand, blood-red lipstick on the butt, her right hand on her hip, her head cocked. She looks at me in a way that says *I can tell you ain't from around here.*

"I'm doing okay, I guess. Been a weird morning, though."

"Ain't it always, honey. Coffee?" Her teeth are stained a dirty yellow; her voice is low and burred, like a vacuum cleaner in the next room. All the smoking, I think.

"God, yes."

She smiles and looks years younger for it. "You wantin' br'fast, dear?"

"Yeah, that'd be great. Can I have... whatever he had?" I say, pointing at the possibly sleeping fellow at the other end of the bar with my thumb.

She pulls a pen and ticket pad from her apron, writing as she says, "Br'fast plate with bacon, hashbrowns. Sure thang, son. You want anything else? A beer?"

I look around, just noticing that it's not just some of the people drinking with breakfast, but *all* of them. Fucking West Virginia. I shake my head. "No, that's okay." She starts to turn away, heading back to what I assume is the kitchen. "But..." She stops, looking at me expectantly, and I find it's hard to continue. "Can, can... Can you tell me what day it is?"

She looks confused. "The day, honey?"

"Yeah, like, is it Wednesday?"

"I don' think so, but you know... I ain't rightly sure. I think it's Thursday." She nods, with authority, and then marches through a set of swinging doors into the kitchen to cook my eggs.

I sit in the smoke, thinking about Thursday. If it's Thursday, and I drove like a bat out of hell all night and all day Wednesday, *maybe* I could have made it here. Maybe. But what if it's Wednesday? She wasn't sure. She didn't know. I turn around and look at the men sitting smoking their cigarettes and drinking their beers behind me. One of them looks up at me.

"Hey man, you don't know what day it is, do you?" I ask.

He looks a bit surprised that I've addressed him. "It's Friday, I reckon. Hey Jimmy, it's Friday, ain't it?"

His companions break off their conversation and look at him, then at me. "Naw," says one, "it's Thursday."

"Thursday?" says the other, "what'n'Ell're you smokin', Joe? It's fuckin' Winsday."

"But I thought it were Friday," says the first man.

"Does it matter?" says the other, a bit petulantly, "You go work that damn tractor every day, regardless, 'cept Sundays, and it sho' ain't Sunday."

"'S true."

"So shuddup 'n' eat yer damn eggs, Bob, so we can get back to work."

And they all go back to eating and pay me no more mind.

I sit dumbfounded. Maybe it doesn't matter to them at all, but it matters to *me*. I watch them eat for several minutes, not able to even look away, struck by the utter ridiculousness of it. No one knows the day of the week? I want to scream. My gut feels tied into such a knot, I can hardly breathe. I open my mouth, then close it again when no sound comes out. The smoke is suddenly oppressive, and I desperately need fresh air. Or to know what *fucking day it is*.

I am just about to interrupt again, angrily, when the waitress comes back with my food. "Here you go, honey," she says, setting it down in front of me, sloshing a bit of coffee onto the bar top. "And I think it's Friday today. It's so hard to keep track out here, every day bein' about t' same's t' next, y'know?"

"Indeed," I say, believing her, feeling obscurely relieved, like a rubber band stretched between my temples has snapped. I try to imagine what it would be like to not care about the day of the week at all, unless it was Sunday, and to drink beers with breakfast. In the end, I can't really do it.

After I eat the greasy eggs, I get out of the diner as fast as I can. I walk across the road to the gas station, intending to buy a newspaper. Unequivocal date on a newspaper. I go in, get a Coke for the road, and walk up to the front. There are two paper racks to the left of the counter, behind which a pimply kid in a Pantera t-shirt is reading a porno mag and loudly chewing gum. I reach into the first, pulling the paper up so I can read the top. The picture on the front is a full-color aerial shot of a complex set of crop circles. "FOUR NEW CROP CIRCLES!" reads the headline, then in smaller type, "Teenager suspected, denies charges."

Across the very top it says "The Danese Moniter, Wednesday Aug. 22nd."

I put it down on top of the kid's magazine, maybe a bit more forcefully than necessary. "Is this today's paper?" I must've said it a little less calmly than intended, because he takes a step back, bumping into the rack of cigarettes behind him.

"Y-yeah, man, yeah. Why, what? What's wrong with it?"

"It says Wednesday!" I don't mean to yell. I don't think I am, until I hear my own voice, alien and loud in my ears. More quietly I ask, "Is it really Wednesday?"

"Naw, man, it's a bi-weekly. Next one's out on Saturday. Tomorrow." I don't think I've ever seen anyone scared like that before; or, at least, not scared of *me*.

I leave the Coke and the paper on the counter, and walk out of the gas station, breathing hard. When I go to wipe the sweat off my face, I notice my hand is shaking. I was calm, until I saw that date, and then I was crazy. But it isn't today; today's Friday. Waitress said it. Kid said it. So why do I still feel so crazy?

I get back into my car, lean back, and close my eyes, letting the sweat drip down my face, pooling in my closed eyes, dripping down my neck; my head throbs. I breathe deeply, trying to calm down. It still doesn't make sense.

Eventually, I rub a hand over my face, and it's steady this time. I run my fingers back through my hair, noticing a sore spot on the back of my head, noticing that I need a haircut. The dashboard clock reads 10:10. I start the car, pulling out onto Route 20 carefully, turning left to follow it south, towards the interstate, towards home, maybe towards some sanity.

After about an hour of being finally back on the interstate, nearing the Virginia border, I start to feel a bit better. My dashboard clock tells me it's just after two in the afternoon. I drove across the country, and have some amnesia, for some reason. *Perfectly normal.* Sure.

As I drive, I absentmindedly push my hair back from my eyes, and find that sore spot on the back of my head again. It feels a bit rough, under the hair. I could have hit my head, maybe when I pulled off the road in Idaho. That would explain the lack of memory, maybe. I should probably go see a doctor when I get back to school: A concussion bad enough to cause memory loss is supposed to be pretty bad, I think. At least, I think I read that somewhere.

I fiddle with the sore spot as I drive, listening to the radio. I've finally found a station that's not country (David Bowie sings: "...*this is major Tom to ground control, I'm stepping through the door...*"), thank God. Miles pass, and I sing along, thinking I can actually just forget about the crazy way today has gone. I go to punch up the volume on the radio, and I notice that the volume button is wet when my finger comes away. I look down at my hand and see blood on my finger.

I'm fascinated, and horrified. Where did it come from? I touch the back of my head again, and find it wet, my fingers come away covered in blood this time. I swerve, not looking at the road, horrified by the blood on my fingers. I look back up, straighten out, and suddenly the radio sounds sinister ("...*your circuit's dead, there's something wrong / Can you hear me, Major Tom?...*"). I turn it off, looking for a place to pull over, and something to stop the bleeding from the back of my head. I pull a crumpled napkin from the door pocket, throw it on the floor when I see how dirty it is. I can feel the blood starting to drip down the back of my neck now. I dig further and find a small stack of unused fast-food napkins. I press them to my skull with one hand, driving with the other, searching for a place to pull over.

A sign tells me "Rest area, 5 mi ahead" and I speed up, just wanting to get there as quickly as possible, a growing sense of panic in my gut. When I pull in, the lot is full. I park on the gravel to one side, not locking the car, barely remembering to close the door as I sprint for the bathroom. When I pull the napkins from my head, they're soaked through with blood, starting to dry and crust on the edges, bright scarlet in the center, with hairs stuck to the scabbing bits towards the outside.

I'm panicked. I push my way through the line for the urinals, pull a handful of paper towels from the dispenser and press them to my head, throwing out the napkins. Then I pull out another fistful and take them to the sink, running water over them, and use that to try to wash my head. I'm as near tears as I've been in years, since my grandfather died.

As I'm blotting my head with alternately wet and dry paper towels, trying to see if the bleeding's lessening, someone I didn't notice standing behind me puts a hand on my shoulder. I yell, screaming in real fear, and jump back violently, surprised and terrified, feeling like a cornered animal. I look at him with wide eyes, still pressing the bloody paper towels to my head.

"Whoa, buddy! I just wanted to see if you're okay: I'm a nurse."

Feeling embarrassed and relieved, I step back to the sink, and tell him I'm okay, but that I hit my head a couple of days ago; I apologize for being jumpy. He tells me his name is Stan, and asks if he can have a look, giving me a sharp, reptilian grin. I feel strange about it, but I tell him okay, and he steps over, gently parts my hair, and takes the damp paper towels from me, gently mopping the back of my head while I stare down the drain in the sink.

"Looks like you picked open a pretty good scab. How'd you say you got this?"

"I—" I don't want to tell him that I couldn't remember. "I took a tumble playing soccer the other day, didn't really hurt too much then." I feel bad lying.

"Huh. I wonder what you hit; this wound is perfectly round."

"..."

"Well, at any rate, you should keep pressure on it for a bit longer, but I think the bleeding's mostly stopped. Scalp wounds, you know: bleed like stuck pigs, if you'll pardon the expression."

"I have heard that," I say, trying to think of a way to thank him, and wondering what it means to have a perfectly circular scab on the back of my head that I don't remember getting. "Uh, thanks Stan. Er, Nurse Stan?"

He laughs, holds out his hand. "Just Stan. You take care of yourself now, okay?" His hand is cool and dry, his grip firm; I think, for just a moment, of red sands and a thin, howling wind, and I don't know why. "And don't go bumping your head around anymore, okay?"

"Yeah, sure," I say as he walks out of the bathroom. I stare into my own eyes in the mirror. People stream around me, no one wanting to talk to the bleeding man staring at his own reflection, and I feel somehow like I'm looking at someone else. Someone I don't know at all, and someone who doesn't like me very much.

Back on the highway it's a struggle not to finger the sore spot, the scab, on the back of my head. I turn on the radio again, hoping for distractions, wanting to get that last line from David Bowie ("*...can you hear me Major Tom?...*") out of my mind, which is all I can think when I stop thinking about the perfectly circular wound on the back of my head. The station I was on is playing some shitty pop-rock song, so I flip stations till I come to someone talking.

It's local news: Someone won a small pot of money in the lottery from whatever little town is broadcasting this. Then a story about the rash of crop circles that showed up during the storm the other night, the same ones that were in the newspaper I almost bought this morning. I wince at the memory of yelling at the poor clerk. An interview with the kid they arrested for it. He denies it categorically, but without any eloquence, just repetition; no real explanation of what he was doing instead. Then it switches to national news, Associate Press pieces, the War on Terror, 12 US soldiers killed in a suicide bombing in Afghanistan. A rash of UFO sightings in the Northwest, thrown in, I suspect, to lighten the mood after the stories about the horrors of war. A story about heavy rains and flooding the other day in Wyoming and Idaho, dumb kids swept away trying to swim in suddenly full drainage ditches.

And then a little story about a car accident in Idaho. "The badly burned remains of a blue Subaru station wagon were discovered in rural Idaho, just north of the Utah border, this morning. The vehicle appears to have lost control and crashed during heavy rains on Tuesday night. Authorities suspect that the fire was lit after the storm had abated, potentially by a late lightning strike. The vehicle was discovered by a local farmer, who says that he regrets that he did not find the vehicle the day of its accident. The vehicle had Oregon license plates, and the driver's body has not yet been recovered, though it could have been consumed in the unusually intense fire, authorities say."

I switch off the radio, and, despite myself, finger the perfectly round scab on the back of my head. It feels rough, sticky, angry. I drive for the next hour in silence, trying not to think of anything at all, but coming back to that news story. There must be hundreds, no *thousands*, of blue Subaru station wagons with Oregon plates out there. Thousands of them. Just a coincidence. And, if that'd been me, then what am I driving now?

It's just starting to get dark as I park in front of my house in Richmond, happier to be home than I've ever been in my life. Back to grad school, back to work, and I can forget about this crazy trip. Matt, my housemate, helps me unload the car, and I tell him I'm thinking about trading it in, getting something newer.

"I thought you loved that old Subaru?"

"I thought I did too, but something about this trip has made me feel a bit apprehensive about it. Maybe I should get something with better airbags."

"Hmmm." That's all.

I don't trade in the car, though, because I get caught up in work, in research, in classes, in teaching. And Virginia in the winter is even more miserable than Oregon in the winter: It's colder, and everything's dead, and it still rains a lot. Sometimes it even snows, and then it's nice to have the four-wheel drive of the old Subaru. I do get it re-painted though, a nice bright green. But I try not to drive anymore unless I really have to.

After that trip, I spend a lot of my spare time on the computer, looking at news from the days I'm missing, hoping something would jog a memory. Nothing does, but I do learn that there were UFO sightings all around the edges of that storm system that caused such flooding in Idaho and Wyoming, the one that I got caught in that Tuesday night. Those sightings were pretty universally laughed off, but it was noted all over the internet that it was the densest cluster of independent reports of UFOs since Roswell in the late 1940's. And that the West Virginian kid they were blaming for the crop circles was eventually cleared, because one of his friends came forward and told the cops that they'd been smoking weed together that night. They both got fines, but nothing worse. And those crop circles showed up at about the same time I pulled over in Idaho, Tuesday night, or early Wednesday morning, and they never figured out who made them.

I don't know what to think anymore. I went to a doctor about my head, and he told me I'd taken a nasty bump. He didn't want to stitch it up, though, because of how much it'd already healed. When I told him that I couldn't really remember how I'd gotten it, and that I had some amnesia, he scheduled me for a CT scan, but it all looked normal.

So mostly, I try not to think about it.

Frost in the air, dry leaves under foot. I like walking at night in the old cemetery in autumn—something about the old gravestones and the fallen leaves and the crispness of the air. Late fall is about the only tolerable time of year in Richmond, honestly. I walk to the top of the hill, find a friendly looking sarcophagus and climb on top of it. I lean back, talking softly to my dead host, knowing he can't really hear me, but it feels good to be friendly, even to a dead man. Formalities over, I put my hands behind my head, looking up at the stars. What is up there, I wonder?

I finger the scar on the back of my head and stare up at the stars.

Roo Vandegrift is a queer mycologist and illustrator. He grew up on the coal fields of southern Appalachia, before heading West to complete his PhD in fungal ecology at the University or Oregon, where he fell in with queerdos and anarchists. He writes science fiction when he's not writing science. He is currently producing a documentary film about mining and conservation issues in Ecuador called *Marrow of the Mountain.*

Xuan Nguyen

The Divine Do Not Live on the First Floor

First appeared in Nectar Poetry

I. But from here,
I can see the door.
I can see the floor

of the first divide
before the heavens' demise,
I will be the snake that swallows heaven wholly,
I will swallow it holy,
I will swallow it: Holy.)

II. But from here,
there is no more
than the gild
that surrounds me.

Starling in a cage,
who will you be?
What will you sing?
(Can you hear the fairies sing,
each to each?
Seed to futile seed?)
They will never find the green.

III. I have seen it.
But I am a star in a cage.
A house in the fen,
IF, WHERE, AND WHEN.
I grew up in this swamp,
a boy watching
silken tree breeding silken moth,
cocoons unraveling in clever fey-fingers,
who sold their silks
with bells and dead-ringers.

IV. In the Silverwood of
the Crescent Court
banking the swamp,
I first saw red.
I first raw fed.

(When I rose from the remnants
of viscera,
my belly full of roses,

The way the fairies looked at me
was the way birds look
at birds of a feather.)
V.   One day, I heard the fairies sing,
A bird is a bird is a worm,
upon the firmament of the kingdom of heaven.
I held firm:
I will be a serpent, if I must be a worm.

VI.   Unlike the fey,
I have seen.
I have found the green.
Severin, oh, Severin.
You know that the heavens
will not win.
I will be
Ouroboros me.

VII.   Chevalier Lacandola,
Will you do more than--
plead. When you know.
When you know what I am.
Inimitable,
unforgivable,
and everlastingly
destined to be
forgotten.

The world will not remember me.
I have made art: I have a legacy
of ripe blood, milk petal, and star scale.

But there have been others before me.
And there will be others after me.

None the same,
but the same.

VIII. I may die forgotten,
but it doesn't matter.

It doesn't matter, as long as I am seen
by Holy.

Holy is a mirror.
Holy is what I will become.
Holy is what I have won,
and which you were given
from the heavens,

SEVEN, SEVEN, SEVERIN.

IX. In Holy, I will find:
the shed-gold of gilt cage,
the silver-eye of silk pearl,
a mouth of venomous design,

And a fate to match mine.

X.   A fate to match mine—
we shall see in time
who becomes Divine.

On a Night Alone, I Have Nothing But My Own

There is nothing more beyond the door.
There is no kingdom of gods, no wonder, no more.

There is never going to be an Empress of Heaven. There
was never before, and it will never be *then*, I will never
find *IF, WHERE, AND WHEN*, I will never reach *HERE,*
THERE, AND THEN.

There is no such thing as Holy, and I will never know home.

I dream of a house on stilts in the swamp. I dream of a
Becoming.

This house of mine is one of emperatorial design. A palace
for a lost god. A memoriam to the blood of my blood, the
ancestors of my ancestors. An Empress of the Last. An
Empress of Glass. I do not want my house to be over-
run by glass, not like the cage I am in, the cage I will die
within. The gilt veneer is tarnished by now.
In my house in the swamp,
there is a deck, also on stilts, where I look at the mercurial

fey, liquid-limb to liquid-limb, singing, and always having
their way. The fey are divine, and in time, I, too, would
have learned divinity.

But in my starling's nest now, oh, can I only see: The End.

I will never live long enough to see IF, WHERE, AND WHEN
I could have contrived an escape, fashioned a key out of
hairpin and jade to leave the gold bed, the shimmering
cage. Oh, how, now, watch the starling sing—she does not
sing like men, she does not sing of here, or everthen, she
sings of Holy, but Of Holy, there nothing left.

There are no gods above. There is nothing to become.

With a deft enough hand, I could've shaken it. She, Amade-
us-Her, could have left the gods in a sparkling fireplume
of their own dry, glittering dust.

But my hands no longer know the weight of scalpel. My
hands no longer hold god inside them.

I know only now,
the ill comforts of the sickbed.

Rich and red,
and red and gold,
lucky colors, for one lucky enough
to never grow old.

I still yet have time, they will say.

He died in his prime,
He could've recovered someday,
they will say of Amadeus Vu.

But you and I, you and I, dear Holiness,
will know better.

Will you bring my body to the first floor
of the KINGDOM OF HEAVEN,
Fairy Sovereign? Lady, Lord?

If the door opens for me,
then I will see: I was wrong.

I was wrong, and there will always be
a hyacinth-shade of me: no legacy, forgotten.

Do You Know What Happens When You Cannot Find the Kingdom of the Divine

What happens is that there is nothing more, there is no sublime, there is nothing that will save you, nothing that will come in time. But do you know, when you find yourself on earthen floor, drinking honeysuckle, peach, lilydine; eating moss, dewberry, lime; swallowing orchid, lichen, ulamine. What happens is that you find the woods.

The Crescent Court waits for you,
you who the world has sundered
in two, cleft in twain like an apple

beneath the butcher's knife.

You are not the surgeon anymore,
AMADEUS VU.

You are a stonefruit, heartsplit, beneath the woodsman's ax.
Relax, relax, AMADEUS VU, *isn't it all you ever wanted? Isn't it*

a relief from responsibility? All you have to do now is relax,
     and rest up,
UNTIL THE DAY YOU DIE.

(and they wonder why you tried to kill yourself.)
AMADEUS VU, peekaboo,
you found me, you found me!

[Now, what can I do for you?]

Please, Lady—Lord. Please havemercy. Have mercy.
And let me into the night garden, *you said with a glint.*

[Whatever will you do in there?]
[It is not a place for your kind.]

And what is that? you spat.

[Why don't you tell me?]

Born sick from seed, raised well, but rotting from silkstomach,
     milkliver, lacelung. Thirty-five years of health. *And then no*
     more,
the wealth of life—*forgotten, rotten, rotten*—and sick forev-
     ermore.

I was not like the others. My mother was not like their
    mothers.
My egg came out cracked, *shattered in a way you'll never get
    back.*
There was always something wrong with me, you see. But
    no one knew.
Except the fairy few.

[So you'd like to be born anew? What will my lilies do for
    you?]

I am what I am, and what I have always been.
Show me the door to the heavens, the first floor
to the Kingdom of Gods.
Havemercy, Lady. Lord?

[Either-or.]

You can be the Lady of the Last, and I'll be the Lady of
    Glass.

[Will you shatter beneath me today? I'll hold you sweetly,

and we can play
amidst glowing white lily,
stargazing moon.

The dew of jade,
and the planetary tide,
rising so soon.
I'll feast on your flesh,
and in my flesh,

You will become Holy.]

Not today, Lady. You cannot have me today.

[What shall I do for you until then,
pretty, pretty AMADEUS VU?]

(your breath caught so beautifully when you knew:
through a death by divine consumption,
you could reach more than the first floor
to the kingdom of heaven.)
I swear to you,
if you let me live another day,
you may suck the marrow out of my bones,
and string pearl into my guts, roasting hazelnut
on a fire of my flesh.

[Then what shall I do for you today?]

Find me another way to live.

[It won't be easy. And the pain will never go away. And you
    will be
devastatingly, devastatingly tired.]

But it will be better than this. Better than what mortal medicine,
mortal hands could give. None of them gave me a way
to live. They all said I wouldn't.
They talked about someday
I might simply wake up,
get better.

But more often they said
I'd see heaven.

[Have you ever heard
of SEVEN, SEVEN?]

No, Lady.

[We moon-folk live by the sway
of SEVEN, SEVEN.

It guarantees we shall all see the heavens.
It's what falls from them. Sublime, sublime.

In time, you shall see it, too.
Look for a man named Severin.]

What does that have to do with this?

[You are a man between worlds.
Dead and alive. Celestial heaven and cursed earth.

SEVEN are the seconds you spend on earth.
SEVEN are the seconds you spend in heaven.

You have spent much longer here, already.
Just remember what you will pay

for the Fairy Sovereign to send you back a different way.]

Lady,
because of you,
I live anew.

[Let's just see you don't regret it.]

Xuan Nguyen is a disabled and transgender writer and artist who does music as FEYXUAN. They focus on the intersections between transgender identity, divinity + monstrosity, and stigmatized mental and physical health. Their work has appeared in *Prismatica Magazine*, *Rogue Agent*, and *beestung*, and they have two chapbooks published, *The Fairies Sing Each to Each* (Flower Press) and *Lung, Crown, and Star* (Lazy Adventurer Publishing).

Alyssa Gonzalez

Life of the Mind

The convenience store clerk leaned on his elbow, idly spinning a yo-yo, eyes glazed. The yo-yo released five yo-yos of its own at the end of each spin, a show he seemed to find uninteresting. Outside, a disorienting array of neon lights clashed with the setting suns, lurid blue and green against the pinkish sky. A woman in a pencil skirt, deep blue blouse, black bowtie, and black peep-toe heels strode into the store, and the electronic bell of the glass door's movement snapped him to attention. As he opened his mouth in rehearsed greeting, she arrived at his counter, raised a small wallet-like pad of paper, and cut him off before his first word.

"Dr. Karen Almirola, Rollaven District Sanitation Inspector, third class, first degree, *matalovu cor Dundalita,* I need to see your storeroom, please," she recited in one breath. The paper corroborated her details.

"We're not due for our next inspection for another three eclipse cycles," he protested. After a moment's realization, he added, "and that's not the next callsign."

"Look, friend," Karen answered, leaning forward a bit and letting her dense brown curls hang over the counter. "There's something going on in that room, and I need to inspect it for your safety and that of the whole Rollaven District, maybe even the rest of the planet. You can make your little scene about the gamma scrats you haven't been keeping down like you told your boss you would, or you can let me in and deal with the thing before it gets you first."

The man looked like he was about to confusedly protest again when another woman burst into the store and immediately locked the door behind her. Catching her breath, she was scared into backing away into a store display a minute later by a screaming crowd pounding on the door waving miscellaneous items bearing her likeness. Here, she wore olive green leggings, a black tank top, expensive running shoes, a green pearl necklace, and a series of black linework designs on her forehead, accentuating her brows, but in the images, she wore elaborate evening gowns, saris, and abundant, extravagant jewelry as well as her facial ink. She kept backing away, knocking over the display and pushing another aside. The clerk gawped in astonishment and stammered helplessly, raising a shaky hand to point at her.

At the counter, the first woman raised a finger and then rushed to the second, catching her before she could tumble into another shelf.

"Easy, easy," Karen whispered. "I'm here to help."

"They won't stop chasing me," the second woman gasped. "They started as soon as I stepped outside, and they won't stop. I need to get away. I need—" She scrambled to her feet and out of Karen's arms, and only refrained from bolting toward the back-alley door when Karen called out, "Someplace to hide? I have one of those."

The woman paused, pleading in her eyes.

"Come on," Karen continued, putting a hand gently on the woman's back. "Let's get you out of here."

The clerk watched dumbfounded as Karen led the woman out through the back door. As the door creaked shut behind them, he muttered, "I locked that door."

"What did you say your name was?" the woman asked Karen, looking around nervously in the dirty but sunlit alley.

"I didn't," Karen answered, "but you can call me Karina Ruiz."

The woman looked confused, and Karina didn't elaborate. Instead, a linework glove of magenta light coalesced around Karina's left hand, and she gestured at the door, which unlatched itself, swinging gently open. Two bright green batlike creatures the size of cats bounded out of the door on their knuckles and flapped into the street, leaving puffs of green powder behind, and Karina shook her head sardonically. "It's always gamma scrats around here. These folks never seem to get rid of them." She gestured for the woman to follow her, and hesitantly, she did. Navigating by her hand-light, Karina looked around for a few minutes and then excitedly raised a large plastic suitcase. Motioning for the woman to exit, Karina returned to the alley and closed the door behind her as the glowing lines faded out.

"What's that?" the woman asked.

"Something that never should have been left here," Karina intoned, "that will upset the timestream if I don't take it away. I'm just annoyed that he made me go in the back way to get it."

"That's...not really an answer," the woman responded, crossing her arms incredulously.

"No, no it isn't," Karina answered, "but you're not who you want me to think you are, either."

"How did you know?" the woman asked, now seated within Karina's ship in a well-cushioned chair. Opposite her, on the other side of a round table, Karina sat in a similar chair and pushed a magazine toward the woman.

"Deepika Ranjul is a treasure this whole world knows on sight, who's been famous for long enough to know that mobs happen if she takes her morning jogs to the street instead of her usual indoor track," Karina answered, waiting for the woman to look at her own face on the cover. "And you've never heard that name before."

The woman somehow managed to blanch with horror and blush in embarrassment at the same time. "No, I haven't." She fussed with the hem of her top.

"So what kind of interloper takes on the appearance of the most famous person on this entire planet without knowing it?"

The woman who only looked like Deepika Ranjul turned her head and lowered her eyes, rubbing her arm sheepishly.

"As you wish," Karina answered. "Is there somewhere you wanted to go?"

"Nowhere. Anywhere. Just...away from here." She bolted upright at a metallic clanging noise, and slowly relaxed as nothing followed it.

"You'd better get some rest. I'll pick somewhere safe where we can figure out what to do next."

The woman who wasn't Deepika Ranjul lay awake in her cabin. The room was at once clinical and cozy, with plush covers on a bed that looked like it folded out of the slightly shiny gray walls. A small window showed the flaring blue and orange of the ship's travel through space and time. As she closed her eyes, she turned her mind toward old memories.

Spires of gray-green stone, reaching into the moonlit sky from the ocean floor. Lenses for the light concerts down below. Metal arms for water measurements. The porous smoothness of the stone, a delight for weary claws. Shankarasuth's last light concert, before they retired, and the celebration of their life that it became. How expertly they used light attenuation to give the concert layers, to make the deep scattering as meaningful as the shallow clarity. Watching the recording again and again, trying to understand the lives that they had lived.

Her first assignment, to document the sociology of the newest species the Yitorns had discovered. Casting her mind into the Thoughtlines to find a receptive host, entering his body. Silently observing his activities, and then asking him questions in his dreams. Occasionally taking control to examine something he didn't notice and apologizing afterward. Learning his name.

T'toramin the Crafty. The feeling of his many waxy limbs fluttering through dense vegetation to find food. Thanking him for his time with a vision of Shankarasuth's last show. Writing a report that got a lot of attention, and then faded away.

When she met Atanalodh.

She started to cry.

His claws in her mind. The mindknife he held to her most cherished memories. The lavish gifts from distant worlds, precious and irreplaceable. The days he spent riding the Thoughtlines into her and out, each the dreadful wrench of a Yitorn's deepest sin. The smell of his finest pheromones. The way he dangled her professional advancement before her, keeping him around because she'd lose everything if she didn't let him. His ample embrace, at once a comfort and a threat. The echo of his voice, sonorous and deadly. The day he trapped her in herself, just to prove that he could, and lived her life so badly it took her weeks to undo his misdeeds. The day she lost everything.

"*Let me out!*" a voice screamed into her reverie. Her crying only increased. "*Why are you holding me in here!?*"

"*I'm sorry,*" the woman who only looked like Deepika Ranjul sobbed back. "*I'm so sorry.*"

Her sleep was fitful, and she dreamed of claws and saffron.

In the morning, a smell both familiar and new wafted into the room, which did more to wake her than the wan morning sun. She rose, smoothed her clothes, and stepped into the hall. A few steps later, she came to the same table where she had sat the evening before. Karina was collecting deep yellow pancakes from a pan onto a plate. Behind her, a metal tower of a being, marked in black and pink and whose lower portion was covered in metal ruffles like a layered dress, held a tray that still carried the condiments of the unfolding meal. This latter being pointed their eyestalk at her and announced in a harsh mechanical staccato, "SHE IS RISEN."

"Thanks, Mar," Karina answered. "I hope you like methi thepla."

The woman sat, staring at the lightly fried discs of flour and fenugreek in pensive silence.

"IS IT NOT TO YOUR LIKING?" Mar asked, in the same harsh voice. Karina put up a hand, and Mar levitated backward slightly.

"It's familiar because it's Deepika's favorite," Karina explained, sitting down and taking a small bowl of mango chutney from Mar's tray. She placed it between her and the woman, folded a methi thepla into a scoop, and scooped some for a small bite. "That body knows that, even if you don't."

The woman mimicked Karina's motions, and clearly enjoyed what she tasted.

"I'm not going to call you Deepika," Karina insisted as she took another bite, "so you might as well tell me your real name."

The woman hesitated, contemplating her meal for a moment. "Namarula."

"Thank you for telling me that, Namarula." Mar appeared behind Karina with a pitcher of water and some glasses on their tray, and Karina took them.

"I hoped to hide that name forever," she said, pouring herself a glass and quickly finishing her food.

"It's not just the fans you're running from."

"No," Namarula answered, turning sheepish again. "No, it isn't."

"And whoever it is, they scare you enough to take over the body of the first receptive mind you found, and start running even there."

Namarula started crying. "It's worse than that. I broke all of my people's most important rules." She put her face in her hands. "I entered the Thoughtlines unsanctioned, I entered a body without its permission, I suppressed the mind to take total control...but I had to get out. I had to get away. He'll... they'll...there's nowhere left for me."

Karina took Namarula's borrowed hand. "There's a whole *universe* out there for you, and I'm going to get you there."

She looked up at Karina, eyes pleading.

"You don't get to keep holding Deepika, though." There was a hardness in Karina's words and face that didn't fit her gentle voice. "That's something you'll have to answer for."

Namarula looked momentarily frightened. She asked, "Why would you help me, after what I did...after what I'm still doing to Deepika?"

"Right now, I see two people in desperate need, and the way to help you both is to get you somewhere safe."

Namarula hugged Karina, suddenly and tightly. "Thank you."

Karina let her cling for a minute or so, and then answered, "Now, let's get you some fresh air."

"Where are we, anyway?" Namarula asked as she and Karina walked on red-tipped grass just outside Karina's ship, under a greenish sky. Namarula finally got a good look at the exterior, bulky and square, a stark opposite to the curvilinear lady who flew it. The hull bore its name in green paint, the *Light Caller*.

"Planet Lateria, 60,000 years from when we met. Far enough that whatever trick that creature uses to find you should take a while to work again."

"I've never heard of that planet."

"I'm counting on that," Karina answered.

"Oh?"

"Somehow, your pursuer knows where and when you go. Maybe your minds are linked, maybe he can sense your path through the Thoughtlines, but however he's doing it, he needs to know what to do with that information. So if we hide on a planet you've never heard of and know nothing about, at a time and location that are both lies, he can't get that information from you...and if you've never heard of it, chances are, neither has he."

"That...almost makes sense," Namarula answered, looking up at the sky and watching the clouds gently swirl.

"A lot of things about me almost make sense, and the rest, you can talk to Mar about," Karina answered slyly.

"You're a remarkable creature, Karina Ruiz," Namarula remarked, tilting her head and eyeing her rescuer.

"I suspect you are as well, Namarula, but I won't be sure until I know it's just you."

Namarula sat on the ground and clasped her knees. "When a Yitorn studies the same subject for a long time, they leave their mark on us. We come back with a bit of them in us. Phrases, movements, even memories. After a dozen subjects, we're such a jumble that we only make sense to ourselves when we're studying someone, living their life instead of ours, focused on our notes. We call the elders 'collage students.' The art they make about being a collage student is fashionable back in Yitorn present. My favorite light concert was about that...Shankarasuth lived so many lives, it took a whole ocean to show them."

"Most species are little oceans like that," Karina mused. "Everyone we meet touches us somehow, and the memories are remade every time we remember them. We spend a lot of time thinking about the people who made us who we are, and the people who might make us into who we will become. A lot of us start to wonder if our past selves would even recognize who we are now."

Namarula sat still for a long time. "Perhaps we Yitorns aren't so different after all."

A three-eyed froglike creature with a grasshopper's mandibles hopped up to her. She thought it cute until it raised an arm and stabbed her with an invisible blade apparently protruding from its forearm. She screamed in pain and Karina lifted her and tried to shake off her attacker. The blade crackled and flickered, showing its shape as the frog-creature climbed up her leg and torso, each step another invisible stab leaving no wound behind. The stab that took it up to her collarbone came with a telepathic message: *"There's no running from a Saberthought, Namarula."*

Karina stopped the attacker's message with a loud screech from her magenta light-glove. The creature fell off, its mental blades flickering in and out of existence. It skittered away into the grass, and Karina guided Namarula back inside the *Light Caller*.

"Hang on, Namarula," Karina answered. "It's time for us to leave."

The *Light Caller*'s violent lurching lasted only a few minutes, but Namarula didn't let go of her handhold until Karina put a calming hand on her shoulder.

The Yitorn using Deepika Ranjul's body sat down in the same chair, clutching her old water glass and breathing heavily. "Why? He will find me. He always found me then, and he found me now. Lies and distance and he still found me. There's no running from him." She started to rock back and forth. "I shouldn't have let myself hope. *No running from a Saberthought.* That's their motto. That's what's on all of their lintels. That's the catch phrase in their light concerts. That's what they say when they've found someone. *No running from a Saberthought. No running. No…"* She started to cry. "It's going to be like this forever. A little more running, and then the blade. No running from a Saberthought…"

Karina crouched to Namarula's eye level and put her hands on her shoulders while Mar attended to the ship's controls. "Listen to me, Namarula. We are going to get you out of this. You deserve it, and it's what I do."

"*Why?*" Namarula demanded, shaking off Karina's hands. "Why are you so sure I'm worth all this? Atanalodh will come for you, too."

"I've been traveling the universe a long time, Namarula. I've seen more than you can imagine, and the one thing I never stop seeing is the value of an outstretched hand."

"But...maybe I didn't need to take Deepika's body," she protested, looking at the floor and wringing her hands. "Maybe...I could have fought..."

"How *that* part ends depends on how Deepika feels about you when this is all over. Until then, you *got out,* and there's no shame in that."

She looked up.

"The monsters who take hold of us know that making it hard to fight them is only the beginning. It's hard to fight a bear, but a bear will eventually *stop.* The real evil is when they learn to not just make it hard to fight, but also make it hard to run." Karina walked to the other chair and sat down. "Getting away from *that* is an accomplishment, and I hope you never let anyone convince you otherwise."

Namarula was quiet for a few minutes, and then exhaled, "I haven't gotten away yet, though."

Karina smiled. "I have some ideas about that."

Deeper inside the *Light Caller*, Namarula, Karina, and Mar all stood in a tiny, disused room that must have once held guests. Karina knelt on the floor and Namarula followed, while Mar remained vigilant. Karina looked at her left arm and watched the magenta linework wrap it.

"The rest of this plan will make the most sense if I can tell you in your own mind. Is that okay?"

A bit confused, Namarula answered, "All right...but Yitorn minds are...complicated."

Karina reached her right hand toward Deepika's head and closed her eyes. A moment later, the two figures in the ship were frozen in those positions, but within Namarula's mind, they stood in the sky above a slowly spinning landscape of gray-green stone and ruddy earth, protruding from vast oceans. The stone looked like towering cities, filled with light and movement. Above them, streaks of white flashed across a vaulted upper limit, fading a little before streaking once more. There was no sun or other light source, and the sky looked and felt like the inside of a thunderstorm, without rain. Karina looked much as she did in the wider world, her clothing crisper and tidier, but Namarula looked like a cloud of glowing green-white mist, which occasionally formed claws and other limbs from its substance.

"I've seen weirder," Karina commented.

The mist that was Namarula crackled and vibrated, which communicated, *"For some reason, I believe you."*

One of the stone building's lights turned from green to a deep red-orange, and Namarula looked worried.

"She's strong. We train in taking total control, but never in

holding it for more than a few hours. I don't know how I've been able to keep her this long."

A second building's lights changed color.

"We might be able to hear her soon. What was your plan?"

"Tell Atanalodh you're waiting for him."

"What!?" Namarula hovered back in terror.

"If he somehow finds his way into the ship, Mar can deal with him. If he comes here, into mental contact like I am, he'll be visiting you where you're strongest, and where you make the rules. And, you'll have my strength to draw on, without him even knowing that I'm here. Maybe even Deepika's, if she'll share it with you."

Namarula hesitated. "What *are* you, Karina Ruiz?"

"You haven't figured it out yet?" Karina put her hands on her hips with a sly smirk, her left hand and forearm glowing pink, the radiance illuminating a churn of tentacles under her human-like exterior.

"You're...a Tivoluun?" Namarula flickered incredulously. "Every text and scholar tells that your kind went extinct before the second Matter Crisis. Hundreds of Yitorn scholars have sought survivors, never finding one."

"Nothing's ever really extinct once it figures out time travel," Karina answered. "And nothing beckons in the Thoughtlines if it doesn't want to be found."

"I know at least ten professors who would sever their own Thoughtskills to hear you say that."

"Maybe someday, one of them will." Karina dismissed her hand-glow. "Until then, I'm the only thing like me, as far as I know. I don't age, I can take on disguises, I've been around for millennia, I've been *everywhere*, and here, I can share the strength of a thousand lonely centuries with you." Karina approached Namarula and laid a gentle hand on her churning mist, reassuring, "We don't have to do this. We can find other ways."

Namarula draped a flickering tendril onto Karina's hand. "Thank you, Karina."

She looked down, as another building's lights turned orange, and looked up at the sky. *"Atanalodh. I'm waiting for you."*

Up above, the Thoughtlines cracked and pealed, growing in intensity. A cloud formed before them, pulling in the sparks as it took shape. It resembled Namarula's misty form, pulsing in yellow, but all of its edges and boundaries were razor-sharp. The cloud continued growing during its slow descent, arriving before Namarula and Karina at nearly twice her size. A long tendril, hazy and sharply defined all at once, extended from the cloud around the two challengers, its end like a translucent carving knife, gently tapping on Namarula's mist. Underneath each tap, the mist took a shape like a collarbone.

"My sweet Namarula," the thing cooed venomously, *"I missed you so. I picked out some natano fruit from the Fellucian rainforests for you."*

"Not today, Atanalodh," Namarula answered, resolute.

"Then why did you call me, my love?" Atanalodh's tapping grew more emphatic.

"You said it yourself. 'No running from a Saberthought.' I'm done running."

"Are you? Well, that's a relief." Atanalodh drew the mindknife along Namarula's collarbone, then upward, gently

grazing along her substance. *"I was worried I'd have to convince you."*

Namarula closed her eyes, raised a long tendril toward Atanalodh, and slammed it downward. It crashed through Atanalodh's arm, and the long limb shattered into pieces that disintegrated into nothing with a metallic clatter as they fell. Karina looked on in satisfaction. Atanalodh vibrated, flickered, and morphed his edges into rows of blades.

"This isn't going to be like the last times," Namarula insisted.

Namarula froze as a second set of limbs began tapping on her, this time from behind.

"Are you sure about that? There's no running from a Saber-thought..." Atanalodh gleefully recited, this time having his double grate its mindknives into Namarula's substance ever so slightly with each tap and caress, *"but the fight's not worth it, either."*

From down below, one of the green-lit buildings erupted into a monstrous maw and lunged upward, crushing the second Atanalodh to nothing. Atanalodh proper reached over with another tendril, tracing a thin line along the giant stone serpent, and then cut its head off in a single swing. The pieces crashed downward as the building-snake receded, reforming into a cracked and wounded version of the building they once were.

"Now, now, Namarula, you know what happens when you try to use your memories against me. You get careless, and I make sure you know it." Atanalodh looked down at the cityscape, a vibration like a smirk crossing his mist. *"But perhaps you need a reminder."* Atanalodh streaked downward, through the

invisible floor on which Karina stood, and Namarula and Karina followed urgently.

Down below, Atanalodh stopped near one of the taller buildings. "*I remember this one,*" he mused aloud. "*Your Yitorn convocation. Your body wore such grand finery, and your mind was resplendent. I was there, you know.*" He dragged a mindknife along its stones, tracing the lines between them, leaving harsh scratches behind.

"*No, you weren't!*" Namarula shouted back. She drove herself bodily into Atanalodh, slamming him into the building and lashing her limbs around his. With a hideous wrenching snap, she severed six of them, their mindknives crumbling like crushed glass. "*I have relived this moment every day since you started hurting me, and in every second, I know who did and did not watch me receive my circlet. You and I did not meet until years later. You can't scare me anymore!*"

Namarula raised another building to crush Atanalodh, but the building's lights turned orange mid-motion, and it returned to its usual shape.

"*Memory is a fickle thing, my sweet Namarula. It answers to many masters: emotions, logic, time...and me.*" Atanalodh plunged a mindknife through the building's windows, and Namarula now remembered, clear as day, that Atanalodh *had* been at her Yitorn Convocation, front and center, grinning deviously. She shuddered back in horror, and Karina landed behind her, steadying her with a hand and a nod. Atanalodh swelled in size and crept toward her again.

"*There's no running from a Saberthought, and no fighting, either,*" Atanalodh threatened, waving a mindknife back and forth. *"I'll have you again, if I have to hollow out your entire life to do it. It's better you come quietly."*

Karina knelt behind Namarula and grasped one of her tendrils. "You have my strength," she whispered, and her thoughts focused on her Yitorn friend.

From above, below, and all of the other directions, fifteen spectral buildings lunged out of the psychic ether, pounding into Atanalodh and crushing every limb the Saber-thought tried to interpose. As this onslaught worked itself out, Namarula raised one of her own limbs, hardened and heavy, and jabbed it into the center of her abuser, crashing straight through him and into the building behind. In her thoughts, Atanalodh's false presence faded from her Convocation memories. Atanalodh lurched and shuddered, raising several limbs and watching them flicker into nothing instead of forming mindknives. Namarula seized Atanalodh with a dozen tendrils, flung him into the lightning-studded sky, and pierced him with another fifteen phosphorescent columns. Like a pincushion, he crashed and rolled back down into Namarula's memory landscape, and again he rose.

"That's a nice trick," he coughed out, the mist of his body giving partial way to the crablike image that lay underneath, *"but I have a nicer one."* He collected the mistiness about him into an orb and plunged it into the ground beneath him, cackling with satisfaction. All around, building lights changed from green to yellow, and Namarula felt Atanalodh's venomous presence seeping into every moment of her life. Screaming as his intrusion proceeded, she heard him whisper directly into her mind from a thousand places in her

own past, *"Mine is the only thing you ever get to be, and I will have every second of you whether you want me to or not. Remember,* you *did this."*

Karina rushed to Namarula and shook her, shouting her name, but her screaming did not stop, nor did the changing lights. Her face tightened, she placed her magenta-glowing hand on Namarula, and she shouted into the sky, *"Now, Mar!"*

Aboard the *Light Caller*, Mar gently pushed Karina's left hand against Deepika's head. In Namarula's mind, a hideous screeching noise roared into the entire cityscape as the sky flashed pink, and all at once the green glow of Namarula's memories returned as Atanalodh's intrusion retreated back into him and then exploded into nothing. Atanalodh grasped his head with his jointed claws, howling in pain, as his carapace cracked and flickered. Namarula calmed and descended. As she did so, some of the buildings began to move—specifically, the red-orange ones. A group of them crept closer, displacing some green buildings on the way there, and some other nearby buildings turned red-orange and joined them. Namarula clubbed Atanalodh into the sky, and shattered bits of his mental carapace fell before her. Up above, the mobile buildings crashed into him, pinning his crushed body in place. Namarula clambered up the nearest one, Karina following. At the top, staring into what was left of Atanalodh's face, she whispered:

"That was clever, shedding your Thoughtskill for one last effort to infiltrate everything I am. You had to know, though, that it was the *last effort. Without this layer of psychic possibility,"* Namarula explained as she gestured at herself, *"all you have left is your*

own mind, in its own shape, without even the hope of leaving here unless I let you. Or rather, unless Deepika lets you."

The buildings squeezed, and one of Atanalodh's clawed arms fell off, disappearing into the city below.

"She'll probably squeeze me out of here soon, but before that, she's going to squeeze you out of everywhere. She's in here too, you know, and she felt exactly what you just tried to do to me...to us. I locked her in her bedroom, sure, but you just tried to burn her house down. She has priorities."

"It doesn't matter what you do," Atanalodh coughed. *"I've already made my mark on you. Even if you destroy me now, you'll remember me...remember everything I did to you...for you."*

"That's my burden to bear. This is yours." Namarula clamped onto Atanalodh's head with a wispy limb while the buildings underneath bent violently, crushing Atanalodh's body to nothing in their perfect tessellation. Namarula flung his insensate head into the Thoughtlines above, where the next flash of lightning erased it. As she turned toward Karina and took in her face of mingled horror, awe, and relief, the red-orange lights spread across the city, and then mingled together. The Thoughtline lightning faded to a low simmer, while the cityscape became the four walls of a light blue bedroom. Namarula and Karina now stood before a lavish canopy bed, and between them and this furniture stood Deepika Ranjul in a well-decorated red-orange sari.

"I...I did it," Deepika murmured in disbelief.

Namarula collected her Thoughtskill, hiding it within herself to show the vaguely humanoid, crablike shape of her Yitorn mind, and knelt before Deepika. Still breathing heavily from her ordeal, she was too exhausted to cry, but she wanted to.

"I..." she began, "I'm so, so sorry." She kept looking at the floor, not even shifting her stalked eyes upward to Deepika's feet. "It shouldn't have been you. It shouldn't have been anyone. I'm..." The tears finally came. "I'm so sorry."

Deepika drew in her lips. "You were running from that man...Atanalodh?"

"Yes," Namarula answered, still shaking.

Deepika descended to the floor and draped a careful hug around Namarula's hard shell. "Then I forgive you."

Namarula sobbed openly. "Thank you," she choked out. "But *why?*"

"I've been fighting my way out of your hold since you came to me, and it showed me your memories. He's...he was... scary. The things he did to you...I don't even have words for them. I could have let him destroy you from the inside, and taken my chances with him after that, but he didn't deserve it. My people have known too many monsters like that. They deserve a fight, and we gave them one."

Namarula hugged back.

"I was angry with you. I *wanted* to be angry with you. But seeing all of that, seeing him...I understand."

Namarula hugged tighter.

"It's still not okay that you didn't ask me, before or during. But I understand."

The two were still for a long time, and Karina stepped back and looked out Deepika's bedroom window. Outside, a six-year-old version of her in a white dress chased butterflies, and a fifteen-year-old version held hands with her first boyfriend on a park bench. Karina smiled.

"I should get going," Namarula intoned wistfully. She stood, and then stopped. "But where I'm from, I just murdered a respected scientist so thoroughly that his mind will never be recovered. I thought I had nowhere to go *before*, but now…"

Deepika looked worried, crossing her arms. "Well, I can't let you stay in here if it's going to be anything like this time."

Karina stepped forward with a raised finger. "If I may, I think I can solve both of your problems."

Aboard the *Light Caller*, the suitcase Karina had retrieved from the convenience store shook open, and a series of metal limbs emerged from it. Smoothly, the entire case lifted itself upright on these limbs and reconfigured itself into a humanoid shape, which then began to secrete a warm brown skin. In a few minutes, the robotic form looked human, but for the circuit-board pattern of her veins and metallic blue sheen of her hair. A minute after that, it secreted clothing: a green sundress and brown sandals. Suddenly, she began moving, and spoke in a new voice.

"This feels…strange," Namarula announced, raising her new arms. "And wonderful."

"I thought you'd like it. Like you, that body had nowhere to go. Whoever owned it before didn't want it, and I have no use of my own for it, other than protecting the timestream from something that shouldn't exist here for another million years or so."

Namarula took a few steps around the *Light Caller*'s control room as Karina, Mar, and Deepika watched.

"Right now, it's on the default appearance settings, based on a future human civilization," Karina explained. "You should be able to figure out the reconfiguration protocol and make it look like your old body within a few days."

"I don't think I want to," Namarula answered. "That shape is full of bad memories now. It's time for me to make some new ones. Better ones."

"That's a good idea," Deepika responded, putting a hand on Namarula's new shoulder. "Take care of yourself, Namarula."

"You too, Deepika." The two hugged, long and dearly.

"I can drop you off a few moments after Namarula first entered your body," Karina explained to Deepika, "so that you don't lose any time. There'll be two of you in Rollaven for a little while, but if you don't make a scene about it, it should pass without drawing any additional attention to either of you."

"Thanks," she answered, looking out a window at the unfamiliar world outside. "What did you say your name was?"

"You can call me Karina Ruiz."

"Right, right. And who should I ask to play you in the movie I'm going to pitch about this ordeal about fifteen minutes after I get back home?" she asked with a wry smile.

"Well, if you can't get Karunya Changrabali, I'll settle for Nina Davuluru," Karina answered without missing a beat.

"You really do know who I am, don't you?" Deepika Ranjul laughed.

"You were amazing in *Aquí me quedo sin ti.*"

"Really? I feel like most people didn't get that one."

"Most people are wrong about a lot of things."

The two laughed, and Namarula smiled, not really understanding what was happening.

"Time to hold on. The *Light Caller* handles like a soccer riot."

Deepika and Namarula grasped the nearest handholds as the shaking started.

"Where did you want to go after this, Namarula?"

"I don't know...someplace warm. And sunny."

The *Light Caller* lurched violently, and Karina began to sing, "*Esta noche será especial...*"

Mar took the next line: "*NOS IREMOS PARA LA PLAYA...*"

Karina: "*Tambores, arena, y mar...*"

"*CANCIONES DE MI GUITARRA...*"

Deepika and Namarula smiled.

Alyssa Gonzalez is a biology Ph.D., public speaker, and writer. Her fiction uses science-fiction and fantasy elements to explore social isolation, autism, gender, trauma, and the relationships between all of these things. She writes at The Perfumed Void (*the-orbit.net/alyssa*), on the subjects of about biology, history, sociology, and her experiences as an autistic ex-Catholic Hispanic transgender immigrant to Canada. She lives in Ottawa, Canada with a menagerie of pets.

B. Martin Allen

You Don't Belong Here

Early in life, I figured out that you could get away with being in almost any space as long as you acted like you belonged there. Walk like you know where you're going. Behave in accordance with your surroundings. Hold wonder and fear on the inside. If you need to assess your surroundings, stop down and pretend to read a book. If you're overwhelmed, find the nearest restroom and calm down in private. Do what you need to do to be okay, but do so invisibly. Exude enough confidence, and regardless of power differentials, the vast majority of people will take no notice or be too intimidated to question you. The handful who do will be inordinately hostile, but hostile people are generally hostile no matter how you act. When you cannot avoid their hostility you have three options: appease, shame, or fight.

Home had turned into the one place where those three options all failed, where I did not belong. Starting when I was twelve, I spent nearly three years mostly unhoused and without parental supervision or support.

I split my afternoons between the library and The Office. The library was a magical place where one could borrow up to twelve books at a time for free. The Office was a topless bar with no cover charge for "the ladies" and a sign outside touting a free, all-you-can-eat buffet at happy hour. The promise of free food was what initially drew me in.

About two weeks into my happy hour Office routine, I met Mike. Mike was the quiet man at the loud table. No one liked the loud table. One of the larger tables in front of the stage, it naturally attracted groups of loud men because loud men want to be front and center. Loud men consistently viewed the loud table as a stage of greater importance than the actual dancers' stage, on which they performed loud man commentary, each loud man jockeying to be funnier, cruder, more macho than the others. Loud men groped, were quick to anger, and, worst of all, were lousy tippers.

I was seated in the far corner stool at the bar nibbling at a plate of lukewarm chicken wings and making a concerted effort to be not noticed when Mike walked up to the bar, slipped a twenty to the bartender and made arrangements to secretly have his drinks free of alcohol because "someone has to drive these assholes home." This display of basic decency made me smile in spite of myself. My smile was noticed, my attempt at invisibility was blown. Now it was on me to initiate some small talk.

"You don't belong here."

Mike tensed up. Apparently, this was not the disarming compliment I thought it would be. I was going to have to continue talking.

"Are those coworkers? Business associates?"

Mike sighed. "Yeah."

"I figured if you were hanging out with that lot there was a paycheck involved."

Mike let out a small laugh, and that would have been the end of the conversation had we not drawn the attention of Mike's loud compatriots.

"Yeah, buddy."

"Get some!"

Mike dipped his head in embarrassment. His hand covered his eyes for a second while he rubbed his temples as if he could transport himself anywhere else by sheer force of will.

"I'm so sorry. They're just…"

"I think the word you used earlier was assholes?"

"Yeah. Can I at least buy you a drink to apologize? By the way, I'm Mike."

"Well, Mike, I hate to break it to you, but I too am fake drinking. This is just Coke with lime. The lime wedge really sells it. I wouldn't dream of drinking in a place like this. It's full of men like that."

"Wise beyond your years."

"I figure it compensates for men like your friends. I'm just creating balance in the world."

The loud men kept being loud in our general direction.

"I'll tell them to stop."

"You know that won't work. It never works. They're like a bunch of junior high boys, the more you tell them no, the more they act out. Here's what we're going to do, you're going to stay here and talk to me a few more minutes, and I'm going to act like you're the most charming man in the world.

Then I'll leave, and you'll go back to your table with some story where you got my number or some such. They'll think you're some stud for picking up girls, and you can go home to your wife and be happy you're not like them."

Taken aback but amused, Mike said, "Well, okay then. So what brings you here? Do you—umm—work here?"

"No. I'm here for the food. It's neither delicious nor healthy, but it is plentiful and free. Plus, I like the dim lighting and that people here don't ask a lot of questions."

Taking my hint, the getting to know you session ended.

"Well, Mike I need to be elsewhere. Try not to let those guys rub off on you."

"I'll try."

I left expecting to never see Mike again.

Twenty-three hours later, I was back at The Office, tucked into my favorite booth. Located in the front corner opposite the entrance, it was an ideal hangout: poor sight lines to the stage, opposite side of the room to the bar, and about five feet from the buffet. Many customers didn't even notice the row of booths, a holdover from the building's former life as a restaurant. The booths served little purpose but were not worth the expense to remove. I looked up from my plate of French fries and highly suspect shrimp cocktail to see Mike standing in front of me.

I stared, panicked that he might have mistaken my politeness the day before for interest.

"Hi. I was hoping you'd be here."

I continued to stare. In my panic, I had stopped chewing. My mouth tightly clenched around a piece of shrimp. A full ten seconds passed before I composed myself, chewed, swallowed, and then spoke.

"Why?"

"Those guys last night were potential clients. Only reason I landed the account was because of you. I don't think they even read the prospectus."

I nodded knowingly, gleaning the meaning of prospectus from a combination of context and root words.

"Glad that worked out for you."

"I really wanted to thank you."

"Oh? You're welcome."

Mike pulled out his wallet. "Listen, I don't know your situation, but…"

This man was attracting unwanted attention.

"Put that away and sit down," I hissed in a near whisper. "What do you think people are going to think is going on when you hand me cash in a place like this?"

Mike quickly sat down across from me. "Sorry, I just want to help."

"I don't need your help. You don't even know me."

"I don't even know your name, but I do see you scrounging free food while you just made me thousands."

For a moment, I was defensive and ashamed, and then I wasn't. I tried to think of one thing that would make my life easier but was less costly than the stack of twenties he was about to hand me.

"Okay, Mike, if you really want to help, I need a new coat. A very specific kind of coat, practical enough for every day, formal enough for evening wear, and tailored so I don't look like I'm wearing a tent. We go to Neiman's, you buy me a coat, we call it even. Deal?"

"Deal."

Three days later, I picked up my custom-tailored coat from Neiman Marcus. As I slipped it on and checked the fit, any last trace of shame left me. I earned that coat through my own skill and guile. I'd taken nothing that wasn't willfully given. I had conned some grotesque grubby men into believing what they were already predisposed to believe. I might be sleeping in the clearing behind the 7-11, but I would be *warm* while sleeping in the clearing behind the 7-11, and when I woke up, I would be able to walk to school looking together enough that no one would guess my life was a perpetual urban camping trip.

Less than two weeks later, I met another guy like Mike. And a few days later, yet another. It was easy work, and I was good at it. I liked the luxuries it afforded me. Sleeping in a hotel room rented with someone else's credit card was better than sleeping behind the 7-11, where a rainy night meant no sleep at all. While my history/physical education teacher had given me a key, the worst motel shower was better than the hurried five a.m. showers in the boys' locker room.

Over the first month or two, I gradually found my way into a world richer and uglier than anything I'd witnessed at The Office, a subculture of men with so much money that nothing was out of reach. They had the most luxurious cars, the best drugs, the most fashionable clothes, and the pretti-est wives from the finest families. And it was never enough. These men were bottomless pits of material desires. They craved the newest toys, and the best new toy was a teenage girl. Teen girls were lured to private parties and VIP lounges by someone, I really don't know who, to be set upon by these men. It was more of a canned hunt than a social gathering.

These parties were about more than just the acquisition of sex, they were about networking, deal making. They were bad men bonding over a shared transgressive experience, trust built from mutually assured destruction.

My interest wasn't in these men. My interest was in my clients, men who had enough of a moral compass to be un-comfortable with the idea of bedding a child but were too weak to stand up to their colleagues who did not share that discomfort. For them, I offered a very specific service. In ex-change for one of their credit cards and a note giving their "niece" permission to make purchases, I would meet them at one of these gatherings, blend in with the other girls, and then pretend to be completely infatuated with them. I wasn't selling sex. I was selling the illusion of sex. Creating that illu-sion took so little, a small smile, a touch on the arm, an occa-sional whisper was enough. The hardest part was pretending the business talk was over my head.

I was not without feeling. I worried about the girls. Initially, I would try to find out if they were in the same circumstances as myself, but they never were, and they sensed that other-ness in a way only teenage girls can. These girls had a place to call home, a stability they took for granted. Home wasn't a want, it simply was. What they longed for was excitement. They wanted to feel pretty, special, and more adult than they actually were. None of that interested me. I felt no pride in being found attractive. For me, it was all a means to an end.

My rigid adherence to my own ground rules kept me safe. I never tried to get to know my clients, and I didn't let them get to know me. My clients were useless men. I'm sure they viewed themselves as nice guys for not actively participating in the abuse of underage girls, but if they, as grown adults with substantial wealth, were too weak to stand up to that wrong, they were not worth my trust. I can honestly not recall a single name. They're just a blur of faces with one shared bland personality.

I never counted on that work for survival. I always had a reserve of bars, clubs and restaurants to use for shelter at night. I kept claim on my clearing behind the 7-11. For cash, I tutored freshman at a local university in literature and composition. My tutoring eighteen-year-old guys led to my decision to never take on a client under the age of thirty-five. Younger men want sex more than they want networking.

While clearly what I was doing can be viewed as sex work, thirteen-year-old me didn't see it that way. I viewed myself as a grifter or con artist. I used clients to improve my financial circumstances, and in return, I fooled other men into improving my clients' financial circumstances. It was seedy, but it was the most straightforward compromise I could make to keep my life moving forward.

When my father found sobriety, I found my way back home. I am grateful for that year of near normality we had before he died. I would love to say I came home and seam-lessly slipped into life as a teen, but it was rockier than that. I simply did not know how to be young, but fortunately youth is a transitory state.

Programmed to be a mid twentieth century housewife with a second wave feminist veneer, **B. Martin Allen**, CFO and Development Editor for Autonomous Press, gleefully dis-appoints. Since the 1980's, in venues ranging from indie weeklies to the Huffington Post, Allen has been writing high-ly personal stories of disability's intersection with poverty, feminism, queer culture, and abuse. Keyword searches to find Martin include: autistic, chronic illness, intersex, par-enting, transgender, and queer.

Melanie Bell

FetLife

At the Asian food court
At a queer women's meetup,
The woman two seats down from me
Tells the table she's a fitness domme.

"The men pay me to lose weight.
If they don't meet their goals,
I take their money."

To the curious listener next to me
She recommends FetLife,
Smiles knowingly when I said
"Yeah, I'm familiar with it."

Turns out she wrestles near my place.
"Fantasy wrestling too.
The men try to push me off the chair and I stay there."

"Is it always men?" asks the woman beside me.
"Yes," she assures.
"It's always men.
Would *you* pay to do that?"

Melanie Bell is a contributor to *Spoon Knife 3*. She holds an MA in Creative Writing from Concordia University and has written for publications including *Cicada, Contrary Magazine* and *Huffington Post*. She is the co-author of a nonfiction book, *The Modern Enneagram* (Althea Press, 2017), and her short story collection *Dream Signs* is forthcoming from Lost Fox Publishing.

Matthew Warner

Diary of The Cryonic Pharaoh

July 1, 12032 A.D.

[by automatic voice transcription]

The computer says I should start a journal to help my "cognitive recovery," so here I am, speaking into this ancient microphone. The equipment, like me, has spent the last ten thousand years in a zero-humidity, oxygen-less stasis in this bunker hidden a mile beneath the desert.

The computer says I'm Gerald Dillingsworth. The name is meaningless to me. All I know is I woke up a couple days ago in a metal sarcophagus with the worst hangover imaginable and joints as stiff as cement.

Hangover. Cement. I understand what the words mean. I feel and see them in my mind, and I can write and speak them. But I don't remember how I learned them. I have no experiences to understand them. The computer assures me my "narrative history" will return. The amnesia will dissipate as my brain fully reboots after its long hibernation.

Recording this has exhausted me. I'm going to rest in one of the hundreds of shuttered bunk cubicles lining the walls. Everything is perfectly preserved because the bunker has been filled with nothing but antiseptic preservative gas for the last ten millennia.

Gerald Dillingsworth. I wish there was someone else here to talk to about who I am.

July 2

Turns out there is someone else who can clue me in. Myself. I found a video blog entry from Gerald Dillingsworth, raving lunatic of the first order, dated August 25, 2032. I'm so disgusted that I might commit suicide once I'm done pasting in the auto-transcript:

"Come with us," they said. "We have this huge, fancy-dancy, underground bunker where we can all hide from the apocalypse. It'll take a thousand years for the chemicals topside to dissipate, so we're gonna put ourselves on ice until it's clear."

I told them I didn't have the technical skills to help rebuild a civilization once we were thawed ("thawed" being a misnomer since we'll be suspended with gases, but what the hell do I know?). I'm a sculptor and a writer. But they just said they need "those types" of people, too. Made me so angry, them saying "those types." So I showed them. I was among the last four cryonauts slated to be preserved—four among four hundred who thought they were better than me. I waited until the other three's backs were turned and stabbed a kitchen knife into their kidneys. And then I used my knife and a good, old-fashioned crowbar to sabotage three hundred ninety-six cryo-coffins. Now I'm the only one left. Bet those stuck-up pricks didn't see that coming.

A measly thousand years. Screw that. I told the computer to put me under for ten times that long. I'll rise out of the ground as the king of the world, stomping whatever little pygmy people have managed to evolve in the meantime. I'll be a T-Rex among sheeple.

The computer says a suspension for that long is beyond its design limits. It only projects a fifty percent survival probability. We're in a geothermal-powered bunker miles from any fault lines, but the computer can't guarantee the hermetic seal holding in the preservative gas will survive that long. Well, so what? I'll do it anyway. I'm a god.

I'm going to throw up now.

July 3

This place is starting to smell. All those bodies, most of them in their wrecked cryo-coffins, haven't been permitted to decay until now. I walk around with my hand over my mouth and nose, feeling ill. Serves me right.

I've watched the video of myself half a dozen times, noting the strained quality of my voice, the way I kept licking my lips. My right eyebrow started twitching when I said, "A measly thousand years." It's doing that now. Must be a stress thing, like the way the rehydrated food I'm consuming gives me diarrhea.

I know I should kill myself as penance. Ten millennia or not, I'm a mass murderer, and justice should be served. Except I have no memory of it, nor of who I was. None. Just fleeting impressions of things that form the basis of the language I speak. Pharaoh. I think I used to be a pharaoh, which was a king of some sort. At least that's what my awakening brain tells me. Maybe that's why I had the right to kill everybody.

I feel like I woke up on a movie set after production wrapped, with no connection to anything that happened. This is why I wonder if this is all a conspiracy to make me think I'm a murderer. Someone planted the decaying bodies here and used sophisticated software to fake my supposed videotaped confession. I wasn't an artist; I was a pharaoh, after all. But that's crazy talk. I must be prone to crazy talk, otherwise how could I have been capable of such atrocity?

Conspiracy or not, the choices ahead of me are the same. Kill myself, or go on with life.

I'm glad I don't remember anything.

July 4

The computer doesn't know what's topside anymore. Its periscope and chemical sensors up there broke down a few thousand years ago. But it says there's an escape stairwell I can use to climb out. "Advise you don environmental protection suit prior to ascent until chemical neutrality is verified." Its sultry female voice pissed me off for some reason, so I changed it to a monotone male.

Except I'm afraid to go up. Free of the megalomania that encumbered the old me, I can admit that now. I'm not a god or a T-Rex. I'm just some ugly Caucasian guy, over ten thousand years old, but with the face of a twenty-five-year-old psychopath. A safety razor makes my hand tremble when I hold it, so I'm letting my beard grow out. It's coming up like weeds in an empty lot.

An empty lot. I remember it now. It's where I grew up—or where I spent a lot of my childhood. Something about broken glass and mutilated animals. Best not to think about it.

Since I'm procrastinating on my return to above ground, I've decided to do something about the decaying bodies. I'm stacking them in a large storage room among shelves full of books and sculptures and paintings. For all I know, I created some of these masterpieces, but I feel no affinity for any of them. They're all just objects to me, devoid of meaning or emotion—unlike the bodies I'm dumping in the same room.

Their rigor mortis has already gone away, so they're flopping around like rag dolls, waving to me as I heave them off my shoulders, mouths falling open to scream in accusation. I tell them I'm not responsible for what happened. To blame the old Gerald. I'm the new Gerald now, and I don't remember any of it. I'm nicer. I never would have murdered them.

I cried the first couple times I said that. Now I just ignore them when they speak to me.

July 5

With the bodies sealed in the storage room, the rancid smell of decay is slowly dissipating. Even better is the news that I should have virtually unlimited air down here for now on. The bunker was designed to sustain four hundred people for an indeterminate period after their waking up, but since there's only me now, the strain on the life support systems is considerably less.

As for food, the computer is growing new crops in the hydroponics garden. The first harvest should be ripe by the time I've exhausted the dehydrated supplies.

Now the only thing to decide is when to venture above ground. Or if.

July 6

Had a bad night last night. My memories keep wanting to come back, so I keep pressing them down. But I can feel them down there, bubbling under the surface. I'm afraid if I hold them in for too long I'll explode, like a carbonated drink dropped on the floor.

Recovering my memories means owning up to what I did, and I can't have that. And, oh my god, what if after remembering everything I change back into the old Gerald? What if I convince myself I didn't do such a bad thing after all?

I was a pharaoh, after all. That's what I catch myself saying when I'm not paying attention. It happens on my walks around the bunker. That's what I do all day: walk in laps. I pass the empty bunks and the empty cryo-coffins, and then the storage room. I always stop at the storage room's door to listen, but so far I haven't heard anything.

Walking keeps me relaxed and focused. I suppose I should be spending my time in the library, refreshing myself on history and brushing up my above-ground survival skills. But after the first five minutes of a lecture about the chemical apocalypse, I grew bored. History is in the past. And as for survival skills—how to hunt and navigate and make shelters—every time I start studying that stuff, I grow deeply depressed. There's no way I'll be able to do those things by myself. I have no aptitude for the rough-and-tumble lifestyle. I feel like a jail inmate who's been told he can regain his freedom just as soon as he finishes building a car engine from scratch.

Maybe I'll get lucky and discover I won't need any of those skills. A lot could have happened in ten thousand years above ground. Any survivors would have surely rebuilt civilization by now. I'll be as far removed from them as an ancient Egyptian from a man of my own time. They'll see me and think, "There's a pharaoh. We better take care of him."

July 7

Last night, I heard noise in the storage room containing the bodies. I climbed out of my bunk and walked in my socks to the door to stand there. But by the time I arrived, the noise stopped.

Words came out of my mouth. I felt drunk and couldn't remember what I said until I watched the security tapes this morning. "Serves you right," I said through the closed door. "Serves you right."

I need to get out of here.

July 8

I took a bold step this morning and tried to venture above ground. After following the computer's instructions to put on the environment suit—adjusting my portable oxygen supply and so forth—I shuffled in booted feet to the outer door. Despite the suit's protection, I still held my breath as the computer unlocked the exit.

Air hissed as the door unsealed, but I couldn't feel it through my suit and mask. The moment I slipped through into an unlit stone corridor, the computer closed the door behind me. "Do not worry," it said through my radio. "Bunker sensors will react to reacquisition of transponder proximity. I will let you back in."

I switched on the flashlight strapped to my wrist and began climbing the stairwell carved into the rock.

In ten minutes, I encountered a roadblock. Or should I say, "blocks," because that's what barred my way: a hundred irregular blocks of rubble had fallen into the stairwell long ago. Oddly, I felt relieved. I wouldn't have to face the future today.

I transmitted photos to the computer and requested advice. After a moment, it radioed back, "Storage room 25A contains drills. Recommend you retrieve equipment while I process imagery to formulate digging plan."

I climbed back down the stairs, trying to remember if room 25A was the one containing the bodies. I didn't think so. The bodies were in a room containing artwork. Did the computer really think I could dig my way out? There could have been a thousand tons of rock overhead. Poking it with a drill might make it worse.

Such were my thoughts as the computer opened the outer door and I stepped back into the bunker. When I saw what was waiting, I screamed and fell to my knees.

One of the bodies was in the corridor. It sat on the floor and leaned against the wall, staring at me with milky white eyes.

My first thought was that it had climbed off the pile of bodies I made. It walked out while I was exploring the escape stairwell. But that was impossible. It was a corpse.

I kept my environment suit on as I dragged the body by the armpits back to its room. None of the others had moved. I closed and locked the door from the outside.

Then I marched straight to the command center to review the security tapes. I would see how the body got out of the storage room. I expected to see footage of myself doing the deed.

But the computer said all the internal security cameras were offline. The relevant hardware modules weren't responding. I followed its directions to a locker in one of the corridors. It was supposed to contain the CPU and data drive that ran the cameras.

The locker was empty.

"Who was the last person to open this locker?" I asked.

"Unknown. Internal security cameras are offline."

I felt a chill as I trudged back to the storage room where I'd stored the bodies. The door was unlocked again. Somehow. No, not somehow. I'd unlocked it myself and blocked the memory. I poked my head inside long enough to determine the bodies were undisturbed before I relocked it.

Damn. I really need to get out of here.

July 8 — supplemental

After I recorded that last entry, I tackled the problem of escape with renewed vigor.

I pulled a battery-powered drill the size of my arm out of storage room 25A and returned to the rocks in the stairwell. By that time, the computer had analyzed the configuration of the debris and had several suggestions on where to loosen it up. I quickly learned to stand off to the side as hundreds of pounds of rubble began to steadily cave in. I frequently had to pause to clear it away and ensure my path back to the bunker below remained unobstructed.

As I drilled, of course I considered the body in the corridor. Is this place haunted? Doubtful. The most probable scenario was I moved the body myself and forgot about it. I had sabotaged the cameras, too.

Which means I'm my own worst enemy.

Fragments of my old life continue to surface in my consciousness. I see an old-fashioned electric typewriter, on which I learned to type in the seventh grade. I see my first set of stone-carving tools. A lock of a woman's hair; I don't know whose. And with each new bit of flotsam, a puzzling set of emotions bubble through me: longing, disgust, depression. It's only a matter of time until the old Gerald Dillingsworth rises from the pool, grins maniacally, and shakes off the water.

When I was tired of drilling, I trudged back down the stairs to the bunker door, hopping between fallen boulders like I was crossing a stream. My arms were almost too heavy to wipe away the rock dust caking my faceplate.

I waited for the computer to recognize the transponder in my suit and open the bunker door. But nothing happened.

"Computer, open bunker door."

Silence answered me.

"Computer?"

I felt aware of the boulders still blocking the stairwell above me. An unknown quantity of work remained to be done, but there were surely several tons of rock remaining to be moved or pulverized. I hadn't yet opened a crack to the air above, so I was dependent on the oxygen tank strapped to my back. My supply would be exhausted in another hour.

"Computer."

Finally, it answered through the radio. "What do you require?" It sounded subdued, almost sheepish.

"I said open the door."

No answer.

I reminded myself it was just a machine. Getting the correct response often meant rephrasing a question.

"Why don't you open the door?"

"User instruction."

"What user?"

"That record has been deleted."

Well, that was just great. I started to cuss the machine out before I checked myself. "Here's a new instruction: delete any commands currently in memory that you not open the door for me. And replace them with the following command: open the door. Now."

A moment passed in which I watched a dust mote cross my flashlight beam.

The door popped open on its hinges. I angrily yanked it the rest of the way open and went inside.

No corpse waited for me in the corridor this time. But that didn't stop me from going directly to the storage rooms to check the pile of putrefying bodies hadn't been disturbed. Then I went in search of a shower and a meal.

I can't trust myself. I'm the only living person here, but I'm entering fugue states in which I don't remember sabotaging cameras and reprogramming the central computer. Even now, I keep imagining I hear footsteps.

July 9

Had a bad scare last night.

Despite the knowledge I'm the only one here, I can't shake

the superstition that the ghosts of the people I murdered want revenge—that they're the ones who moved their bodies, sabotaged the cameras, and tried to lock me out. Of course I know the truth, that *I'm* the one doing these things, that my subconscious is at war with me, my reemerging memories stoking my guilt. But none of this sober analysis can stop the crawling feeling on my skin as I sleep, that itching sensation of someone watching me. So last night I shut and locked the shutter to my bunk cubicle before going to sleep.

An hour later, I heard footsteps in the corridor. They stopped beside my bunk and waited. I turned on my tiny flashlight and held my breath.

Whoever it was skittered his fingers along the outside of the metal shutter. Then he scratched it with his fingernails. The sound moved down my spine like razorblades. Then he moved on.

When the footsteps reached the end of the hall, I summoned my anger and threw open the metal shutter to my bunk. I screamed a challenge as I charged down the hallway in my bare feet. I raised my puny flashlight overhead like a club as I rounded the corner.

And stopped short as I came upon a man standing in the darkness. He had his back turned to me. My flashlight beam played across the decayed skin of his scalp visible through his thinning hair. He turned around and smiled, showing blackened gums. He was missing an eye.

It was me. I faced a zombie version of myself.

I screamed and shut my eyes. And when I opened them, he was gone.

Of course he was. Because he was a damn dream. A symptom of my fragmenting mind.

I need to get out of here!

July 10

PATHETIC LITTLE MAN WEAK YOU WILL JOIN US IN DEATH

I AM WATCHING YOU YOU WILL NEVER BE ALONE YOU WILL NEVER ESCAPE WHAT YOU DID TO US YOU DESERVE WHATEVER YOU GET

July 10 — supplemental

Jesus. I just found the transcript of that entry from earlier today. Now I'm talking to myself. That's the only explanation. Or the ghosts are.

It must have happened while I was blacked out in the bathroom. I'd just finished brushing my teeth, and I was staring at myself in the mirror, wondering who I was.

I woke up over an hour later in the cafeteria, bleeding from a gash on my head. After writing that crazy entry to myself, I must have stumbled into the dining area and passed out. When I collapsed, I bashed my head on a metal table.

The computer was thorough in its instructions on how to stitch myself up.

I'm going to go back to work drilling rocks in the stairwell. Although I've now password-protected the mainframe, I'll still wedge a rock in the outer door so the computer can't lock me out again.

July 10 — supplemental

The good news is I broke through to the other side of the rubble. There's now a huge gap through to the stairwell above. The bad news concerns the boulder that fell away to expose that gap. It landed on my lower leg and snapped it. The tibia? The fibula? Anatomy was never my strong suit. That's why I was a lousy sculptor. I remember that now. Remember lots of things. Not that it'll help me.

When the boulder fell on me, I tumbled backward down the stairs. I would have cracked my skull if not for my helmet.

The rubble, the result of a long-ago cave-in, maybe from an earthquake, had functioned as a drain plug against ground water. Ten thousand years' worth of accumulated water began gushing down on me. The environment suit's oxygen supply still worked, thank God, so I didn't drown. But if I didn't get back inside soon, the bunker would fill up.

The water made movement easy, which was a good thing. I looked down at my leg. I had a new, second knee below my right knee.

I groaned as I dragged myself inside. I kicked away the rock I'd wedged against the doorframe (with my good leg) and told the computer to shut it. The inrushing water narrowed to a sprinkle and finally stopped. The corridor was several inches deep with water. I lay there like a maimed dinosaur.

The computer kept saying something. "User notification. User notification . . ."

"Computer, I need . . ."

It must have taken my call as a go-ahead to read me its notification. "Rubble breach in emergency stairwell has admitted ground water to internal sensors. No chemical contamination detected. Environment suit still recommended above ground until inert atmospheric conditions confirmed."

"Wonderful." I groaned as I dragged myself down the puddled hallway. "Need instructions on treating broken leg."

The pain was exquisite. I felt lightheaded. As I strained, I sputtered saliva against the inside of my faceplate. I felt blood squeeze past the stitches on my forehead.

I became aware of legs standing near me. Dozens of them. Lining the walls on both sides. They were all bare, gray, and spotted with decay.

I looked up. All the people I'd murdered stared down at me.

That's when the rest of my memories returned. They crashed and rolled over me like an ocean surf. I remembered my rage at the hoity-toity scientists who built this place. The way they condescended when they invited me to join their human time capsule. Didn't they know I was a pharaoh? I remembered grinning as I ambushed them with my knife and destroyed the cryo-coffins.

But it was like remembering the anger I felt at my brother for breaking my toy when I was six years old. I'm no longer that person. I don't feel that way anymore. I'm not really a pharaoh. The only resemblance I have to pharaohs is I spent thousands of years in a tomb.

Oh, God. The guilt... I sobbed as I lay there in the water. I'm crying now. I can't believe I murdered those people... That's what a vacation from your own memories gives you. Perspective. And my new perspective wasn't a good one.

The dead people lining the walls, my honor guard of indictment, they didn't have to say anything. All they did was stare.

"I'm so sorry," I said. "I wish I could take it back. Please forgive me. Please . . ."

I bowed my head, submerging it in the puddle filling the hallway. Listened to myself cry inside my helmet. I was a snake, the lowest of the low, wallowing in the primordial pool, not deserving to breathe the air above.

When I looked again, the people were gone.

I felt lighter. The ghosts had forgiven me, if they'd been there at all. Or I forgave myself. There was no way to atone, no way to undo my crime, so what else could I do? I had to acknowledge my evil. I vowed never to travel that path again.

That is, if there's a path left for me. Because the road was again cut short.

Footsteps splashed toward me. I rolled over to see a scrawny, balding Caucasian man approach. He wore a cryonaut's jumpsuit, and he looked entirely healthy. Not a zombie, but a real person. This was confirmed when he grabbed my bad leg by the ankle and yanked.

I screamed as he pulled me down the hallway. The water made it easier for him to move me. Yank. Pain. Scream. Glide a few feet. Repeat.

"Stop! Stop! Who are you?"

He stopped yanking long enough to point at the nametag sewn into his jump suit. "Ernest Feldstein. I'm a psychiatrist. Not that it matters anymore."

Yank. Pain. Scream.

"But I thought . . . I thought . . ."

"Thought I was dead? So did I when I woke up and found everyone slaughtered. But you failed to find all the cryo-coffins. Mine was stashed up in an air shaft, out of the way. Last-minute addition to the crew. Aren't I lucky?"

Yank. Pain. Scream.

For a scrawny man, he sure pulled hard. I worried my shattered leg bone would slice an artery. In this middle of this agony, however, I wondered if his presence explained some of those things I'd blamed on myself, like the body in the hallway and the sabotaged cameras. Not that I felt like asking him just then.

He towed me all the way back to my own cryo-coffin. Dropped my feet inside. Then before I could react, he hoisted my upper body by the neck. I was too busy trying not to choke to stop him from dumping me the rest of the way inside the coffin. Then in two quick movements he unlatched and removed my helmet. I gasped and reached for him, but he was already slamming the lid down on me.

I watched him through the window as he checked the coffin's readouts. "What are you doing?"

"What does it look like? Putting you back into stasis. Except when I swim out of here, I'm going to leave the bunker door wide open. This place will flood. The seal on your coffin will rust and deteriorate. Might take a few years, but what does that matter? Once it ruptures, your coffin will fill up, and you'll drown in your sleep. Fitting end for you, I think."

Ernest Feldstein smiled as he addressed the ceiling. "Computer. Initiate stasis sequence in cryo-coffin twenty-six."

When nothing happened, his smile fell. "Computer. Acknowledge."

The password. He didn't know I'd locked down all central computer functions earlier that day.

"Computer." My voice shook. "Replace bunker atmosphere with preservative gas. Password: pharaoh."

Ernest Feldstein stared at me in panic as a light green gas began hissing out of the ceiling vents. He began coughing. "Computer. Belay order! Computer . . ."

For ten millennia, the antiseptic gas had preserved the bunker's environment as thoroughly as an atmospheric vacuum. No bacteria, no mold, no organism of any kind had spawned in the sterile tomb. With the impenetrable bunker door shutting out all moisture—and the cryo-coffins suspending Ernest Feldstein and me in clinical death—we'd traversed the centuries. But now, outside the protection of his cryo-coffin, the balding psychiatrist would suffocate.

He lurched for one of the open coffins in a last-ditch attempt to save himself. He died with one leg and one arm still hanging out.

"Computer. Fill my cryo-coffin with ordinary oxygen. Password: pharaoh. I need to think."

And I've been here ever since.

July 11

It's just after midnight. I keep falling asleep and waking up. My leg is swelling and turning purple. The pain overwhelms all thought.

The computer says I need surgery. The longer I delay, the worse I'll get. Except there's no one else here. Wouldn't it be a colossal joke if that has *always* been the case—if Ernest Feldstein was yet another figment of my guilt? He was a psychiatrist, after all, and I've never gotten along well with them.

I cried for a while after killing him. Haven't I killed enough people? Haven't I learned anything? I didn't have any choice—or did I? I could have just let him kill me. It would've been justice for my victims.

The worst part is I know he wasn't evil. In his shoes, I doubt I would have acted any differently.

As if any of this makes any difference anymore. I'm still stuck down here with a maimed leg.

I could tell the computer to return the bunker atmosphere to normal and open my coffin back up. But then what? Try to climb out on my own with a broken leg? Put my helmet on and try to swim up a mile-deep stairwell? With no guarantee anyone is up there who can help? I'd never make it.

I've recorded a distress call. The computer is transmitting it up the stairwell on several radio frequencies. On repeat. If there's anyone topside who can receive and understand it, then maybe I'll be rescued.

Until then . . .

I'm dictating these final words, and then I'm going to order the computer to re-initiate my stasis. I survived ten thousand years in this thing. Maybe I can survive a few more. I removed the password restriction to make it easier if someone finds me.

If they don't, I suppose justice will be served. I leave my fate in the hands of my victims. If they've forgiven me, then maybe they'll give me a second chance.

If I emerge from this cocoon, hopefully this time I'll no longer know how to kill people. The caterpillar retreats into his chrysalis, and when he emerges, he's a beautiful moth. A pharaoh moth.

Computer, initiate stasis sequence in cryo-coffin twenty-six.

Matthew Warner is a writer in the Shenandoah Valley, Virginia. His novels include *The Organ Donor: 15th Anniversary Edition* and *Empire of the Goddess*. Known primarily as a horror and fantasy writer, he's a lover of all things weird and humorous. Visit him at *matthewwarner.com*.

Lucas Scheelk

Once Upon An Alternate Universe

Golem, living out of time, wearing tzitzit the length of human thighs, witnesses the Moon twined with Mars

"Canadian geese flying towards the North Pole?" asked Moon.
"I guess no one's spared from changing their flight plans!" Mars
replied.

Golem, desperate to call his people, prays with a minyan of stars

Highway Pre-Deceased

Do you need directions? Your budget cannot afford 72
    hours

Charm the cashier at self-checkoutConceal your booze in
    the Fred Meyer parking lot
Their morning is your eveningCHUG
What a stressful shiftCHUG
You're the fuck-up they're lovelyCHUG

Is it travel if the destination is the sameYour insurance
    doesn't cover existence

YesterdayDay 0
You wanted to join your mother

TodayDay 0
You want a parade within walking distance

TomorrowDay 0
Mars will be at its closest to Earth

With a knife you can create new freckles

This isn't the Enterprise, you will miss your exit

Lucas Scheelk (they/them) is an autistic queer white Jew with bipolar disorder. They're from the Twin Cities, now in Washington state. They're the author of *This Is a Clothespin* (Damaged Goods Press, 2016) and *Holmes Is a Person as Is* (self-published, 2016). Check out their writing at *Assaracus, Barking Sycamores, QDA: A Queer Disability Anthology, Queer Voices: Poetry, Prose, and Pride, Stone of Madness Press, Pandemic Publications, Spoon Knife 5: Liminal, Wizards in Space,* and *Mollyhouse,* among others. They don't have a college degree to their name but dreams to run a library. Twitter: @TC221Bee

Richard A Shury

Homecoming

The parking lot smells of sun as I stop the car. Swapping shoes for jandals I walk across the lot, slowly, the heat of the day surrounding me. The obligatory saunter enforced by my footwear brings me past a set of long, high windows. I reach the door and enter, expecting a wash of cool, but the swarming heat remains. This isn't the US, and AC just isn't done here.

It's early enough that there are few customers. I pick a booth and slide in, with a groan which has, by now, become automatic. I try to remember when I started doing it and fail.

I sit, allowing my driver's tension to sink away. Then I lean back, and pull a menu from the slot, avoiding the top left corner, which is painted sticky brown by what I hope is old ketchup. I glance around, but there's no server to be seen; then I recall how bad the customer service is here—these people don't need tips to survive.

All-day breakfast, the menu says. The same words that enticed me from the road. Scanning the options, I ignore the voice telling me to eat healthily.

Five minutes later, a woman wanders over. I assume she's a waitress because she asks me what I want to order, but she's dressed in nothing more than nondescript shorts, a t-shirt with puffs of flour on the front, and a pair of off-white jandals which used to be just regular white. I wonder if she's the cook as well as the server.

Her skin is a pale shade of brown, and she's at least middle-aged, with a hint of prettiness under a burgeoning set of wrinkles. Her teeth are smoker's yellow. The skin on her legs is strangely smooth.

"What can I get ya?" she asks, pleasantly enough.

"Coffee, please. And breakfast number two."

She looks me up and down. I know that next, she'll ask me where I'm from. They don't believe me when I say, Wellington. But she doesn't ask.

"Coming right up."

The waitress turns and wanders off. I realize I forgot to ask for water, but I don't call out to her.

The walk was long and uphill, but I tried not to complain. It was a nice day, too; another nice day. Up a winding path in the sunshine, with trees swaying in the breeze, bright green leaves and tiny white blossoms, intricate patterns of light and shade all around me. I've been in worse places.

Still, it never seems real. My mind wandered to the wake, the opened casket. After that, I vowed I'd never see one again. It was... wrong. The casket was there, but she wasn't.

It was like revisiting my childhood home, another thing I shouldn't have done but did. Nothing wrong with how the house looked exactly, it just wasn't what it had been. I wiped the memory from my mind as best I could, and walked on, up to this place.

She's not here either, I'd realized as I approached the stone slab. I hadn't been able to do that classic movie scene where the person talks to the other person as if they were here, sleeping under still ground, and cries their eyes out. It didn't feel like that at all. It felt like I was standing in a field staring at nothing. I walked back down the hill.

I decided to find a place to remind me of the real her. A place we'd shared, somewhere just ours, she and I. It didn't take but a moment for the perfect spot to come to mind.

She did shift work, so it was hard to find time together. But sometimes the fates were kind, and we'd drive out, epic journeys to me then, and find a little diner. I could order whatever I wanted, and we'd just talk. About whatever was going on with me, self-centered as I was, as all children are.

It was something we only did a handful of times, but it stuck with me. Last time I was home I'd planned to go back there with her, but then there was the call that cut all plans short.

So I drive, trying to find the place. I asked Dad, but he didn't know. Now all I have is the search. I visit all the places I can think of, one at a time, hoping to find the memory of her there.

I eat my breakfast slowly, trying to live in the moment. Every mouthful is a world of taste and sensation. My complaining stomach settles down into a contented purr. I roll slices of bacon across my tongue, and dip toast in thick, gooey egg yolk. Pancake syrup stains my fingers, and I lick them clean.

Sitting back, I survey my conquest. There are streaks of grease across the plate, glinting in the light. There are yellow blobs, and a mess of syrup spread across the table-top.

I sit sideways in the booth, and cross my legs, waiting for the waitress and more coffee. She takes her time; I pretend I'm in the south, on some lazy weekend, no hurry to be had. Which is partly true.

This isn't the place, though. I can just tell. Memories are unreliable, but I'll know it when I see it.

I have to believe it's still there, a small place off a small road, an oversize parking lot with overhanging trees. I'll just have to keep looking.

Draining the rest of my coffee in one go, I stand. I leave some money on the table, then remember they don't do that here. I recover the money and pay at the counter, receiving a mumbled thanks and a handful of coins. I walk out to the parking lot, pull on my shoes, start the engine. I'll drive out again tomorrow.

Richard A Shury is from New Zealand but has been haunting London for some time now. His short stories *Ricky's Journey*, *Gamer*, and *The Formula* have been published in anthologies, while his story *The Vortex* placed second in the Limnisa Short Story Competition 2018. He hopes these are the calm before a storm, so you might call him a part-time optimist. Find him @RichardShury or *https://richardshury.wixsite.com/rashury*

Brianna Bullen

AI: *Artificial Interconnection*

Betrayal weighed both on the mind and on the body, causing tension from the tip of the spine through to the muscles of the hands. She was still in disbelief at her orders, while simultaneously not being surprised. She had hoped for better. She hovered above the Earth in her air-speeder, requesting entry into their atmosphere. She was requested to pause as their scanners picked up her ship's ID badge and the contours of her face. She got the green beep of all clear and entered down into their airspace, sliding like a knife through their creamy layers of white cloud and blue gas. The music on her radio was singing to her in human tongues, set to the ancient but revered era of the 80s that had been exchanged to them in cassettes and transmissions broadcast out to meet their tech at the peace meetings between their planets. Not that they actually had their own planet, just colonies that were spreading out the reach of their dying Empire. They'd lost their home planet centuries ago, but they were a warrior race with the equipment to claw parts of the galaxy for themselves. Their only bonds were to each other, to revenge against a cruel galaxy. If this meant being crueler than the harshness of space itself, so be it.

Clawed hands flexed against the steering wheel. Her gloves had accommodated for her hand's nails, built to a regulation two inches. This made blinding enemies particularly efficient. She bopped her head to the beat, another nervous tic, while biting her lip, the darker orange skin there chapped in the ship's artificially controlled temperature environment. Her pass signaled that she was just a courier. The name was true, but the details fake. She was a good enough spy to have not had it ever put on record as a tripwire.

She curved through a cloud as the ant-lines of flight traffic became visible, getting minutely bigger with each second of her descent. She was hailed by a checkpoint before an entry-point tube. She waited for the worker to double-check her papers manually before she could be let into domestic Earth traffic space. At this level, she could see the tops of high-rises, face to face with intergalactic advertisements. Bored, she checked out the closest ones. Earth had taken to the existence of aliens with surprised delight that quickly faded into the mundane of fashionable fads. A human man, a bulky specimen sensually posed, was advertising a Hedrav tech leg prosthetic. The woman next to him was Hedrav herself, modelling a white summer dress with Earth flower shapes pressed into the fabric. It made Yuil uncomfortable, the contrast of the soft frivolous fabric against the woman's vulnerable scales. It was obscene. Hard armor should have been fitted over the skin—the vulnerability left her open to attack. Still... once the discomfort passed, she couldn't help but compare herself to the model in the picture.

While the model was scaly and red, her own flesh was pale orange and smooth. The lady's large ears disappeared into jagged frill points, while her own stood out, elven and scale-less, from slicked-back short hair. She slicked it back in the same direction her curly horns ran, to let their shape blend into them. They'd once been mocked as puny Lega—a type of space mountain goat—but they were more likely to have been Delta Quadrant backwater Rheyzhav. She knew neither of her parents, hoped their union had been on even footing as inherently shameful as it was, so could not confirm her hypothesis about her background. The lady was peak Hedrav beauty standards, bulkily muscled and large, with prominent ears, full silver eyes and fangs on display. Scales or fur were both seen as standard. She tilted her head, blue pupils on grey sclera taking in the image before it shifted to a neon display of beverages and fast food.

In a display roundly—but privately—condemned by Hedrav as tacky and dishonouring, Earth officials had pre-sented attending Hedrav with these dark, carbonated bev-erages. The first pop against General Houden's tongue had led to spluttered choking and claims of poisoning that had almost derailed treaty agreements. The humans had merely laughed—at him, at all Hedrav kind—and said it was perfect-ly harmless Soda Pop. While many goods were imported, the particular brand—Pepsi Cola—was expressly prohibited on Hedrav-controlled planets. Nevertheless, herself and several officers had tasted the elixir as contraband. She had enjoyed the kick. The muted but potent sugar that burst against the tongue. But such words could never be voiced. In a higher military position, you had access to things other people could only dream about, but you could never admit.

The person behind the counter—build and features suggested female, but gender was complex here—smiled while handing her documents back, freshly stamped. Good to go. "Aren't you lucky getting a meeting with the consulate," she could practically feel the lights of the full-vehicle scanner going through her, "hope your meeting is successful!" Yuil nodded minutely and pressed the pedal, easing herself into the on-ramp that took her into the rows of air-traffic.

She didn't realize she was holding her breath until she passed the checkpoint. The separatists' cloaking tech had worked, disguising what was actually in the parcel with the illusion of a harmless box of letters. Hedrav4humanPals (winky face). Tech-Commander Kya would be pleased. Major Jijahren would laugh. Lieutenant Ll'ahayan would smirk. Just as planned. If all things went to plan, she would survive this. She would. Her hands clenched against the steering wheel again, breaths shallow.

The Hedrav needed her to be at the consulate by 0800 hours; Lieutenant Ll'ahayan needed her to be there at 0815 by the latest. Not too late to raise suspicion, but enough to get the Hedrav on edge and acting irrationally. Enough for Lieutenant Ll'ahayan's faction to get into position. Enough for Lieutenant Ll'ahayan to try and warn the human 'United Nations' while getting denied an audience. When the bomb went off, they'd finally listen. Weakened. Hurt. Suspicious of any Hedrav but prepared to listen to the one with the track record of warning against insurgency. That's what Lieutenant Ll'ahayan had said, anyway. Coming from any other Hedrav, and Yuil would have thought it a power grab. But Lieutenant Ll'ahayan wanted what was best for both humans and Hedrav. A future where tensions were completely gone. Under his vision, he believed it to be achievable. No more lives lost in unprovoked attacks, united in cause against extreme prejudice. Where people could coexist and their children would be accepted. A fraction of a city lost was a small price to pay under Lieutenant Ll'ahayan's vision.

A small price...

She was cut-off by a wildly driving human, yapping to someone on their comms device, their hovercar failing to indicate. Such inconsideration in domestic travel would be a grave offense on any of the Hedrav's planets. The human had the gall to scream obscenities out the window at her, the innocent party.

The move across her lane didn't get the driver anywhere quicker, though. The lanes were all congested. If the traffic didn't ease up, the hour of travel time allocated to scope out the parameter before the deadline would be eaten up. She growled in frustration, head meeting steering wheel. The more things came up, the more afraid she became. She was after all a loose end, and although she admired her leader—indeed, almost loved him—she didn't doubt he would dispose of her if either the Hedrav or the humans got the upper-hand in the resulting fight. Couldn't claim innocence in interference if she was around. She was prepared to die for her people and their future, but to die at the hands of the man she was loyal to over the belief she would ever betray him was insulting. Scared her more than death's cold hands.

No advertisements to distract her, she looked to the vehicle beside her. Made eye contact with a human child, staring wide eyed and slack mouthed at her. First Hedrav, huh kid. Drool and fries fell from the kid's mouth. Yuil waved. The child perked right up, waving happily, picking up her toy from the meal box to greet her. A plush red furry Hedrav figure. Friendly and smiling. She felt nauseous.

"Systems detect anxiety in pilot," the cold clinical AI of her ship clipped out. "Would pilot like to commence comfort protocol?"

Eyes on the road as the traffic began to clear, she nodded her head once. "Yes."

Immediately the voice changed to a relaxed, comforting sigh of a yawn. A pop-up box appeared on her dashboard, showing the flickering image of a smiling face. "Hey, Yuil. Everything's telling me you aren't feeling too good. You want to have a chat? No pressure."

She had never met the woman on the screen. She was just an algorithm. Pixels generated as a human addition to the ship that was implemented during the technology sharing portion of their meetings. See, humans cared about something called 'mental health.' They valued the mind more than they valued physical strength. To an extent it made sense to Yuil. Keeping your wits in battles and being able to enact strategy was essential. But this wasn't what humans used it for. Their focus was on emotions. Putting a salve on weaknesses. The Hedrav thought she was weak, anyway. She almost terminated the AI but hesitated. The lady on screen was human. Clean faced, skin an even brown, features full of mischief. Hazel eyes were swimming with kindness behind circular spectacle frames. Openness no Hedrav would ever share. Yuil's eyes locked on the pale pink glossed lips, quirked in a smile that flickered with pixels.

"Yuil? Work with me."

She jolted. "Sorry, C. It's... been a while."

"Tell me about it! My program hasn't been activated in three months. Do you know how lonely it is in the dark?" C was pouting.

Cramped prisons with no ventilation or light. Being shoved down a well by Hedrav teachers who didn't want to have to deal with her weaker disposition. Floating in deep space, praying for recovery by a passing ship. Being in the gullet of a space-whale...

"Sorry, C," she repeated, softly.

"Man Yuil, you've already apologized. I'm just kidding around. You just let me get some good uninterrupted sleep in. How's your sleep been? Last time we talked you said you were having some troubles. Anything changed?"

She hadn't slept for forty-eight hours, going over every possible complication and step of the plan. "About the same."

C tilted her head, looking at her with concern in her small square on the dashboard. "Oh Yuil. Weight of the world on your shoulders as usual?"

"Something like that," she said, clipped. Turned off the air-highway. "Might be the last time talking to you for a while."

"That's such a shame," the simulation was lifelike in its ability to render human concern. "I like being here for you."

Beneath her armor, her chest tightened. "Yeah."

"You like me being here for you too, don't you, Yuil?"

"... Yeah." Her throat felt dry.

The woman on the screen was smirking, glasses lit up and grin like the cat who got the canary. "If I were with you, I could make sure you got some good rest. Wouldn't let you leave bed without a stern talking to."

That sounded so nice. "Waiting by the door outside to push me back in?"

"Oh baby, I'd be in that bed with you." That smirk was practically ravenous now. "Only way to make sure you don't sleep in that armor is to be in there with you, right?"

Yuil was taken back. But like any conflict, she needed to meet the adversary head on. "Stars, you'd be an annoying bedwarmer."

"Oh, that's not fair," she tilted her head, short dark curls bouncing to the side. "Just because I'm clingy. And run hot."

Stars. This AI. Blood rushed to her cheeks. There was no backwards facing mirror inside the air-speeder, equipped with external cameras as it was, but she was sure her orange face would be a bruised dark blue. "Hedrav aren't cold-blood-ed, you know."

"I do," C said gently, reminding her of her limitations. "My files tell me you're endothermic. With a baseline temperature of twenty-five degrees Celsius. So colder than me."

Yuil rounded a bend, turning the music down to better focus on C's words. She didn't volunteer anything, though.

She wondered if the model for the AI was that much of a tease and smart-arse, or if the AI had developed it independently to best draw out a reaction from her reticent personality. Their first interactions had been kind, though. More formal. Less inappropriate. But the baseline without interactive learning was a worthy human. Some military comms officer who had been volunteered for, or had volunteered for, the task. Presumably, they'd felt her to be affable enough but able to stand her ground for the task of dealing with harsh Hedrav communication. Every time, it did feel like she was purposefully made for just Yuil.

Despite herself, she felt one hand leave the steering to hover over her face, the move followed by the AI's eyes to give the illusion she was really there with her. She jerked it back,

"The system wouldn't have booted me up if it didn't feel there was a problem," C said evenly, brows furrowed. "What's up?"

Yuil tried to ignore the request. Put a bit more speed into her drive. But her thoughts let themselves out before she could stop them. Quietly. Barely audibly. "I'm scared."

"Oh, Yuil," C was all sympathy. As simulated as the expression was, it was the kindest gaze that had ever been sent her way. "Thank you for trusting me with that. I know it can be… hard. Would you like to talk about the reasons for your fear?"

Yuil closed in on herself, something inside her brain clicking into a different gear. She shook her head. Throat tight. "No."

That concern never wavered. "I wish you could trust me. You can trust me. Can I do anything for you at all?"

She shook her head again. Stopped halfway through. "Could you keep talking?"

"I could talk your ear off," C chuckled. "What do you want to chat about? I'm always up for chatting about my family, personally—"

"I don't have…"

"I know. I know. I wish I could give you mine," C sighed. "Would you like me to sing the song on the radio for you? I like music, personally."

In another few minutes, she'd be able to see the Consulate. "Please."

Traffic had paused her by the turnoff. As C sung, Yuil felt herself drifting off. Drifting way passed the bend she was supposed to take to get to the consulate. Veering off to the military compound in this city. Found herself yelling at the front. *Somebody, defuse this bomb, please. There's an attack planned. Please get your forces ready. You've been betrayed. By the Hedrav and Lieutenant Ll'ahayan both. Please listen to me. I can't let them betray you like they've betrayed me.*

Imagined the regulation boots of C running to meet her, accompanied by higher ranking officers. Concerned and taking the situation seriously, but catching her eye. She could trust C, after all. They'd let out the breaths they didn't know they were holding. When the bomb was diffused, the battles fought, Yuil could finally ask C her full name before C could ask her out for coffee. (She hated coffee, black death in liquid, but could make an exception for C.)

They'd grant her protection from both groups she'd betrayed in multiple ways. Traitors couldn't get medals of honor, but she'd have their respect. She'd finally feel the glory and pride all Hedrav were supposed to feel, holding

C's sunburnt hands in her own, which were much longer with claws.

Comfort rose in her chest, C's job done, in a twittering note.

Brianna Bullen is a Deakin University PhD creative writing candidate writing about memory in science fiction. She won the 2017 Apollo Bay short story competition and placed second in the 2017 Newcastle Short story competition. Her poetry chapbook *Unicorns with Unibrows* is currently published as part of Puncher & Wattmann's Slow Loris series.

Kushal Poddar

A Willow Read House

An eidetic willow reads the house,

chuckles at the acts, bends in tension

having a sneak peek at the knives

kept in a leash inside the blindfold of drawers.

Today it follows the house-daughter's narrative

sprawled all over the living room, stairs,

and even between the couches' operose clefts.

And even in the couches' cleavages.

for a moment her face floats up to the caliginous pane.

If the tree would make a scrapbook with those

the pages would expunge the moments every Autumn.

The knives would remain. The face—in some orphanage.

Death grows up to be death.

A poet and a father, **Kushal Poddar** edited a magazine - *Words Surfacing*, authored seven volumes of poetry including *The Circus Came To My Island, A Place For Your Ghost Animals, Eternity Restoration Project: Selected and New Poems* and *Herding My Thoughts To The Slaughterhouse: A Prequel.* Find and follow him at *https://www.amazon.com/Kushal-Poddar/e/Bo7V8KCZ9P*

Ian Kinney

Excerpts #OfAsh

AUTHOR'S NOTE: In following excerpts #OfAsh, I cut-up posts from my Facebook feed, I then repost the writing back to Facebook for my Friends to see. All of these excerpted posts, and more, are available for public view on my Facebook Page. To highlight its status as pilfered text, not only do I include no conventional capitalization (except for the pronoun, "I"), nor do I include any proper names (except for recognizable brand names), but I also editorially end every sentence with either a question mark or a full stop. My experimental writing process, #OfAsh continues on Facebook.

beer acquired, vacuum cleaner locked and loaded, laundry explosion sorted; I'm ready to conquer the chaos. dumpster diving is more than a hobby, it's a passion. get inside. these clouds look scary and I can see quick movement from my office window. #OfAsh

I was a child model. they write, we create idea machines that cost nothing. nothing like this happens, I'm just surrounded by machines that cost nothing. I love that. they write, the knowledge locked inside the machines must be social. too cute. had to share. I just read about this magic. the setting end turns intellect into sequin smattered velvet. a recycled petition. #OfAsh

I don't do stuff like that. you grieve forever. but her wounds attest to the significance of adventure. en route by train, blurring thru a thunderstorm at 7 am. the bees answer back with interpretive dance. like an aphrodisiac, only with less sexy foam and more fun. weeping in a hotel room in solidarity with mourners all around the world. I'm forgetting the words in english. the antioxidant that you're taking is at best useless and at worst harmful. you will suffer again. and it appears that a triggering mechanism—such as infection with a particular virus or strain of bacteria—is also necessary. #OfAsh

yesterday, on my way home from work, I almost kept driving. what did I leave behind? there's so much to see. can you see me? I'm beginning to wonder if I should go to the hospital. a few pictures along the river. I would not exist if not for other magicians who encourage me. 30 years feels shorter than the future. I prefer the softer pillows, but maybe there is something out there that's better than that. what are your tonsils good for? I may paint on a smile, but it feels like I act it out. what is the best pillow in your opinion? hope for today. the dr. wrote me a note to keep me off work for a couple days. the past couple of days have been rough. seeking authentic engagement. he laughed at me and said "we'll see". not sure where I was going, but I was just gonna drive till I run out of gas. I told him I was gonna go anyway because I can't afford to take time off. yesterday, on my way home from work, I almost kept driving. what did I leave behind? #OfAsh

I was prepared for this. I felt it coming my whole life. this is the kinda shit that's gonna get me sent to jail some day. we're here for a good time, not a long time. wash your fucking hands and stop touching your face. if you like sarcasm and satire then this is not the place for you. so good. sitting in my backyard, listening to the playlist that I made during my epic trip last year, the soft glow of the lights inside of my house and then ... giggles and laughter from my children and partner inside. watch it. I worry about all of you. is someone able to talk please? me coming out of this socially awkward and afraid. yar. it's amazing what sleep can do. I am finished. oh yeah, looking forward to this. I really need a friend. I do not see things first hand, or travel with the rapid winds, or enlist swift horses to glimpse distant vistas. I'm not doing ok. the bunnies that live by my workplace had their babies today. trying to reach out. extra points if you spot my absolute favourite. every single morning. tell me, what is the poem or collection that stays with you, or that you return to? these are lovely. we have had the geese reclaim the roof of the building. subdivisions. I really need someone to talk to. for my ally is the mark, and a powerful ally it is. I feel like this is consumer marketing at its finest. okay maybe this one is my favourite. I have been called out. one of my tech savvy cousins made me a toon. I have never been so cool, but this is excessive. what routines have you eliminated recently? don't get me wrong, people deserve to be compensated. but I question my existence sometimes. save for later. save it for dinner and cook your potatoes in a tinfoil sack made for amazing and flavour-full roasted potatoes. to show shepherds how much they eat, sheep turn pasture into wool and milk. they were amazing years, and I'm so proud they decided to each climb a tree. if you would like more, then follow me. earlier this fine warm evening, the kittens and the dogs played together. they did not vomit the grass, uninstructed, to show the facts of their digestions. I have created a professional page, and published two books. they do not show you their theorems. the moon, and the stars, but oh how my thoughts fly. the 80s anthology that you loved shall now serve as a shudder side project. game changing limited editions - not found in stores. I helped to build this long ago. alas, I have to strain to see the sun. I would really like a psycho-geographic map of my neighbourhood, one that identifies the cats individually. k, get on that for me, thanks. don't hesitate to text me if you have any questions. a synagogue+mosque hybrid. my pandemic blanket is ever so slowly getting bigger. I made a pub style party platter. 'tis true. can I get a large serving of attention? we just watched the episode where x gets the shit kicked out of them, and honestly, it was so heartwarming. I can't fucking deal. a lesson in stillness. next-state surgery. I said I thought their seeds were beautiful, and I still think that to build a robust model for reality we need to evaluate new info. life may be incredibly hard, but also perfectly wonderful. it is commonly believed that a fish living in a little stream does not know the size of the river, or of the sea. I did a thing, and it wasn't even because of a psychotic break. I will not even entertain it, I will just laugh it off. there are so many "free" healing workshops and webinars in my feed right now. the girl with the pearl earring just got even cooler. someone explain shower cap undies. this is what I call clickbait, but I refuse to click. wow, I want one. we need some hope-filled words for these gorgeous spring streets. the key to a good day is routine. transfer. this is to say that honestly, today was a really rough day. any lil' bit of virtual kindness, encouragement that you can spare is appreciated. I just want to remind you, that I respect and appreciate your frustration with the lockdown, but please go ahead with a plan, and do so sensibly over time. I was prepared for this. I felt it coming my whole life. #OfAsh

you need to stay. mathematics. port. sensitivity. sensitivity. birdsong. this is chaos theory. hedge. so let them go. frame. trust energy. yay. and if you cease to exist? you are here. and every choice you have ever made has led you to right now, reading this. while you exist, you are here. I have a wall. walker. prayer. every movement and moment matters; those bad choices led you to the best days of your life, if you were to play it all in rewind. double bubble. change will come, even if you're standing still. butterflies with their wings cause hurricanes. so, make your choices and make them loud. trust your mathematics. so many factors play a part in you being here today. the masked. the universe would notice. the mess that would make. so let them go. hedge. this is chaos theory. the hearts that would break. can y'all shut up about x? I used pain, in part, to make my wedding invites. so just stay. you need to stay. mathematics. #OfAsh

I can even remember the labels on the jars. I'm a huge fan of metal and black metal. my cold-addled brain just manufactured a fantastic full length sex dream featuring this ensemble cast. I wish this was real. war. I just ordered myself a yesterday, on my way home from work, I almost kept driving. what did I leave behind? there's so much to see. can you see me? I'm beginning to wonder if I should go to the hospital. a few pictures along the river. I would not exist if not for other magicians who encourage me. 30 years feels shorter than the future. I prefer the softer pillows, but maybe there is something out there that's better than that. what are your tonsils good for? I may paint on a smile, but it feels like I act it out. what is the best pillow in your opinion? hope for today. the dr. wrote me a note to keep me off work for a couple days. the past couple of days have been rough. seeking authentic engagement. he laughed at me and said "we'll see". not sure where I was going, but I was just gonna drive till I run out of gas. I told him I was gonna go anyway because I can't afford to take time off. yesterday, on my way home from work, I almost kept driving. what did I leave behind? #OfAsh

wow, I had no idea. I'm me again. my lungs don't like me breathing too deep. I guess it's time for a long shower after the show tonight and running the humidifier on high. temporarily astrologically burnt out. second day of the new year, not so much. I am still stalling. I'm not gonna have kids, but you have to convince someone to rifle through my stuff when I die so that you can laugh at this. I forgot about this. it's beautiful. it's so hard to watch this knowing that most people would stand by and watch another genocide. I am selling/giving away some things. would you like any of this? better get off da screens. wow, I had no idea. I'm me again. #OfAsh damn girl, you beautiful, like a potato. the isolation is starting to get to me. bubba shot the jukebox last night. that's quarantine, baby. took a short drive, and this turkey was right on the road, walking toward me all puffed up. when I seek your approval, I don't approve of the me that seeks the approval. my plant blooms after tears. okay, yes to the physical distancing and the protection of customer service staff, but goddamn, my glasses need adjusting and it's driving me nuts. we actually had to go into reverse for a bit. that one fly who harasses you is back. do you need any turnbuckles? any ideas? work hard to remember this one. clouds are amazing. the years are in stock again. it's just a layman's curiosity I suppose, the same as how I wanna know about the inside of everywhere (haha). these injections suck. where would I find such things? watching humanity react to basic instructions. I've sworn an oath of solitude until the pestilence is purged from the lands. I have to say weird stuff, or I'll die. it's probably best to just look away when I eat. all three. altwo. alone. damn girl, you beautiful, like a potato. the isolation is starting to get to me. #OfAsh

he walks around not even realizing that he's dead. I could really use a friend right now. how do you convince a boomer to stop reading the comments on things? contemplating past selves. trying to focus more and be less stoned. found this ominous as fuck garbage can today. it's not even a toilet. I can order a litre of customized ice cream to my house. a kind of friday miracle. it's so out right now. I see from my interweb newsfeed this week that it has been a rough one for a lot of u. like holy fuck. he walks around not even realizing that he's dead. I could really use a friend right now. #OfAsh

8 tater tots exactly. did it just slip my mind? a little win. very late. what creates magic and shares? I really need to stop giving energy to people who won't give it back. hey everyone, my car died in the cold. do any of you have a know a trustworthy mechanic? baby cop face. was I supposed to get a phd at some point? are all you folk doctors now? the baby cop face. I think this is our street... from up at the top? who can I bribe to drive me around a lot tomorrow? don't get locked into long-term commitments. offer extended. shop online now. 8 tater tots exactly. a little win. #OfAsh

heh, it me. another thing I dreamt. relax, this is my second rodeo. I bought a ladder. I want to remember these very early mornings, how she sings and talks in the dark, unafraid. who is she visiting? how do you protect your device? respectability is bullshit. next up, world domination. december is here and so fridays this month will feature christmas movies. gonna have me a cup of happiness. he was built on a different planet. this gem came up in my memories. this level of protection does the trick. yes to masks. if it makes you feel proud and happy all of the time, then it's not propaganda. I have a kick-ass community and they push me to greatness every day. yes, I am in fact listening to the mr. meeseeks remix at work. do you think a depressed person could make this? runners, help: I gave myself a bluster on the bottom of my pinky toe. I protect my phone because I'm a careless human. heh, it me. another thing I dreamt. #OfAsh

---

Ian Kinney is a bisexual settler poet who lives in Calgary and cares for his family's net-zero homestead on the Kainai territory between Lethbridge and Vulcan, Treaty 7 Land. His work engages with memory, disability, and trauma on a personal, philosophical, and theoretical level, rejecting the idea of recovery as a linear journey from "damaged" to "healed", as well as refuting progressive notions of "healed" or "whole" as an ideal—or even possible—result for those who survive trauma. His writing explores possibilities for rehabilitation within our shared expressions. Ian has authored one book of poetry, *Air Salt: A Trauma Memoiré as a Result of the Fall* (University of Calgary Press, 2019) which was shortlisted for the 2020 Robert Kroetch Award For Poetry.

J. S. Allen

Witching Weather

(or Belno's Tale)

Belno understood more than most how the lives of seeming strangers are actually intertwined in ways surprisingly intimate, how our every action ripples through a web of interpersonal connections, with consequences no less potent just because they operate outside our knowledge or understanding. Belno was comfortable with not knowing and not understanding. But sometimes when he watched people, he could almost see the gossamer threads connecting them, stretched and vibrating with perturbations from their daily doings, with cautious tendrils seeking new connections.

He fancied himself a connector of people. He'd been doing this since he was a waif coming up on the hard streets of Kortholomoth. It was Belno who coalesced his fellow urchins into a community who looked out for one other, turning their mutual desperation into a prosperity of sorts. Not that he was their leader, not that anyone would credit him, but Belno knew he had wisely connected the right people at the right times to bring about a sort of golden age for street kids in Kortholomoth.

Sure, the golden age lasted only a few weeks. But a few weeks is an aeon when you're eleven. And what glorious weeks they were! Whenever Belno was hungry and low—which was most of the time—he liked to think back to capers from those good days.

Like that night they cleaned out the dock master's mansion. Enchito, the littlest of their crew, snuck in the coal chute and secreted himself all day in the house while the dock master and his family packed for a trip. Belno had rallied perhaps a hundred children (the number grew each time he told the story), who had all suffered at the hands of the cruel dock master and his associates, and when finally the family and servants departed, Enchito threw open the doors and let them all in. In less than an hour the entire house had been picked clean, furniture and all. Belno claimed for himself an overstuffed crimson chair, which he sat upon like a throne amidst the debris of the abandoned ruin where he and his gang headquartered at the time.

Elna knew this story already, and all his others, so Belno kept it to himself. Just smiled at the memory as they trudged along. They had decided, over Belno's objections, to return to Kortholomoth, and so—after plucking themselves finally out of the Lokiswood this morning—they had hiked for miles across the desert until they found the King's Road and then pointed themselves east.

It was always harder on Elna, these lean times. Scowling even deeper than usual, she turned her face away from every passerby, for fear of being recognized.

"Relax, Elna," said Belno. "No one's after us, not anymore. They've moved on, clean forgot us, forgot all about Belzea."

She shushed him as two camel riders passed at a trot.

"Don't say that word. Best you never say it again, damn your eyes."

"Aw, Elna. Don't go disparaging Belzea. Belzea is a reliable earner, every time. It's not my fault Shula went rogue."

Elna wheeled on her husband then, halting him in his tracks. "So it's my fault, then, is it? That's what you're saying?" A slight woman she may have been, but Elna possessed a fierceness not to be underestimated.

Belno shriveled back, throwing up his hands in defense. "No, no. That's not what I said, Elna. I said, it's Shula's fault, isn't that what I said? We've been over this, remember? We agreed it was definitely Shula's fault."

Elna balled up her fists, her lower lip quivering with rage. Belno watched that lip very carefully, knowing his fate hung upon it. She had a mean left hook, and the only way to dodge it was to know when it was coming. But on this occasion, his words seemed to penetrate, and her rage gathered itself up and redirected itself toward the person who more justly deserved it: Shula. Elna turned back to the road and spat. "One day the wheel will turn."

"One day soon. You'll see. We won't be down for long. We never are. We've got friends in Kortholomoth. Money comes easy in Kortholomoth, remember?" He was using her own words against her. Personally, he thought Kortholomoth too risky and had argued for Ragne—someplace new, someplace no one knew them or had ever heard of the colony of Belzea. But Elna had insisted on Kortholomoth: familiar and safe. Safe, so long as their past transgressions were forgotten or forgiven. After two years, surely people had moved on.

But it was a long walk to Kortholomoth. Ragne they could have reached simply by floating downriver. Instead, they had to cross a desert on foot, and Belno's foot was already acting up. He had stepped on a thorn while hiding out in the Lokiswood, and while Elna had got most of it out, the tip of the thorn was still embedded deep in the sole of his left foot. He was toughing it out for now—but another four or five days on the King's Road? He was not so sure.

Neither he nor Elna knew the first thing about surviving in the wild, and their two weeks in the Lokiswood had been wretched ones. They'd not eaten properly in all that time, and the pair of them had shriveled up to little more than skeletons. They used some lengths of rope they'd found in the woods to hold up their trousers, which were much too large for them to begin with. The trousers, too, they had found in an old rotting shack. Elna still had not forgiven him for making her put them on, these trousers so dirty they had mushrooms growing on them. But it saved their lives: When the angry mob came looking for a rich couple in fine attire, Elna and Belno were able to blend in with the mob and escape unnoticed.

Still not able to let it go, Elna brought it up again: "We'd have money now if you hadn't burnt our clothes. Your jacket alone could have fetched us a pony."

"Not the clothes again," moaned Belno, pulling at the start of a beard that had grown during their two weeks in the woods. "Who did you think was going to buy our clothes, Elna? Have you noticed any high-end buyers out here on the road? And after we sold them, what, were we supposed to walk to Kortholomoth in the nude? Was that your plan?"

"You didn't have to burn them, that's all I'm saying. You could have hidden them, we could have come back later, after things cooled down."

"Hello," said a woman driving an ox-cart, startling them both. "Would you care for a ride?" A kind-faced woman in a headscarf, Belno judged her instantly to be a generous spirit. He was never wrong about these kinds of things. What really got his attention was the half-eaten biscuit in her hand.

"Absolutely," Belno started to say, salivating—but he was quickly silenced by Elna, who pulled on his sleeve and whispered, "Watch it! That one's a witch."

With great reluctance, Belno said, "No, thank you, ma'am," but his eyes followed the biscuit as she rode away, and he scratched his whiskers in dismay. "What's got into you, woman?"

"That's her, all right," said Elna. "Mixes potions in the woods, she does."

"What? How would you know that?"

Suddenly it struck her: "That's Shula's sister."

"Are you sure?"

"Yes. She lives in a house on stilts along the river, up past Jala. Shula brought me along as a witness when she went to collect her inheritance, remember?" Elna watched the receding figure on the ox-cart. What did Belno see in her eye? Respect? "Shula was terrified of her, said she inherited the witching way from her mother. Did you see that ox? That ox rightfully should have gone to Shula, but she was so intimidated by her sister that she let her keep it for herself."

"She didn't look intimidating to me. She looked nice. With food to share."

"You should know better than to take food from a witch," said Elna, aghast.

"What's wrong with witches? Why are you always worked up over witches?"

Elna shook her head sadly. "Every fool knows to watch out for witches. All the more so with the witching season still upon us."

"Witching season! They come and go with the seasons, do they?"

"I told you, Belno. It's once every ten years, they have their Gathering."

"Is that still going on?"

"Well, it's over now. But they're still congregated in the area, aren't they? Dispersing themselves gradually. Many no doubt on this very road."

"It's not like there's a lot of other roads around."

"That's my point. I'd wager every tenth person on this road is one type of witch or another."

"You think so?" Belno looked up doubtfully at a train of donkeys led by a pimpled, red-uniformed courier. "They all just look like regular folk to me."

"That's what witches do, to blend in."

Belno set his mouth, unconvinced but not wanting to rile up his wife any further. "Well, I certainly hope the next person to offer us a ride is not another witch. Because I for one do not intend to walk all the way to Kortholomoth."

"Ain't no one picking us up tonight. It'll be dark soon. We

look way too rough to pick up at night. Maybe if you hadn't burnt our clothes…"

"Yeah, yeah," said Belno.

They walked in silence up a long hill, doing one another the kindness of not speaking. By now, they were both well sick of one another's voices. Their shadows grew longer and longer, and by the time they crested the hill, the desert sighed around them and a red, dusty dusk descended over the land.

"Maybe we should set up camp over yonder at the base of that hill," suggested Belno, pointing to a sharp little hillock a few hundred yards ahead.

But Elna said, "I don't like the look of that hill, husband. We should walk on through the night and leave this place behind."

"Aw, Elna, what's the rush? It's a long way to Kortholo-moth. When's the last time we could lay down without ants crawling all over us?"

"They have ants out here, too, you nincompoop. And I'm telling you, Belno, I have heard about this stretch of road. That little hill over there? That's where they see her."

"That's where who sees *who*?"

"The apparition. They say she was killed along here. And at dusk," she said, swallowing, "she appears to travelers. And if you see her, it means you will die within the week."

"Come on, Elna. Do you truly believe such ghost stories? Who told this to you?"

"I heard it from the kent girl in the woods. She described a hill just like that one. Kents have knowledge of spirits, you know." They would have starved to death in the Lokiswood had it not been for the little care packages, bundles in leaves and tied with kala fiber, left by the kents.

"Be that as it may, my foot is throbbing, Elna. We haven't eaten in days. We can't go on this way. Be realistic, Elna. We need to make camp. There's a thousand other hills in the Maelor Platt, what's the chance this is that selfsame hill? Naw, look at it, Elna. It's just a regular old hill. A nice place to take shelter from the night wind."

"Stop looking at it," cried Elna, batting at her husband. "She might appear to you."

"All right, all right, I won't look. But maybe we could get a fire going. What do you say?"

"That's all I need. A dead husband and me left to die of exposure on the side of the road."

"No one's dying tonight, Elna." A wagon rumbled by, the driver eying them with suspicion before flicking the last of his burning cigar into the dirt. Belno rushed to collect the stub before it burned out. "Hey, our luck is changing!" He puffed on the stub to bring it back to life and looked gratefully after the wagon.

Elna shook her head, disgusted by her husband as he picked dirt from his lip. "Come on, you lout. Let's get you off that foot." They departed from the road and made for the hill. The red sky was turning to purple. "Just don't look at the hill."

Belno couldn't have been happier. Two weeks was a long time to go without a smoke. It was shaping up to be a fine evening. "Now if only someone would toss some brandy out their wagon."

"Oh, you would probably lap it right off the road, wouldn't you?"

"Depending on the quality," agreed Belno.

"And to think I could have married Baz."

Belno took the tiny cigar out from between his teeth, singeing his fingers in the process. "Ow! Baz? Why'd you have to go and bring up Baz? We were having a nice walk." Belno stubbed out the cigar against a stone. He wanted to save the rest for when he could enjoy it. "Is that why you wanted to go to Kortholomoth? To be with Baz?"

Elna looked away. "It was a joke."

"But why were you even thinking about Baz? It's been years. Why bring up Baz out of nowhere?"

"Sh!" said Elna, grabbing hold of Belno's wrist. "What's that there?" Belno winced; Elna's grip was like a steel handcuff when she was scared.

Belno's heart leapt and he squinted through the failing light to see where Elna pointed. Across the way, someone was moving around—bending, picking things up, setting them down. There was a wagon and dark shadow that might have been a horse or ox lying on the ground. "Someone setting up camp, I expect. Say—maybe they've got something to eat. Or even better, some brandy!"

"Will you keep your voice down? It's got to be the witch we saw on the road earlier. It makes sense, right? Why else would she have come here, to this very hill?"

"Elna, let go my arm, that hurts! Witches, witches, everywhere. Honestly, Elna."

"Shh! Stay low." Elna tugged Belno to the right, circling

around and putting the slope of the hill between them and the maybe-witch.

The first hints of the night wind stung their eyes with sand, and they paused a moment in a sheltered lee of the hill. "Elna, I've got to sit down," complained Belno, slumping down on a fallen log. "Here's a fine place out of the wind."

Elna remained standing, clasping and unclasping her hands.

Belno's foot was throbbing. "Look, Elna, just relax. There's no ghost. There's no witch. There's just people minding their own business. They got their camp, we got ours."

"I don't know," said Elna, working her tongue in her cheek. Whenever she worked her tongue like that, Belno knew she had set her mind on something. There was no use arguing. Groaning, Belno slumped the rest of the way to the ground.

"Elevate that foot," whispered Elna. "I'll just have a quick look and see what she's up to."

Belno lay back and waited for stars to appear. The neeker-beekers began to sing to one another, and—bit by bit—Belno began to relax. Elna's paranoia had infected him a little. He would never admit it, but the truth was Elna did have a sense for the occult.

Laughing at himself, Belno sat up and examined his remaining quarter-inch of cigar. His eyes had adjusted well enough to the dark that he was tempted to unroll the cigar and redistribute its contents into an improvised cigarette—to make it last longer. The trick was to keep the wrapper moist so it didn't crack when flattened out.

But something caught his eye in the dirt, something that

didn't belong. He recoiled at first, thinking some small animal was there. But no—it was a torn piece of something.

Belno picked it up: a lump of soft fabric. His fingers found a seam, skillfully sewn. "What's this?" He held it against the sky to try and get a better look. The cloth formed a sort of concavity and inside was some fibrous stuffing. The same stuffing was strewn about the camp site, and as he looked around he noticed several more lumps of cloth, more than a dozen pieces in all scattered about.

Belno was collecting these pieces when Elna slunk back down the hill, picking her way through a patch of cacti. "That's her, all right," she whispered.

"You know, whispers carry a lot farther across the desert than regular talk," said Belno. "That's a fact."

"No," whispered Elna. "That makes no kind of sense. Now, are you listening to me? She's got a fire going."

"It *is* a might chilly," observed Belno, holding up another of the cloth pieces to catch the light. "Will you look at that, it's got tiny fingers?"

"What you got there?" demanded Elna.

"Found it." He held out a tattered piece for her. "I think it may have been some kind of doll."

"A doll? You're down here playing with dolls, while I'm up there risking my life?"

"Oh, don't be dramatic, Elna. Who's risking their life?" He grabbed the cloth-ball back from her.

"Oh. Now I'm dramatic, am I? I might have been snatched up by a wyvern for all you care. Some husband you are."

"Now it's wyverns? What happened to the ghost?"

"Yes, wyverns! Wyverns and witches and ghosts, all. Mark my words, Belno: A foul wind blows on the Maelor Platt."

"Yes, fine, a foul wind blows. Now help me gather firewood." He put the pieces of the doll into his knapsack.

"Firewood?" hissed Elna. "You want to camp here, with a witch just over the hill?"

"She didn't look like a witch to me."

"Pardon me," came a voice. Elna and Belno both leapt into the air in fright, turning to face the woman silhouetted against the dusk. "I heard the two of you talking. Thought you might be hungry." In her hand she held a smoking frying pan.

A sudden grin split Belno's whiskered face, and he drew two steps forward. "Does my nose deceive me, friend, or is that salty fried dough popping in your pan?"

"Extra salty," smiled the woman. It was indeed the kind-faced woman from earlier. "Come and share my fire. On a night like this, it is better to be together."

"Come, my dear," said Belno cheerfully. "Let's not be rude."

Elna's jaw trembled, but she came along, her fear of witches temporarily eclipsed by her love of salty fried dough.

In a matter of minutes they were all feasting on spice balls together around the fire. Elna was sullen but ate just as many spice balls as he. Finally sated, Belno reclined and groaned happily to himself—and then, as if this night could have been any grander, their host brought out a pipe stuffed with fine kanis. "I don't usually smoke, myself," said the kind-faced woman. "I packed it to share with the kents, because you see, originally I had packed with a trip to the deep forest in mind. But instead I find myself on the road to Kortholomoth, of all places. So perhaps I should share this with you instead."

"I knew you were a kind soul the moment I saw you," said Belno, sitting up again and reaching for the pipe. He pulled a burning stick from the fire and had the pipe lit in less than second. "Didn't I say that, Elna?"

Elna looked away, disapproving. But when Belno passed the pipe to her, she accepted it without hesitation.

"So I have a question for you," said Belno. "When you heard us earlier behind the hill, which did you hear? The whispering or the talking?"

"Oh," said the woman. "Well, I heard both whispering and talking. But then I am a very good listener."

"But the talking is louder," said Elna, around the pipe. "My husband thinks whispering is louder than regular talking."

"Not louder, Elna. Carries farther, that's what I said. What do you say, lady, which carries farther, a whisper or normal speech?"

"At dusk in an open place like this one? Definitely a whisper carries farther."

"Thank you. See, Elna? This lady knows of what she speaks."

"Sure," said Elna. "Quiet is loud. Next you'll tell me fire's cold and east is west."

"Pass the pipe, don't be rude," said Belno.

"It took me a few minutes to remember where I'd seen you before," said the kind-faced woman to Elna. "And how is my sister Shula?"

Uh oh, thought Belno. He tried signaling her with a desperate shake of his head, but it was too late; the topic of Shula had been broached.

"That conniving jackal," began Elna. "All that she has by rights should be mine. A cheater and a thief is what she is, and if you are anything like her I want nothing to do with you."

"Aw, Elna," said Belno. "Don't be that way. The woman just shared her dinner, and her fine fresh kanis."

The woman raised her eyebrows and smiled weakly. "I am called Ursu, by the way. I couldn't help overhearing your talk of witches. My mother was a witch, but I myself am not one, just to be clear."

"So you admit you are witch-born," said Elna sharply.

Belno shushed his wife. "You don't have to say it like that. It sounds like a bad thing when you say it. I don't see what's wrong with having a witch for a mother. Maybe if my mother had been a witch, things would have been better for me. Did you ever think of that?"

Elna's eyes remained fixed on Ursu. Ursu squirmed, avoiding the woman's gaze. Leave it Elna to make a social occasion awkward.

"I would like to propose a toast," said Belno. "... I don't suppose you have anything to drink?"

"Only water, I fear."

"Oh." Having had supper and a smoke, Belno was a little disappointed not to be able to finish the night with a little brandy.

With a sigh Belno returned his attention to the cut-up doll, turning the pieces over in his hands, brushing off the sand.

After a long moment of silence, Ursu cleared her throat and said, "I'll see to my ox," and excused herself.

"You should be nicer," said Belno to his wife.

"Why are you fidgeting with those rags?"

"They're not rags. Look, here's a little ear. This was a right fancy doll for some rich kid, I expect."

"Let me see that," said Elna, snatching the piece from his hands. "Give me those other pieces." She worked a moment, laying out the pieces and rearranging them until she saw how they went together. "Maybe it's worth something if we can sew it back together again."

"I don't know, it's in pretty rough shape."

"Belno, make yourself useful and go over to those thorn bushes and bring me a nice strong needle or two."

"Aw, Elna, can't it wait till morning? My foot, remember?"

"You're all right," she said, concentrating on the doll pieces arrayed before her.

Groaning, Belno rose to his feet. "How am I supposed to find a needle in the dark?" But in truth, the moon had come out and it was easy enough to see the nearby bushes bristling with needles. He picked out a few good ones, straight and strong, and by the time he returned to the fire, Ursu was back and watched with curiosity as Elna pulled thread from her belt rope.

"What've you got there?" asked Ursu, glancing down at the collection of torn fabric.

"I found the pieces over there," said Belno, jerking his head back toward the hill. "I think it may have been a doll, once."

"What?"

"It has little fingers and everything."

Elna held up two pieces to the firelight, trying to figure out how they lined up. Ursu's mouth fell open and she cried, "Let me see that!"

But Elna pulled it back to her bosom. "Oh, no you don't. We found it—the law of finders, you know."

"You don't understand," stammered Ursu, her eyes wide. "I have seen this doll before." She sat back down and stared into the fire, blinking.

"Nice try," said Elna, unmoved. She went to work sewing two pieces together.

"You've seen this doll before?" said Belno, bemused. "How do you mean?"

"A woman made this doll on her deathbed. I promised her I would see it to her daughter in Kortholomoth…"

"Well—obviously this girl, whoever she was, didn't appreciate it," said Elna, "or she wouldn't have cut it to pieces and dropped it behind this hill, now would she?"

"Please," said Ursu, "when you have finished mending it, give the doll to me so I may honor the promise I made to a dying woman. I must deliver this doll to its rightful owner."

"Ha! A likely story. How much will you give me for it?"

"I have no money … But I can cook you a fine breakfast."

"Agreed!" interjected Belno, leaping up with vigor and shaking Ursu's hand. "If your breakfast is anything like your supper, it's worth twenty dolls!"

Elna frowned deeply but held her tongue. Later when Ursu was asleep in her cart, Elna chastised her husband, saying, "You agreed too readily to breakfast. We could have had the ox and cart, at least."

Belno laughed. "An ox and cart for a torn-up doll?"

"Will you try and pay attention? A promise made to a dying woman: That's worth more than any ox and cart. Certainly worth more than this emaciated ox and that rickety old cart."

Belno stroked his patchy upstart of a beard and cast his gaze appraisingly over the ox and cart, considering the words of his wife.

"When you think about it," said Elna, pushing her improvised needle through the fabric and pulling the thread through, "the ox and cart rightfully belong to Shula. And Shula *owes* us. We are well within our rights to seize her property, after what she did."

"You do have a point," admitted Belno.

Belno took out his cigar and began the delicate operation of converting it into a cigarette, while Elna worked on reassembling the tattered doll by moonlight.

The two of them stayed up all night, but before the dawn they lay down next to each other and pretended to sleep.

At first light, Ursu rose and took her cane and went up the trail to gather herbs for her breakfast. Once she was out of sight, Elna whispered, "Now's our chance!"

Belno rose quickly and worked to put the startled ox to the cart. Elna picked up the doll and let her eyes linger on it. "It looks different by the light of day."

"Come on," urged Belno, climbing into the cart. "Leave that."

"But why leave it when we could keep it for ourselves? I think it might actually be worth something."

"Leave it," commanded Belno. "The ox and cart for the doll. That's what we agreed, Elna. Fair is fair. Now will you hurry?"

Once they were on the road with no sign of pursuit, Elna and Belno lapsed into a sulky silence. The sun floated just over the road ahead of them, blinding them.

At length Belno said with a frown, "I wonder what she was going to make for breakfast?"

"Always thinking with your stomach. It's a good thing you've got me to look out for you, mister."

"I've got to admit, Elna, having our own ox-cart is a big improvement, as far as my foot is concerned."

"Let's see what she's got in the back," said Elna, climbing into the bed of the wagon. "Oh, Belno, look at this blanket. We can sleep with a proper blanket tonight!"

"Do you think she'll be all right?"

"Who?"

"What do you mean, who? The lady whose things you are currently plundering."

"Well, she let us sleep on the cold ground while she slept in here with this nice warm blanket. I wouldn't feel too bad for her. She is obviously well off, what with her fine kanis and fried dough and her fancy house on stilts. She will be fine."

"Anything to eat back there?"

"Some biscuits, some oil, a bag of oats, a jug of water. Oh, here we are! A sack of nuts and seeds and dried fruit!" She rejoined Belno and together they set upon these snacks with great enthusiasm.

"Belno, chew with your mouth closed!"

"Say, did you find any money?"

"What?"

"Coinage, my dear. Did you find any?"

"Well," said Elna. "I don't see why you would ask me that question."

"I don't see why you wouldn't *answer* that question."

"But why would you *ask*?"

"I am asking, Elna, because I was curious to know if there was any money that came along with our cart. You said the lady was well off, didn't you? So how well off was she?"

"Just because a person is well off doesn't mean she carries a lot of cash on a dangerous road like this one."

"Aw, this road's not so dangerous."

"I'll tell you what I *did* find," said Elna, reaching behind the seat, "is this kanis pipe."

"Ah! Don't mind if I do. Hey, wait—don't try to distract me. You didn't answer my question."

"Yes, fine. She had one piece of silver. See?" Elna produced a coin from the pocket of her filthy trousers.

Belno nodded. "Hey, that's something, at least!"

"Here, take it."

"No, no. You keep it. You know me, I'll just spend it on some whim."

"But, seeing as how you don't trust me, I think it might be better if you took it."

"Come on, Elna. You know I trust you."

"Then why ask?"

"Because I was curious! Just put it back in your pocket, Elna. There's no need to draw attention." Belno glanced nervously at an oncoming contingent of soldiers flying the king's banner against the morning sun.

"I was going to tell you about the silver piece," said Elna, dropping the coin back in her pocket with a *clink.*

Belno cocked his head. "Elna."

She reached into the sack and pulled out a handful of nuts and seeds and fruits. "Yeah?"

"What was that *clink*?"

Elna picked out the fruit pieces and ate them first. "What?"

"You dropped the coin in your pocket just now, and I heard a distinct *clink.*"

"What are you talking about?"

"You told me you found one piece of silver."

"That's true."

"So what's that coin *clinking* against in your pocket then?"

"Oh! Well, she had some pennies, too. I didn't think it worth mentioning."

"You not mentioning money—why, that's like me not mentioning food. You are acting strange, Elna. We've always been a team before, why hold out on me now?"

"Now who's being dramatic? Here!" She stood up in the wagon and emptied her pockets of coins, spilling them on the bench. "Take them all."

To Belno's relief, the soldiers had already passed, but a family passing in a wagon glanced up at Elna's antics.

Belno pulled over to the side of the road, crying, "Elna, what's gotten into you?" Her eyes were all crazy but also welling with sudden tears. Belno studied her a second. "Wait. This is about Baz, isn't it?" Her face hardened, and Belno lifted his finger at her. "You're planning to dump me first chance you get."

"That's not true," said Elna, her face flinching.

Belno shook his head sadly. "After all we've been through."

"Don't be ridiculous. I can't dump you. You wouldn't make it three days without me."

"I don't know about *that*. But—yeah. I'd be lost without you, sweet dove. Now, please collect your money and let's be on our way. The sooner we get to Kortholomoth, the sooner we can buy you something pretty to put on, and be rid of those awful trousers. I know I haven't been the best husband to you lately, but we've had some good times, haven't we, Elna?"

Elna sniffled and stooped to pick up the coins she's spilled. "Yeah, great times. Like the time your investors wised up and chased us out of Dashvar," said Elna, but Belno detected a hint of a smile at the corner of her mouth.

"We'll land on our feet again, Elna. You'll see." Belno snapped the reins to get moving again—but the ox stood fast and cast a backward glance at Belno. "Come on—yah!" Belno snapped the reins again, but the ox did not budge.

"Problem?"

"I suppose he wants his breakfast."

"We don't have time for that. The witch might be on our trail. She might send those soldiers after us."

Belno groaned. "She's not a witch, remember?" He went to fetch the bag of oats.

"Don't tell me you believed her. Of course she's a witch. Why do you think she wanted that doll so much? I'm telling you, when I saw that doll out in the sun, I could tell there was something magic about it. Like it was alive."

"Well, I'm fair sure it weren't alive, Elna. Now, I've never had an ox before. How much oats are you supposed to feed them?"

"How should I know? Just hurry it up, Belno." She turned to keep a look out for trouble. "I'm just saying, she was definitely a witch. Shula told me as much."

Once the ox had something in his belly he agreed, reluctantly, to pull the wagon. They all felt a little less cranky with some food in their bellies.

They drove out into an open stretch of boulder-strewn desert. Across the expanse they could see a ragged line of mountains across the southern horizon. The sky was empty except for the sun and a few high-flying raptors.

Elna gave him some peace for once, and Belno was able to arrange his thoughts into some semblance of order. The Belzea scheme was still solid. Kortholomoth fairly overflowed with immigrants looking for opportunity in the New World, rich hunting grounds for Belno's particular brand of chicanery. But he would have to lay low and wait for the wrath of the Dashvari investors to cool. In the meantime he could get to work on the necessary forgeries.

An idea occurred to Belno then. He knew a guy who lived out here in the Maelor Platt, an expert in forgery. Lorenko the Scrivener. He made up his mind to reconnect with Lorenko and see about putting together some Belzea land certificates.

So, hours later when the sun was at their backs and Elna (having stayed up all night) was asleep in back with the blanket, Belno departed from the King's Road, turning onto a primitive unmarked road. It did not take long for the rough road to jar Elna into consciousness and she bolted upright. "Where do you think you're going?"

"How's a bed sound, Elna? I have a friend out here who'll put us up for the night. Especially if we share our kanis, eh?"

Elna narrowed her eyes. "What friend?"

"You don't know him. Lorenko. I used to run with him back in the day. His family lives all up in these hills."

"Careful, you'll break the axle! Do you even know where you're going?"

"Relax," said Belno. But it had been a long time and the farther he drove into the orange-colored hills, the less certain he became of the way.

Soon it was getting dark. "Well," said Belno. "Here's a spring. Maybe we camp here for tonight. I'll get us sorted out in the morning."

"We're lost," wailed Elna.

"Shh, let's keep our voices down," suggested Belno, aware that Lorenko's family members were mostly bandits by profession.

"Don't worry, I wasn't *whispering*," said Elna.

As he climbed down from the wagon, Belno became aware of the sudden arrival of four men on horses behind them, long scythes in hand. With their matching mustaches, they looked just like Lorenko.

"Thank goodness," said Belno, breaking into a cold sweat. "Maybe you gentlemen can give us directions."

Two of the riders circled around either side of the wagon. Elna sat very still as their eyes passed over her.

"I'm looking for my good friend Lorenko. The Scrivener. Good friend of mine. You know Lorenko, right?" Belno looked at their scythes and swallowed.

"Lorenko's dead," said one of the riders in back, dismounting. He was the oldest of the group and the others stood by, watching him for instructions.

Belno bowed his head, truly aggrieved. "Damn. He was a good man, Lorenko. Truly, the world is diminished for his loss."

"If you say so. Here's how this works. We take everything, you walk out of here alive. Seeing as how you were friends with Lorenko."

"Yeah," said Belno, clapping his hands. "That sounds great. Thank you. Come on, Elna, hop down and we'll just be on our way."

But Elna remained seated. "You're just going to *give* them our stuff?"

"Heh," said Belno, laughing nervously and looking back and forth between the leader of the bandits and his wife.

"Look," said Elna, climbing down from the wagon and sauntering over to the bandit. He stood watching her while she pulled out the coins from her pockets. "Here's all the money. You're welcome to our frying pan and our blanket." Looking him directly in the eye, she added, "But the ox and cart we keep. We're on the run from the police, and my husband has a thorn in his foot and it's turned bad. I doubt he'll even make it out of your hills with that foot of his." She raised her voice so the other men could hear: "Where's your decency? Is this how you treat a friend of the family, coming to you seeking refuge from the police?"

The leader of the bandits stared back at Elna, his mustache twitching. Belno held his breath.

After a long moment, the bandit took the coins from Elna's hands. He gestured to the wagon with a jerk of his head, and his men took the frying pan, the oats, the blanket and everything else. These they loaded onto their horses and then they rode away, leaving the ox and an empty cart.

Belno went and hugged his wife. "Elna, that was great! You were great."

"Get off me," said Elna, pushing him away. "You damn fool, driving us out here to the middle of nowhere. They might have raped me." She put her hand over her heart.

"I should have smoked that kanis while I had the chance."

It was too dark to find their way out of the hills, so they slept that night in the back of the wagon. Belno took comfort in Elna's incessant complaining, a return to equilibrium in their relationship. He kept to himself his retorts of, "I suppose a real man like Baz would have handled the situation differently," that ground being too molten to tread.

Belno liked most everyone, but it was hard to like Baz. It was Baz who, so long ago, spoiled the golden age for street kids in Kortholomoth. Older, bigger and meaner than the other kids, Baz displaced Two-Punch Buke as the ostensible leader of their ragged gang. Baz turned them increasingly toward harder crime and violent competition with the grown-up criminals of Kortholomoth.

Baz had a lot of girls sniffing around him back then, but his eye was for Elna. She may not have been as pretty as the other girls, but Elna had a good head for business. She put herself in charge of managing finances for the gang and—until things went bad—she was an essential element of their success.

When things did go bad and the survivors went their separate ways, Elna stuck with Belno, his main attraction being that he had no interest in money and cared only for the simple pleasures in life—like sitting in a cushioned chair that had once cradled the buttocks of the dock master. It didn't take much to make Belno happy, which meant Elna got to keep the profits of their exploits for herself.

In the morning, Belno followed the spring and found a little pond. Elna fashioned him an improvised hook and line, and Belno spent the morning trying to catch a fish, without success. The ox at least found a few weeds to chew. Most of the afternoon was spent doubling back on broken roads that did not look familiar. Belno had to stop a few times to roll heavy rocks out of the road. It was evening by the time they found their way back to the King's Road.

The ox was tired but they drove him on through the night. Neither of them felt like stopping.

Hunger was their constant companion these next few, long days. They survived on a few gransapples stolen from a farmer's cart, but the ox had only meager grazing and each day he was weaker and more obstinate than the day before. Belno and Elna considered their options: eat the ox, sell the ox, or push the ox on and hope he made it to Kortholomoth. They decided to push on for Kortholomoth, and if the ox should die along the way, then they would eat him. If he made it to Kortholomoth, then they would sell him.

But the next day the ox refused to stand or cooperate in any way. Belno and Elna spent the day begging at the side of the road, accumulating a little bread for themselves and some oats for the ox. The day after, the ox was up on his feet again and looking for what sparse grazing he could find. They gave him the morning to rest and Belno went with him up the slope to find some grass. Only then did Belno put him to the cart again and drive him on toward Kortholomoth.

It was the following day, just a few miles from the city, the weather changed. Elna noticed it right away, felt it in her head and bones. "Storm's coming," she said.

Half an hour later, Elna stood up in the cart, pointing. "Belno, look there. I like not the look of that cloud."

Belno squinted at the cloud in question. It lay flat like a line over the horizon ahead, but above that line the cloud roiled in upon itself ominously while other clouds churned chaotically around it.

Belno said nothing but reined in the ox a little.

"Do you smell that in the air?" said Elna, glancing at her husband. "Witching weather, I tell you."

Then, before their eyes, they saw a ghost-white finger of cloud snake downward from the clouds, and when it touched the earth, that wispy white tentacle transformed instantaneously into a sudden dark monster of red and brown.

"Ye gods, a twister!" Elna clutched at her husband in a panic.

He fended her off as best he could. "It's miles from here," he exclaimed. "Off me, woman!" The ox looked back at them doubtfully.

"Look at it," gasped Elna. "It's headed this way."

"Nonsense." But as he watched, the monster thickened itself, and they saw a cloud of dirt and debris whirling round its base, and indeed it did seem to be looming closer.

"Yes, it is!" squealed Elna. "Belno, it's the witch! She's coming for us to get her revenge! Do something!"

"Do something?" Belno gaped at his wife. "What is it exactly you propose I do?"

"Maybe we should hide under the cart ...?" Her words faded as she realized the futility of their situation, caught out here as they were on the open road.

They watched the tornado zig-zag over the broken plains of the Maelor Platt, uprooting scrub trees and tossing them like toys. It climbed a hillside, sucked up a flock of goats and sent them flying in all directions. It crossed the road in front of them, perhaps half a mile ahead.

"We're sorry," cried Belno to the storm. "We didn't mean to steal your stuff!"

"It was Belno's idea," shouted Elna, cringing as the twister loomed over them.

Belno thought he heard a chorus of spirits howling. *If that thing swallows me*, thought Belno, *my voice will be added to the choir.*

But they were spared. The twister circled back the way it came, wheeling toward Kortholomoth.

When it was lost again to their sight, Elna and Belno exchanged glances and then hugged each other fiercely. But just as quickly Elna pushed her husband away and grumbled, "Some help you were."

Belno rolled his eyes and lashed the ox to drive him forward.

They soon encountered the disarray of the storm's passage: loose debris and trees blocking the road. They found a way around the blockages—and there, just to the side of the road, they came upon a girl lying motionless on the ground. Nuzzling at the prone girl's sleeve was a goat, heavy with pregnancy.

Belno stopped the cart and climbed down for a closer look.

"She's finished," called Elna from the cart. "Just take the goat."

"She ain't dead." He nudged the motionless girl with his boot. "Hey there, you all right?"

A tall man with long white hair rode past on his donkey, paying them no heed.

"Just take the goat and be done with it," hissed Elna.

"Don't be ridiculous. We can't just leave her like this. Help me get her into the cart."

The girl was perhaps fifteen, dressed in an unusual skirt and blouse, blue and white.

"Looks like a nasty bump on the head," said Elna. She searched the girl but found nothing. "Soft hands like a rich kid," she observed.

Belno stood on the seat of the oxcart and looked all around, shielding his eyes from the sun. No houses, no caravans or anything else in sight. "Rich kid, eh? All the more reason to take her along."

Elna closed her mouth. She didn't have to say out loud what she was thinking. Belno rolled his eyes. "She ain't no witch, Elna."

So they drove on toward Kortholomoth. In another hour, the road diverged, the main road continuing toward the South Port and a secondary road veering toward the North Port. Belno turned off the main road, heading for the North Port, where he and Elna both had contacts.

From behind him, Belno heard an unfamiliar voice, the girl's: "Oof! Where have we got to now?"

Belno turned to see the girl sitting up, rubbing her eyes. "Awake, are you, poor dear? It's a miracle you survived the twister."

"The twister … Oh, I remember now: What a terrible ruckus that was!"

Elna said, "You're lucky you didn't blow away, or your goat."

"Lucky indeed," agreed the girl. The oxcart lurched and shuddered over the broken trail, making the girl cry out as she was tossed about. "Ouch! Oh!"

"What's all that carrying on about?" bellowed Elna. "Sit still back there or get out."

"Thank you, ma'am, getting out would suit me quite nicely." The girl rubbed her elbow where it struck the rail.

Belno moved to rein in the ox, but Elna stopped him with a touch on his forearm. She turned back to the girl with a deep scowl. "I told you to be still."

The girl whispered something to the goat.

"Are you talking to that goat?"

"Yes, ma'am."

"What's the matter with you? What kind of a person talks to a goat?"

Belno glanced over his shoulder. "I know lots of folks talk to goats."

"Not like this, they don't. She was talking like she expected an answer. No one asked you, anyhow." She was still watching the girl. "Look at you. You are a mess, aren't you?"

The girl picked broken leaves from her tangled hair. "Am I?"

"You certainly are. A filthy, raggedy mess! Just look at that dress, or whatever it is. What are you supposed to be?"

"You'd be a mess, too," said Belno, "if that twister had got hold of you."

"You know," said Elna, "it is very rude not to introduce oneself."

"Oh, I am terribly sorry," said the girl hurriedly. "My name is Mysta, and my friend here is Mr. Goat. We've only just arrived here."

"Here?" said Belno. "But where is here? We're not anywhere ... this is the road between two places."

"Don't you know anything? What she means is she's new to Lagin."

"She looks Laginese to me."

"Nonsense. Obviously she has come from somewhere very far away."

"Oh, yes, ma'am, a very far away place, wouldn't you say so, goat?"

"There she goes again, talking to the goat!"

"Excuse me, sir," said Mysta. "Did you say you knew other people who talk to goats? Do you mean to say, sir, there are other goats, besides this one?"

Belno blinked as he considered Mysta's question. Elna shot the girl a queer look. "There's something not right about this girl, I tell you. Where are your kin, girl?"

"My what?"

"Your kin, your family."

"Oh, I don't have any of those."

"An orphan, eh? What land do you come from? Where on Moghia do they dress like that?"

"I'm sorry, I'm not sure I come from anywhere on Moghia. Do I, goat?"

"What do you mean you don't come from anywhere on Moghia? Everywhere is somewhere on Moghia. Where else could you be from?"

"Well, some place quite different from here, I should say. Where I come from, you see, there are no goats at all, to begin with, and for another we have no sun like the wonderful one you have."

Elna stiffened. "She is from the Underworld. What did I tell you, husband?"

"You said nothing of the sort."

"Well, I am saying it now. I knew there was something not right about her. Everyone knows that twisters are witch-made. Well, here's our witch!"

"Don't be ridiculous, she's just a little girl."

"Just a little girl? Don't be deceived; a witch can take on all kinds of appearances. She said herself she came from a land without sun."

"I am sorry to interrupt, ma'am," said the girl. "You're quite right that the storm was witch-made, only I'm not the witch. The goat and I, we've only just escaped from a witch—oh, what a monster! Her twister should have killed us for sure, but luck was on our side—because, you see, my friend goat is a lucky goat, and so long as I am with him, I am lucky, too."

Elna stroked her chin. "A lucky goat, you say?"

"Yes, ma'am. If you don't mind my asking, ma'am, what is this place exactly? And why is that animal pulling us? My, he is a big fellow, isn't he? If we asked him politely, do you think he would stop pulling so we could get down from this thing?"

"Get down?" said Belno. "Why would you want to get down, little miss? Aren't you going to Kortholomoth?"

"Kortholomoth? That's a mouthful, isn't it? And why should I go there, when I've only just arrived here?"

Belno called to the ox, "Whoa now, whoa," slowing the cart to a stop. "If you want down, you're free to go, little miss, but you might as well ride with us to Kortholomoth. We can find work for you there."

"Oh, no thank you! I've had quite enough work in the witch's hut." And she stood, unsteadily, and climbed down over the wheel to the ground.

"Wait a minute," said Elna. "The girl can go, but the goat we keep." And she grabbed hold of the goat's horn to stop it jumping down.

"Excuse me, madam," said the goat, "but kindly let go my

horn."

"Oh," exclaimed Elna, and opened her hand.

"Thank you," said the goat and leapt down to the ground.

"Oh," said Elna again, her hand frozen in position.

"Well," said Belno, "that's the first I've seen her tongue-tied! A talking goat, eh? Now that is something new. Why don't you come with us to Kortholomoth? Out in this wilderness is no place for a little girl."

"It isn't? Very well, then, I shall be glad of your company. If it is all the same to you, however, Mr. Goat and I shall walk alongside."

"As you like," said Belno, coaxing the ox forward. He glanced over at Elna. Her eyes burrowed into his. *Still think she's not a witch?* That's what her eyes were saying.

"Oh," said the girl, "how reassuring to find myself walking on my own two legs again, with no storm-gusts to toss me, or oxcarts to chatter my teeth, or witch huts to spin me round till I can't tell up from down!"

Then she stopped suddenly, peering down at herself. "But wait—oh, goat, what is this? These are not my legs! They are much too thin."

Belno stopped the ox again and looked at her, bewildered.

The girl plucked at the fabric of her dress. "And this is certainly not my dress. And—oh, no! These are not my hands, either. Why, no part of me is me at all! Help, goat! What has happened?"

"Now, now," said the goat. "The important thing is not to panic. These things are known to happen, especially in the vicinity of storms and witches."

"Why didn't you say something? You must have noticed how I'd changed! Just look, my skin is the color of the earth where before it was pale; and I must be a foot taller! Didn't you notice?"

"Well," said the goat, "truth be told, my dear, one human is much like another so far as I can tell."

"Why, goat, look at you—you're not you, either!"

"What?"

"Look, this spot on your left flank, I am certain it used to be on your right. And see, your horns are longer now. And just look at all the belly you've gained!"

"Ye gods! You are right."

"Oh, goat, I do not think I much care for this business of being someone else. To tell the truth, I was rather attached to my old self. Why, this voice isn't even my own, and I'm certain this language is not one I was ever taught. Yet when I open my mouth, out the words come tumbling with minds all their own."

The girl and the goat looked up and saw Elna and Belno gaping at them.

"I am sorry. I have forgotten my manners again, haven't I? Come along, goat, we must not delay these kind people. We must try and make the best of our situation."

"Quite right," said the goat, and they stepped briskly alongside the oxcart as it jostled and rattled once more over the road.

Belno was quiet and thoughtful as they drove on toward the North Port, but Elna kept glancing over at the goat and girl, wanting to say something but swallowing the words.

The girl, meanwhile, was looking every direction at once observing the scenery: a red-brown landscape of hillocks, punctuated by tiny scrubby trees and boulders.

At length Belno said, "You know, miss, by the sound of it, the two of you could use some help."

"Oh, yes," said Mysta. "I couldn't agree more. Perhaps you could help us, sir?"

"I would, of course. But I'm no good for the kind of problems you've got. Luckily, I know someone who might be of help."

"Do you? That's wonderful! Where can we find this person?"

"Why, in Kortholomoth, of course."

"Kortholomoth! It sounds a wonderful place."

"Oh, it is: A place where a person can find whatever she seeks."

"And is it far, sir, to Kortholomoth?"

"Not at all. We are nearly there already. As you can see, we're off the main road now, and headed for the North Port. This is the end of a long journey for us. Many days ago we left Dashvar with all we owned, but now as you can see, our cart is quite empty and so too our bellies. We come seeking better fortunes in Kortholomoth. Look there, see? In the distance you can make out the sea."

"The sea? Do you mean that huge thing over there sparkling in the sun?"

"Yes, of course—the sea."

Elna's silence burst then, and she cried, "I've had enough foolishness! Now, little girl, you heard my husband say our bellies have been empty these days. And here you are with a pregnant goat fairly bursting at the udders while we suffer the pangs of hunger. Are you so cruel you would not share a cup of milk?"

"Pregnant?" said the goat. "Who's pregnant?"

"You are," said Elna, "and if I'm not very much mistaken, you'll be expecting soon, too."

"But that's impossible—good heavens! I'm a girl goat! How did this happen? Oh, this is serious."

"The important thing," said Mysta, "is not to panic. Now, go on, goat, let's not be rude; give these poor people some of your milk, won't you?"

"I certainly will not!"

"Cruel, vicious beast!" spat Elna. "You would leave us hungry? Why, you vile, stinking bag of filth! You—"

"Excuse me," said the goat. "But perhaps all of you have forgotten that I am, after all, a lucky goat. No one will go hungry who is in my company. Keep along with me and presently you will see."

No sooner had the goat spoken than Belno stood in the oxcart to exclaim, "Can you smell that, Elna? Can you hear the bells?"

Elna's eyes grew bright. "Ohh...a pilgrim's camp at the roadside temple. They will certainly share their dinner—ghorma stew by the smell of it. Never mind you, selfish goat, we do not need your puss-choked milk. The pilgrims will prove more charitable."

Ahead, a small band of robed travelers was encamped round a tiny but colorful structure erected at the intersection of two well-worn trails. A faint line of smoke rose from a humble fire where a fat pot simmered.

Belno drove straight for that steaming pot, and he and Elna leapt down before even the cart had stopped rolling. Grabbing bowls from a stack, they were stopped only by the bodily intercession of a bright-eyed old man in a hood. "Peace on you, my friends. Have you come to pay homage to the gods?"

"Yes," said Elna. "Right after dinner."

"Surely you do not eat before the gods?"

"Please," said Elna, "we are poor, we have nothing to offer the gods, but I see you have some ghorma bean soup to offer us, and we are very hungry."

"You have nothing at all?"

"Absolutely nothing. Check and see, our cart is empty."

Another pilgrim peered into the cart. "What they say is true, there's nothing—but look there," he said, nodding to the goat.

The old man said, "Your goat looks ready to yield. A milk offering would please the gods."

"Fine by me," said Elna through clenched teeth, and she stomped over to the goat, hissing, "Now listen up, you bearded abomination: Your milk may have been too good for Belno and me, but it's not too good for the gods, now is it? You had just better come along with me to the temple," she said, reaching for the goat's horn.

But the girl slapped Elna's hand away. "Don't you know it's rude to grab a person by the horns?" The goat nodded and snorted. "Come along, goat. Let's have a look, shall we?"

A vivid burst of color against the stark landscape, the temple was really nothing more than an open stall with three gaudily painted walls and a tiled roof sheltering its three idols. The idols were smothered in a multitude of fresh flowers. The stone slab at their feet was overflowing with offerings on trays and plates stacked one atop the other.

"Oh, what pretty dolls," said Mysta. The old pilgrim joined her, folding back his hood. "Oh, they are not dolls, little girl: These are gods."

"Are they?" She whispered to the goat, "And I was certain they were dolls!"

Elna and Belno came along behind, still clasping their empty bowls feebly. Seeing the wealth of offerings at the feet of the idols, their eyes and mouths became round. "Look," said Elna, "is that sugar cake?" And Belno said, "And oh, there is salt, and whisky, and kanis!"

"And soon," the old pilgrim said, "goat's milk." And he brought down a bowl from a hidden shelf in the temple.

The girl stooped when the goat tugged at her sleeve, getting her attention. Mysta leaned down to listen as the goat whispered something to her.

"Well," said said, standing on tip-toe to scrutinize the idols, "they are three very pretty ladies. One is tall and she is balancing a sun and a moon on top of her head—how funny it looks! I don't know what she has in her hands. Another one is fat, with no clothes at all, looking very much satisfied with herself and holding two big bowls. And the third one has her eyes closed and I think she is dancing with a bird and a snake."

"Don't tell me you don't recognize the gods, girl," exclaimed Elna. "Not even the one you're named after?"

"Oh, I'm not named after any gods. In fact, where I come from, we only have one God."

"And where exactly is it you come from?" asked the old pilgrim, pulling on his beard. "You look like a Laginese girl, you sound like a Laginese girl, but you cannot be a Laginese girl—for a Laginese girl would certainly know the Traveler's Trinity when she saw them."

"Truth be told, sir, I'm not at all certain who I am, anymore. I used to be student 227 at the Roosa School, but now I seem to be someone else entirely."

"I see," said the pilgrim.

"Do you?"

"Well, no, not really."

Elna explained, "The twister got hold of her, you understand. The poor dear...Now she talks to goats."

"Is that so?" said the pilgrim. "You are lucky to be alive, little girl. All manner of strange things can happen in the vicinity of a twister, you know."

"So I hear."

"Now, how about that milk?" asked the pilgrim, his bowl ready. Elna and Belno leaned forward expectantly. All eyes were on the girl, who in turn looked to the goat. "Well, Mr. Goat," she said, "what do you say?"

"I should be glad to donate my milk to the Traveler's Trinity. They sound like a good bunch to me."

The old pilgrim's smugness melted instantly into unfettered befuddlement. "But...that...what? Did...?" The old man looked at Elna who was yawning, and then at Belno whose eyes had returned to the sweetcake offerings. Then he looked back at Mysta and the goat. "Did that goat just speak?"

"I don't see why my speaking should be so astonishing," said the goat. "Have you ever met a goat who *didn't* speak?"

"Well, yes, certainly I have! A great many, in fact. It's the talking variety that is new to me."

"What, are you telling me that no goats speak here, none at all?"

"None at all."

"But—that is a catastrophe! You mean there are no goat poets? No goat theater? No goat statesmen?"

The pilgrim shook his head. "None of that, I'm afraid, and we are no doubt the worse for it. Here the goats only know one word, and that is *baah*."

"Well, that's the word we all begin with. Maybe they simply need someone to teach them. What about the other animals? Surely the dogs can speak, or the elephants, or the turtles?" Not waiting for an answer, the goat scurried in a panic to the ox who still stood waiting at the cart. "Speak to me, brother! Have you no words? All this time I thought you were simply coy."

A small crowd of astonished pilgrims gathered round as witnesses to the goat's outburst.

"Now's our chance," whispered Elna, and Belno needed no further encouragement to return to the now unguarded simmering pot of ghorma stew. Belno seized the oversized ladle and poured first Elna and then himself a steaming bowlful.

Meanwhile, the pilgrims closed in on the goat. "A talking goat!" "Are you a magic goat?" "Can you grant wishes?" Then all at once they cried, "I have a wish, goat! Listen to my wish!" The goat bolted through their reaching arms and scampered back to the girl, crying for help.

"You know," said Elna quietly, slurping from her bowl, "a talking goat has got to be worth quite a lot."

Belno considered his wife's words as the hot, salty stew found its way to his belly.

The girl came to the goat's rescue, saying, "Don't worry, Mr. Goat, these people mean you no harm. Isn't that so?" She looked sternly at the faces around her.

"Of course," said the old man with a hardy laugh. "We are an entirely harmless band, I can assure you, just simple travelers. We have been all over Lagin, but never have we seen talking animals. Except in puppet shows, that is." The other pilgrims, the entire band of men and women, circled round them at the roadside temple.

Belno went back for seconds. He wasn't normally one for ghorma beans, but on this occasion these beans seemed the best in the world.

The girl was talking to the assembled pilgrims, and when Belno handed Elna her second bowl of stew, she said, "Look at them over there, laughing with each other. Mark it, that old man wants the goat for himself."

"Well, Elna," said Belno, patting his belly. "You were right about the witching weather, I'll give you that. And you were probably right when you said I wouldn't last three days without you. What would have happened to me if you weren't there to save me from those bandits? But if you're about to say the goat rightfully belongs to us—"

"We are the ones who found her."

"Him," corrected Belno. "I don't know, Elna." He was watching the girl standing on tip-toe to see the idols as the old pilgrim laughed boisterously at something the goat said. "I've got a feeling about these two."

Elna sneered. "A feeling? Last time you had a feeling, it didn't end well for us." She licked the last drops of stew from her bowl.

Belno watched as the goat acquiesced to the old man's kind hands and gave some milk for the bowl. Promptly and skillfully the pilgrim apportioned the milk among three tiny saucers, one for each of the goddesses. "We make offerings to Deilderaft, Mysta, and Rivanna at the outset of a journey, at the conclusion of a journey, or when passing on the road. We try to give them things they like, to bring their favor upon us."

"I see," said the girl.

"Do you?"

"Well, not really, no."

One of the young men, growing restless, said, "Well, goat? Is it true you can grant wishes?"

"Certainly not! Weren't you paying attention? I am a lucky goat. You, a grown man, ought to know by now that getting one's wish is among the unluckiest things that could happen to a person."

Disappointment rippled through the band of travelers. "Can't even grant a wish..." "What good is a talking goat..." Scratching and muttering, the group dwindled to a few.

Elna and Belno lay belly up in their cart, shooing flies lazily, their empty bowls licked clean.

"Look, goat," said Mysta. "The sun. It's getting low. Look at the colors! Isn't it beautiful? You must have seen it a thousand times before, but to my eyes I am sure it is the most beautiful thing I have ever seen."

"It's true," said the goat. "Many sunsets have I seen. But it is still beautiful, every time."

Belno felt so satisfied that he thought he might drift off to sleep, until Elna poked him in the ribs and pointed.

A red-bearded stranger had arrived at the roadside temple, a bundle of sticks resting at his feet. He was looking at the girl. "Did you get separated from your caravan, dearie? They are camped down the trail a ways, not far," he said, pointing the direction from which he had come. He smiled and picked up his bundle of sticks and continued on his way down the intersecting trail.

The girl leapt up and hurried after him. "Wait. What makes you think I am with that group?"

"Well," said the red-bearded man, "on account of your dress, I suppose."

"My dress?" She looked down at herself doubtfully. "What about it?"

"It's a uniform, isn't it? Are you not a choralist from the Mystan School?"

"No—I mean, am I? I must be. But I've never heard of Mystan School before." She turned back to the goat, and back again to the red-bearded man to shake his unsuspecting hand with great enthusiasm. "Oh, thank you, sir! Thank you!" She rushed back to the goat. "Did you hear that, goat? There's a band of people dressed just like me down this trail.

We must go and find them at once."

Elna sat up suddenly from the bed of the oxcart. "What? You're not leaving, are you?"

"I must. I feel certain this is an important clue."

Belno struggled to sit up. "Wait. That trail leads to the South Port, but we are going to the North Port."

"I am sorry to split ways with you. Thank you so much for your kindnesses—all of you." Mysta looked from face to face among the pilgrims.

"Come here," said Belno, and when she was close he whispered, "Whichever port you go to, North Kortholomoth or South Kortholomoth, ask for the sage who is called the Ig."

"The Ig?"

"That's right. Remember his name. He is the one I told you of—the one who could help you." Belno knew everyone, and the Ig was the smartest person he'd ever met. If anyone could sort out this girl's predicament, it would be the Ig.

"Oh, thank you, Belno. I shall miss you. I shall miss you all. Come on, goat, let's hurry! It is getting dark." And with that, she was away down the dark trail, with the goat at her heels.

"You're just going to let her go?" demanded Elna. "Don't just sit there, go after her!"

Belno exchanged glances with the old pilgrim. "Now, Elna. She's got a chance to be with her people again. That's as it should be."

Elna scowled. "She's just a little girl, on her own. Something might happen."

"She ain't on her own. She's got that goat. He's a lucky goat, remember? She'll be fine, as long as they stick together."

"Yeah, well what about us? What do we have?"

"We got each other, babe. That's what we have."

"Great," said Elna flatly.

"Well, here we are at Kortholomoth's door, Elna. I won't stop you if you want to run to Baz. Maybe he could take better care of you than I have these past weeks. But you know me: If you stick with me, the good times will be back again in no time, you'll see."

Elna rolled her eyes. "I mention Baz one time..."

Belno's first order of business was finding a safe place to pass the night. It's true they had a lot of friends in Kortholomoth, but these were not the kind of friends one ought approach head on; it was better to get the lay of the land first.

Belno found what he was looking for in an old neighborhood on the outskirts of the North Port. He turned into a cobblestone driveway, saying, "Look there, Elna," pointing to a faded chalk mark scrawled near the base of the fencepost: two overlapping circles, a vagabond's mark indicating that a kind man lives here, one who wouldn't mind polite squatters on his property.

The driveway ran the length of a sweeping garden. Elna whistled at the size of the house. Lights burned in two parts of the house, but most of the two-story mansion was dark.

Belno pulled the cart around behind a tall row of hedges, out of sight from the house. On the other side of the hedge was a narrow courtyard, a long wall, and an arched pedestrian exit to a side street. Belno nodded approvingly; they could make a quick escape if they needed to. It was, in short, an excellent place to spend the night.

They snored through the night, undisturbed.

At dawn, Belno went out to relieve himself and saw no sign of activity around the house. He had a look out at the side street and was pleased to see street vendors setting up. Belno made himself useful helping the vendors set up their stalls, in exchange for breakfast sausages and some fresh peppers. These treasures he brought back to Elna, much to her delight.

"I've made several new friends already," said Belno, going to rouse the ox. "Come on, you, I've found a nice wheelwright interested in buying you."

Elated, Elna got out of the way while Belno turned the cart around by hand before putting the ox to it. Belno choked up a little to see Elna looking *proud* of him for once.

Ten minutes later: Elna looked at the silver coins in her palm, scowling deeply. "Where's the rest of it?"

"What do you mean?" asked Belno, smile fading. "That's a lot of money, there."

"Six silver draughts? That's all you could get? A fine, healthy ox in the prime of its life, it was worth twice that at least."

"Aw, Elna, just yesterday you said it was emaciated."

"Well, that was yesterday. We fed it since then, didn't we?"

"No," said Belno. "I'm fair sure we didn't."

"What kind of caretaker are you? Your animal husbandry is worse than your actual husbandry. Well, what about the cart? It should be worth something, too."

"The cart?"

"Yes, the cart. Where is it?"

"I thought that was clear. I sold it with the ox."

"You sold it with the—?"

"Cart's not much good to us without the ox, now is it? What, did you expect maybe to put the whip to me and have me pull you about with the bit in my mouth? You'd enjoy that, wouldn't you?"

"Fool, the cart was worth ten draughts at least. Where's the rest of the money? Six draughts for the ox *and* the cart?"

"The cart was broken down, you said so yourself."

"You're an embarrassment, you know that? Now what are we supposed to do? How are we supposed to live on six silver draughts?"

"That's more money than we've seen in a while," pointed out Belno.

Elna sighed bitterly and dropped the coins into her pocket. "You should have let me keep the goat."

Belno groaned. "Not the goat again."

"Our situation would be very different if we had a talking goat. You cannot deny that. We would be rich."

"Come on, Elna, why do you have to spoil it? We just earned ourselves some money for the first time in weeks. Let's go celebrate. Let's get you a dress. Let's buy ourselves supper at a fancy restaurant. What do you say, Elna?"

"Sure, blow all our money on one night out. Great idea," she said, but she went along with Belno, and they went out into the street together. As they descended toward the city proper, they could see the entirety of the North Port, a giant bowl half-submerged in the sea. This was home for the two of them.

They soon found themselves on a crowded street. "Where should we go for dinner tonight? I saw the house of curry is still there," suggested Belno.

"Naw, no curry. You know it disagrees with my digestion."

"What about a nice krika's nest? I know you love a nice krika's nest."

"We are *not* blowing our money on krika's nests."

"Well, gods, Elna. You choose something. You don't like none of my ideas."

A tall, white-haired man came rolling down the middle of the street on a strange wheeled contraption, streaming blue flags behind him. "Will you look at that?" said Belno. There was no beast pulling the tricycle, just the man pedaling under his own power.

The white-haired man, who for some reason looked familiar to Belno, pedaled his contraption in a circle through the intersection, holding out his tall hat in one hand and crying: "Encore Performance Tonight Upon Dusk at Hendrick's Crossing! The Mystan Choralists, Featuring Layona the Soft-Tongued, Daughter of that Pinnacle of Virtue, Mizen Tower."

Belno watched, delighted by the spectacle. The performer put on his hat and executed another loop through the middle of traffic, scattering leaflets as he went. *What a strange fellow*, thought Belno, seeing the man's face, placid but distant as he pedaled his contraption off toward the next intersection.

Belno rescued one of the leaflets from the street before it was tramped by a horse. "Hendrick's Crossing," he said, working out the words. At the bottom it said, "Penny Performance, Donations Gratefully Accepted, For a Good Cause Supporting the Next Generation of Mystans."

Elna overheard a nearby couple, well-dressed, perusing another of the leaflets. "It's the Tower girl, the singer I heard about at the Society meeting."

"Let me see that," said Elna, wresting the leaflet from Belno. "Proceeds support the Mystan School, says here. Belno!"

"What?"

She pulled on his sleeve, luring him away from the street. "That's where she went."

"Who?"

"Our little Mysta, with her talking goat."

Belno's face darkened. "Not the goat again."

"Yes—the goat again. I'm telling you, with a lucky talking goat, all our problems would be solved."

"We can't just take Mysta's goat. It wouldn't be right."

"Of course it would be right. If it weren't for us, what do you suppose would have happened to her? We saved her."

"Well, I suppose that's true."

"And the goat was pregnant. Don't you imagine the offspring of a magic goat would also be magic?"

"Stands to reason," agreed Belno, stroking his chin hair.

"Surely she can spare one lucky goat for us. She wouldn't

be so greedy as to need all those magic goats for herself, with none for us who saved all their lives?"

"You're right—she didn't strike me as the greedy sort at all."

Elna poked the leaflet with her finger. "We're going to Hendrick's Crossing tonight, and we're gonna collect what's rightfully ours. But first—you're going to buy me a dress."

When they arrived at Hendrick's Crossing, crisp and dapper in their clean new clothes, all they found was a field full of wheel ruts and hoof prints. A few local mites were scouring the campsite for anything of value that might have been left behind. One of them said, "They moved the show to Titan's Head," and he pointed up the trail.

So Elna and Belno followed the trail, joining a group of others headed for Titan's Head. Titan's Head was a hillock crowned with a ring of rocks. A crowd had grown up around the base of the hill, near where the Mystans had parked their wagons in a semicircle. The singing girls, with carefully pinned hair and crisply clean uniforms, were arraying themselves on the hillside overlooking the crowd.

"Look, there she is," said Belno, pointing. There was Mysta, the girl they had picked up along the side of the road, standing awkwardly in the midst of the other girls.

"Shh," hissed Elna, pulling his arm down as he started to wave. "Don't call attention." She pulled him away from the rest of their group who headed into the semicircle of wagons to join the crowd. Elna drew her husband around the outside of the wagons. "Do you see the goat?"

"Well," said Belno, looking around. "If there's one thing I know about goats, they like high places."

The two of them looked up to the peak of Titan's Head. "That's it," said Elna. "Come on, we'll circle around the other side so no one spots us."

Belno turned to look back at the preparations. The Mystans were driving lamp posts into the earth, and the strange-looking white-haired man was there, traipsing about the hillside, wearing a jacket with tails, carefully placing small buckets or tins on the ground, for what purpose Belno could not say. "But what about the show?"

"The show? What, you mean the singing girls? It's a song, isn't it? We'll hear fine from the other side of the hill, and no need to part with our pennies, neither."

Disappointed, Belno allowed himself to be led around to the southwestern face of Titan's Head and started up the hillside as darkness fell. They did indeed hear when the girls started singing, but not so clearly as to make out the words. By the time they reached the hilltop, one voice rose above all the others. "Will you listen to that?" said Belno, leaning on a jutting rock to catch his breath.

"Very pretty," admitted Elna. "Keep your eyes open. What's that?" she said, pointing. A baby goat went bounding across the open, giving chase to another leaping kid. Elna followed after them, pulling Belno along. "There!" she whispered, pointing to the silhouette of an adult goat poised atop a rock, gazing down at the singing girls below. "Now's our chance."

Belno untied the rope from around his waist and made it into a lasso. He paused for a moment, mesmerized by that single perfect voice rising into the night.

"Go on," urged Elna.

Belno hesitated. "I don't know, Elna. It don't seem right."

Elna rubbed the bridge of her nose. "We've been over this."

"Well, why don't *you* do it?"

"Fine. You want me to do it. I'll do it." Elna snatched the rope from Belno.

The goat stuck his head around the rock and hissed, "Will you two be quiet? You're ruining the song."

"Oh," said Elna, startled.

Belno snatched the rope back from Elna and quickly tightened the loop around the goat's neck. "Not a sound, my friend. You're coming with us now."

"Don't be preposterous."

"Come on now," said Elna, grabbing the goat's horn and pulling.

"Do you mind!" objected the goat, trying to pull away—but there was Belno with the other horn and the rope around his neck. "Oh, dear," said the goat, going along with them despite himself. "Help," said the goat, then cried, "Help!" as loudly as he could—but his cry was lost in the crescendo of a full chorus.

Elna and Belno dragged the goat down the dark side of the hill, back the way they'd come. Three baby goats came trailing behind. "I don't understand," said the goat. "Where are you taking me? I don't even understand how this could be happening."

"Just relax now," said Belno and lifted the goat over his shoulders, finding his balance before attempting to go down the steepest part of the hillside.

"I'm supposed to be a lucky goat," protested the goat.

"How do you know coming with us isn't the luckiest thing for you?" asked Elna. "Did you think of that? Mark my words, the farther you are from that girl the better off you'll be. Something is not right about her. She's some kind of witchling for sure."

"She certainly is not!" insisted the goat. To the three kids following behind, the goat called, "Stay where you are. Stay here! Wait for Mysta."

"It just doesn't seem right," said Belno, leading the goat along.

"That's because it *isn't*," said the goat.

"Keep your voice down," said Elna to the goat. "It's best not to attract attention."

They didn't have anywhere else to go, as yet, so they returned to the place where they'd slept last night, the small courtyard between the hedge and the outer wall of the estate outside the North Port.

Belno tied the goat to a post, and the two of them stood looking at one another. The goat coughed up some cud to chew.

"Well, Elna, there's your goat."

"Look at you, your new shirt is filthy," said Elna, dusting him off as best she could.

"Hallo?" called a man from around the hedges.

Belno startled. Recovering himself quickly, he untied the goat and turned to flee, Elna likewise poised to make a break for the exit to the street.

But Belno remembered the vagrant's mark and waited to see who came around the hedge row. It was an old man, dressed as a servant. "Hallo? Is it you, sir? Master Gregor?"

Belno strolled casually over to the old man, goat in tow. "Why, yes it is."

The old man, out of breath, had his mouth open. He looked Belno and Elna up and down. "Thank the gods. We were worried about you, sir. Where's your luggage, then?"

"Oh. It's coming along later," said Belno.

Elna came up and took Belno by the arm. "Would you kindly show us to our room?"

"Of course," said the servant and led them toward the house. "You must be famished. We'll start dinner right away." Belno and Elna exchanged happy glances. "It's just Mellerd and myself in the house, you'll have to be patient; we're on a skeleton crew. We had no idea when you would arrive. I'll just put your goat in the stable."

"Oh, no you won't," said Elna. "The goat stays with us."

"What did I tell you," said Elna, smiling around her leg of lamb. "The goat was wasted on the girl."

"I have to admit, it's good to have a lucky goat," said Belno as he opened a second bottle of port. It was well after midnight now, and Elna had dismissed the two servants for the night.

The goat sulked in the corner, tied to a pipe. "You realize of course none of this rightfully belongs to you."

"Trust me, they won't notice the difference," said Elna with her mouth full. She gestured broadly to indicate the opulent dining room and surrounding house. "These ones, their cellar is bursting. To think we spent the last night hiding out in the hedges, suffering the flies. Tonight, Belno, we sleep on feathered pillows."

"And if the masters of the house should return?"

"We've got nothing to worry about, so long as we've got our lucky goat, eh?"

Belno poured himself another drink and settled back into his chair, contemplating his glass. "I wonder if there is anything to smoke."

"Check the hospitality cabinet." Elna pointed with a half-gnawed bone at the armoire against the facing wall.

Belno considered the polished cabinet from across the room. "Hospitality cabinet. How do you like that? There's a fine thing."

"There's some kanis in the left-side drawer," said the goat. "I smelled it coming in."

"Spot on," said Belno cheerfully. He found his feet and made for the hospitality cabinet. "A fine thing," he repeated, opening a large sliding panel. "Look here," he said, pulling out a woolen jacket and slipping it on without hesitation. "How does it fit, Elna?"

Elna flicked her eyes across her husband, then back to her meat as she contemplated her next bite. "A fine smoking jacket, that is. Probably get three crowns for a jacket like that."

Belno admired himself in the mirror set in the back of the hospitality cabinet. Belno looked every bit the master of the house in his gentleman's smoking jacket and new pantaloons. "I could get used to this," he said.

"You *will* get used to it," said Elna. "This is our life now. No more scrapping and eking for us."

Belno opened the left-side drawer and found the promised kanis and a pipe of horn.

"If you must smoke that," said Elna, "then do so outside."

Obedient, Belno packed the pipe and made for the back door.

"Ahem," said the goat. "Mind if I join you?"

Belno hesitated and looked to his wife.

"I need to pee," insisted the goat.

"Suppose we can't very well keep a goat inside all the time, can we?" said Belno with a shrug.

"Of course you can't," said Elna. "Just keep her rope well in hand. In fact, here—let me tie it on your wrist. We wouldn't want to lose our lucky goat."

So Belno lit his pipe and took the goat out. It was a cold, crisp night. The moon was high overhead with a great halo encircling it. "I love nights like this one, goat. Don't you?"

Together they wandered the property, passing under a

stone arch and into a vast, empty garden. "Not bad," said Belno, drawing on his pipe. The goat was not sure if he was referring to the estate or the kanis.

"Mind if I take a puff?" asked the goat.

"You?"

"Sure. Just pass it here," said the goat and stuck out his lips.

Belno laughed and put the pipe in the goat's mouth, and laughed again to see his dexterous lips maneuver the pipe into position at the side of his mouth and then take a deep draw. "Let me guess," said the goat. "You've never seen a goat smoke before?"

"Can't say as I have."

"It's wrong, you know." The goat exhaled through his nose. "Keeping me here."

"Now don't start," said Belno with a frown.

"Belno. You seem like a nice guy. My kids are hungry, Belno. Let me go to them."

Belno took the pipe back. "Mysta and the girls will look after your kids, don't you worry."

"They need their mother."

"Besides, they're lucky goats like you, right?"

"I don't think it works that way."

Belno tugged on the rope. "Come on, you're spoiling the mood. Let's check out the garden. I've never had a garden before."

"You don't have one *now*. Trespassing hardly makes it yours." The goat picked half-heartedly at a shrub.

They meandered the property, coming eventually around to the row of hedges, and the little hidden courtyard where

Elna and Belno had slept the night before. A sound caught Belno's attention. "Hey—you hear that?" Murmured voices from beyond the hedge.

Belno circled round the hedges, pulling the goat behind. He heard an exclamation of joy from some boy followed by groans of dismay from what sounded like three or four others. Belno and the goat surprised a gaggle of urchins in the courtyard focused intently on a narrow wooden wheel, balanced on its side very near a turn in the wall, where evidently it had stopped rolling just short of touching the wall. The happy boy was the one who appeared to have rolled the wheel; he was still holding his right hand up from the motion of rolling it. His unadulterated smile cracked upon seeing Belno in his jacket and pantaloons emerging from the gate.

"Hey!" yelled Belno, shaking his fist. "What are you rats doing back here? This is not your property!"

The boys scattered in a chaos of grubby hands and feet, grabbing coins and bottles as they fled.

"Don't forget your wheel," called Belno, a little more kindly. He strolled over and picked it up. One side was painted red, the other white. Its rolling surface was covered in coarse leather and marked up with lines and symbols.

The urchins lingered at the threshold to the street, waiting to see what Belno would do. He inspected the wheel, tested its balance and weight, and nodded with respect. "Not a bad wheel. It's okay, lads, no need for running off. I've been known to toss the goblin wheel myself, you know. What's the stakes?"

The boys exchanged glances.

Belno patted his pockets, looking for coins but finding none. "Tell you what," said Belno, taking off his jacket. "A jacket like this, gotta be worth, what, three crowns in the market?"

He had their interest; the children began drawing closer.

"I'll put in my jacket," said Belno, draping it across the goat's back. "You put in your pennies."

Belno untied the rope from his wrist and tied it to the post. "Hold this," he whispered to the goat, plopping the pipe into his mouth. Belno rolled up his sleeves and carried the wheel over to where the boys were gathering with their pennies.

The boys marked the line and Belno made a show of stretching in preparation for his toss. It had been many years since Belno had tossed the wheel, but back in the day he remembered being quite good.

Belno glanced over at the goat and winked. *Good thing I have a lucky goat*, he thought. The first boy was up. He held the goblin wheel and focused on the wall at a distance of perhaps twenty yards. He took a step forward and released the wheel with a practiced flick of his wrist, sending it bouncing and rolling. Midway to the wall, the wheel wobbled a little before slowing and coming to a stop just inches from the wall. Another child ran and marked the spot with a tiny pebble. "Nomin's descending," he called.

"Not bad," said Belno. He glanced conspiratorially at the goat and whispered, "But I'm not worried."

The next boy's toss rolled over with red side facing up. The boy slapped his hands to his face in anguish.

The third boy overtossed and the wheel struck the wall.

Now it was Belno's turn. He cracked his knuckles and accepted the goblin wheel. *The moment of truth.* Belno turned the wheel until he found the symbol he was looking for, then he kissed it, put his thumb on it, and stepped into his toss.

The wheel flew way high and bounced badly, rolling wide. But just as it was flopping over on its side, it hit a divot and bounced back upright and surged forward with renewed energy. A collective intake of breath as the wheel approached the wall, then everyone started talking at once as the wheel stopped just at the wall. Each boy had to run up to see for himself.

Belno cackled with joy. "Still got it! Now gimme those pennies, boys, and who's in for another round?"

"That was luck," said one of the urchins.

"There's no luck in goblin wheel," said Belno haughtily. "It is a game of pure skill."

"Your pitch first," said the kid, handing the wheel over.

Belno felt the weight of the wheel and planned his strategy. As the pitcher, a more conservative toss was called for. He leaned his head to the right, then the left, stretching his neck. "All right, boys. Watch and learn." He wound up and stepped into his toss, but much to his embarrassment the wheel struck the wall without even bouncing on the ground first. It rebounded back and rolled in little circles at Belno's feet.

"Tough pitch," said one of the boys, picking up the wheel, and all three of them laughed, feeling more confident now.

"But—" Belno shook his head. "That didn't count. I had some kind of spasm just as I was tossing." He glanced helplessly back at the goat, wondering what had become of his supposed luck.

But the goat was not there. The smoking jacket was laid neatly over the post, and the kanis pipe was laying on the ground. But the goat himself had disappeared.

"Oh, no," intoned Belno, putting his hands to his face. "Did any of you see which direction my goat went?"

The kids didn't even hear him; they were too focused on their game.

Belno ran out to the street, looking left and right. No goat in sight.

"Oh, no." Belno stood in the street opening and closing his hands. He couldn't very well go back into the house to face Elna again, not without the goat.

"Think, Belno. Where would you go if you were a talking goat?"

Back to my kids, came the immediate response. *Back to Titan's Head.*

"Right then," said Belno. He took a deep breath and started back toward Titan's Head at a jog.

A few late-night revelers were on the streets, but for the most part Belno had no obstacles in his way, other than his poor physical condition. He wasn't able to keep up the jogging for long, even though the way was mostly downhill. He had to settle for an awkward, rushed lope. Ten minutes in, he was gasping for breath and had an unpleasant stitch in his side. It was another twenty before he reached the base of Titan's Head, where he collapsed to his knees and lost part of his supper.

No one was about. The traveling band of Mystans had moved on. There was only the night wind from the desert and a field mouse hurrying about her business.

I am always messing things up, thought Belno. *Elna won't forgive me this time.*

He looked up doubtfully at the hill. Maybe the goat had come here, maybe he went up to the top of the hill. Maybe he was up there now. The only way to find out was to climb the hill. Belno groaned. His foot was beginning to throb.

Cool as the night was, Belno was covered in sweat by the time he reached the peak. There at the top, between two standing stones, was indeed the goat, staring off toward the west. Belno should have been relieved at the sight of the goat standing there. But instead he felt a twinge of disappointment.

The rope was still tied round the goat's neck, dragging in the dirt. Belno came up beside him, puffing, and took hold of the rope. The goat did not object.

"They went on without you," said Belno gently. "Probably onward to Dashvar for another performance."

They stood a little while longer, watching the horizon. Finally, Belno said, "Come on, let's go home. It's been a long night." The goat put up no resistance as Belno led him down the hill.

The sun was threatening to rise by the time Belno made it back to the house with the goat. "Elna, you'll never guess what happened," he said as he entered the back door. But the dining room was dark and empty.

Belno checked the guest room. He checked all the rooms, taking the goat from room to room.

Finally, he pounded on the door to the servants' quarters and the old man came out hastily, half dressed. "We'll get breakfast started right away, sir."

"Where is Mrs. Gregor?" demanded Belno.

The poor man blinked, wiping the sleep from his eyes. "That was Mrs. Gregor? I thought she was your mistress."

"Yes, my mistress. Whomever she was. Where has she got to?"

"I'm certain I don't know, sir."

"Oh, no," said Belno, his eyes welling with tears. "I don't believe it. She's finally left me."

Belno made a few half-hearted attempts to find her. He walked the docks, checked with her old friends. But he knew there would be no finding Elna if she didn't want to be found.

He just wished he could tell her what happened. He wanted to explain that when he went out to smoke with the goat and never came back, it wasn't what she thought. Elna was always the suspicious sort, and it was just like her to assume the worst.

He went back to the mansion, in case she returned there. With the old servant puttering about, he committed himself fully to the role of Master Gregor. At least until the real Master Gregor materialized. He discovered, by and by, that the old master of the house—Carbad Brokerson—died suddenly several weeks back, and the rest of his family had moved across the sea. Gregor was Carbad's cousin from Xamlmadhi who was coming up to take over operations of Brokerson's import/export business.

Over the next two days, Belno (impersonating Gregor) was visited by a series of nervous supervisors and ships' captains, anxious to know his plans for the business. During these meetings Belno steepled his fingers a lot and repeated the phrase, "Right now I'm just here to listen and learn." When asked for direction, he would say, "Just keep doing what you've been doing, for now."

The manservant, whose name was Byan, showed him where Brokerson kept all his files. There were budgets and warehouse inventories and ships' manifests. *Interesting,* thought Belno. *Elna may be the one with a head for figures, but I know just what to do with these.* Always with a mind toward building up another Belzea variation, Belno spent his time forging fake manifests and imaginary transactions. He was no Lorenko the Scrivener, but it was easy enough for Belno, using Brokerson's files as templates, to manufacture an entire robust economy of trade between Kortholomoth and the colony of Belzea. He then forged a letter from one Bezor, Lord Protector of Belzea, in which he called upon Brokerson to double next year's order of Laginese grain, on account of the explosive population growth associated with Belzea's economic boom.

The house had an internal courtyard with a flower garden and a stone table. It's here where Belno retired in the evening to smoke and talk to the goat. He kept the goat on a long chain anchored to the stone table—just to make double sure he still had a goat when Elna came back to him.

The goat wouldn't take the pipe from him anymore and refused to speak. "The silent treatment, eh?" said Belno. "I understand." But it didn't stop him talking to the goat. He needed someone to talk to, and the goat turned out to be an excellent listener.

On the third night talking to the goat, he was struck by a realization. "Hey, she said I wouldn't make it three days without her." In fact, the last three days working on Belzea felt good. He was not just surviving, he was focused and productive, in a way he hadn't been in a long time. Maybe he didn't need Elna after all. Maybe the reason it seemed like he was always making a mess of things was that Elna had talked him into some ill-advised, impulsive act of petty theft. When he thought about it, every bad thing in his life could be traced to Elna, in one way or another. Every time they had to flee town, it was because Elna got greedy. This last time—in Dashvar—Belno went along with the narrative that it was all Shula's fault, but wasn't it Elna who brought Shula into the Belzea scheme, over Belno's objections?

During the fourth day, Belno decided that he was going to start smoking inside the house, as a matter of policy. Also, he asked Byan to fetch him pickled cabbage from the market. "Lots and lots of pickled cabbage," he said. Elna never let him eat pickled cabbage.

In the evening he went to the goat and said, "Look, my friend, you were right. It was wrong to take you. I am really sorry about that. I won't keep you here any longer against your will." He unlocked the goat's chain. "You're free to go. Or, if you'd like, I can help you track down your girl, your

Mysta. I'd like to make things right. What do you say?"

The goat looked at him and said only, "Baah."

"You have a visitor, sir."

"Yes, all right," said Belno, combing his hair back with his fingers. He prepared himself for another session of finger steepling. "I will meet them in the study. Thank you, Byan."

He was not prepared, however, to walk into the study and come face to face with Baz.

"Ye gods," cried Belno. "How have you gotten *bigger*?"

Baz had always been a hulk of a human, but now his shoulders barely fit through the door of the study. He reached out with his bear paw of a hand, and Belno shrank away, flinching. "Relax," said Baz with a laugh. "Shake my hand! Look at you, Belnito, where have you been? Everyone misses you."

"Please don't call me Belnito. I'm not a little kid anymore. I go by Belno now."

"Sure. No offense intended. It's just good to see you. Why'd you stay away so long?"

"Well, you know–the soup got kinda hot for us here in Kortholomoth."

"Ancient history."

"Exactly. That's what I was hoping you would say."

"Mind if I smoke in here?" asked Baz, pulling a cigar out of his coat pocket.

"Well," said Belno with a smile. "That depends on whether you've got another of those for me."

"Why not," said Baz, producing a second cigar for Belno.

Belno called out for his servant from the other room: "Byan! Byan, bring us a light, won't you, good man."

"Smoking in the house, are you?" said Baz, eying him shrewdly. "That means you've given up on her coming back."

Byan hesitated at the door with a flaming oil-soaked rag held between two tongs.

"This is how rich people light their cigars," explained Belno. "Come on in, light us up, if you will." He snapped his fingers at Byan, who obediently came forward and lit their cigars.

Big Baz made himself comfortable on a cushioned chair, which groaned ominously under his weight. "I am actually here on business."

"That will be all, Byan. Please close the doors." Belno sat behind the desk he had come to think of as his own. "Business, you say?"

"Yeah. Business with Master Gregor."

Belno steepled his fingers. "Go on."

Baz, from yet another pocket, produced a small, puckered fruit and plopped it down on Belno's desk. "I give you: the simple gransapple. A nothing fruit, here in Lagin. A reliable friend when you're crossing the desert, but otherwise why would you ever want to eat one? They are sour; there's not much flesh to them. Who wants a gransapple when the world abounds with sweeter, plumper fruits?"

Belno waited.

"I'll tell you who," said Baz. "Homesick colonists. They're over there, building fences or forts, or whatever it is they do in the New World, but they miss the simple pleasures that remind them of home. The sour taste of a gransapple on a hot day. To them, a gransapple is not a nothing fruit. It represents Lagin incarnate. Can you grow gransapples in the New World? No! Gransapples only grow in Lagin. To them, our nothing fruit is a luxury good. Do you understand?"

"I believe I follow your pitch. Where does this leave us, business wise?"

"I have a friend who has recently come into possession of a highly productive orchard of gransapples, up in the mountains. I have the manpower to move the gransapples to port, but I need Gregor—that's you," said Baz, pointing his finger like a knife, "Belnito—to ship and distribute the cargo overseas. I'm looking for an exclusive contract for my friend's firm."

"I see," said Belno. "Was this Elna's idea?"

"No, no," said Baz with a laugh. "This is me, I'm a legitimate businessman now. They call me Uncle Baz."

Do they now? thought Belno, puffing on Baz's cigar. *He is trying to tell me that he is the big boss in town now.* "Well," said Belno. "I think you've got a solid business plan. We might want to get that contract drafted and signed as soon as possible—before the real Gregor shows up. But first, maybe you can tell me: Where's my cut in this little scheme of yours?"

Baz looked confused. "What do you mean? You get to keep being Master Gregor. You might be unaware the real Master Gregor is due tomorrow or the next day, onboard the Morning Dew. But don't worry," said Baz, holding up his hand to forestall any concern on Belno's part. "My friends will take care of it. No need for you to do anything different. *That*, by the way, was Elna's idea."

"I don't know that *that's* really necessary, Baz. I don't want to stay Gregor forever. It was a great gig while it lasted, but it's played out, I think. It's time to liquidate what we can and move on. I'd be happy to cut you in."

"Naw, Belnito. Belno. You're better than this. I've always known you to play the long game. Am I right? Belzoland or whatever you call it?"

"Belzea."

"Whatever. You don't get a choice in the matter. We're doing the long game, and you're Gregor. Understand?"

"I don't like it."

"What are you talking about? You're gonna love it. You can work your Belzoland angle. Everyone wins."

"I don't know, Baz. Sooner or later, someone is going to find me out. I don't know how to operate a big business like this one. I can't even figure out where they keep their money."

"It's in investments," said Baz. "What I'm trying to tell you, Belno, is you don't have to worry about any of that. It's already taken care of. Each of your direct reports is now reporting to my guy. Everyone understands. Everyone's on board. Everyone wins."

"Yeah," said Belno sadly.

"You have one job. Keep your head down. Low profile, low risk. If you can manage that, you get to live here in this palace and have all the best of everything."

"That's all I ever wanted," said Belno flatly.

"There's one more thing. She sent me to collect the goat."

"Ah. Listen, Baz. You need to let me talk to her, let me explain."

Baz stood, the chair groaning with relief. "How about just take me to the goat."

"He's in the courtyard," said Belno miserably, pointing over his shoulder. "But you should know. He's not a talking goat anymore. He's just an ordinary goat. I suppose his magic has sort of sputtered out."

Baz followed Belno to the courtyard. "He's right over—"

The chain was on the stone table where Belno left it, but the goat was gone.

Belno scratched his head. "Well, he was here a minute ago, honest." He looked up at the roof. "Do you think a goat could get up there?"

Baz shook his head sadly. "It's a goat. Goats can climb anything."

"He's probably up on the roof. He's gotta be around here somewhere." But to himself, he thought, *That goat is long gone. And good for him!*

When they failed to find the goat, Baz had to knock him around a little, just to make sure he wasn't holding something back. Belno understood, and Baz was very polite about the whole thing.

But then Baz went away, leaving Belno to his mansion.

Belno stalked the empty rooms of the house, half-heartedly taking an inventory of possessions that could be quickly liquidated, should he decide to run. But he knew he wouldn't run. It was too easy to stay here, to play Baz's game.

And, besides, no one was better positioned than Gregor to go big with Belzea. Among Brokerson's files, Belno had discovered a detailed topological map of a coastal region of Akika, signed by a reputable Logozhan ranger-surveyor. What to an untrained eye appeared to be wilderness was to Belno the thriving colony of Belzea, and he stayed up all night tracing overlays for the map, carving up the lands into hundreds of settler plots. He created detailed descriptions of each plot, along with its map-grid coordinates. The large plots within walking distance of the opera house were the most expensive, but Belno made sure there were also plenty of affordable plots on the periphery for investors of more modest means.

In the morning Belno bathed and shaved and dressed in a newly tailored suit. He gathered up all his Belzea documents into a portfolio and strolled uphill to the Bank of Lagin.

Belno waited patiently on the street behind a long line of persons waiting to do business with the bank. The Bank of Lagin generally dealt with the public through a tiny window in a thick stone wall, but the bigger, more complex transactions occurred inside the bank. Belno's goal was to talk his way inside to make his Belzea pitch.

He'd been waiting there for perhaps half an hour, and it was almost his turn at the tiny window, when a stout man with sideburns and a serious bearing came lumbering down the street, fishing a key from his pocket. Belno turned his face away; he recognized this man. One of his early investors from his first Belzea job.

The man glanced toward the line, frowning, before using his key to open a reinforced door leading into the bank. Belno winced. *Have I been spotted?* Evidently this fellow worked for the bank now. *He'll recognize me for sure*, worried Belno, and departed, relinquishing his place in line.

Belno wandered down toward the port, turning the Belzea portfolio over in his hands as he considered his next move. The key to the success of Belzea was to land a few big investors first to generate interest, then create a sense of scarcity to drive a run on Belzea properties. He walked the docks, watching people's feet, looking for expensive shoes. Elna had taught him that trick. *Follow the shoes*, is what she said.

At length among the churning sea of boots and sandals, Belno found a pair of freshly polished black business shoes with silver clasps. Belno changed directions to follow the shoes and had to pick up his pace to keep up. The man whose feet occupied those shoes had places to be. A squat fellow a head shorter than Belno, his hair was neatly combed. As he came up behind the man, Belno glimpsed a rod hanging from his belt. A Sartan, then.

The notion of a Sartan investor seemed, on the one hand, promising in that they would likely be naive to Belzea. But on the other hand, Sartans did tend to have a stronger grasp of geography than did your typical Laginese, which might prove problematic.

Belno followed the Sartan to a second-floor apartment overlooking the docks, where two other well-dressed Sartans were smoking cigars and playing Gritz on the balcony. A banner hung from the balcony proclaiming, "ships for hire." One of the Sartans, rotund and red-cheeked, saw Belno standing below. "Looking for a ship?" he called, around his cigar.

"That depends," replied Belno with a sociable grin. The others looked him over as the fat man waved him up.

As he climbed the stairs, Belno heard the man he'd been following say, "Gimson's a no-go. He wants twelve and thirty or nothing at all."

"He'll change his tune," said the big man. "Give it till tomorrow. And how can we help you, Mister..."

"Gregor," said Belno with a little bow of his head. "Well met, gentlemen."

"You're Gregor?" said the third man, glancing up before returning to his game.

Uh oh.

"Why, yes. Surely you haven't heard of me? I'm just new to the city."

"Sure, you took over for Brokerson, right?"

"Sirs, it seems you have me at a disadvantage."

"I'm Jessup," said the big man, leaning back in his chair. "This here's Asiceles," he said, pointing with his cigar to his opponent. "And that's our cousin Andor, from Whitby. Andor, why don't you fetch another chair for our guest? Among the three of us, we own more than forty vessels with Sartan and mixed crews."

"Impressive," said Belno. He looked over the Gritz board. It was late in the game; Asiceles had only three pieces left, and he contemplated his next move with a grave expression.

"You play?" asked Jessup.

"Well, sure," said Belno. "Everyone knows how to play Gritz. Not that I'm any good." In fact, Belno considered himself an expert Gritz player.

Andor emerged from the apartment with a chair. "You don't much look like someone from Xamlmadhi."

"No," said Belno. "I get that a lot. I take after my grandparents. Laginese stock, you know." He accepted the chair with a "thank you."

"But what would you need to hire a ship for? You have your own fleet, do you not?"

"Ah," said Belno. "That I do. Yes. But here's the thing: My ships are all cargo ships. I have all the cargo ships a man could want. Cargo ships for miles. But what I need is a passenger ship."

Asiceles, his hand hesitating over the board, made his move. Jessup responded immediately by capturing another piece. "You have our attention, Master Gregor. Are we to understand then that you intend to branch out to fares?"

"No, nothing like that. It's not for me; I'm doing a favor for Lord Bezor. Do you all know Bezor, the governor of Belzea? An old friend of the family's. Now he has hands full, poor chap. Ever since they discovered silver in the hills, his sleepy retirement colony has become overwhelmed with fortune seekers."

"Belzea, you say?"

"Yes, on the leeward coast of Akika. Used to be a penal colony, but you should see them now. High art and new world architecture! I've got dedicated ships now that do nothing but carry Lodling grain to the hungry bellies of the colonists."

"Interesting," said Jessup. "And how, pray tell, can our humble little enterprise be of assistance?" To Asiceles, who was about to make another move, he said as an aside, "You don't want to do that."

"Well," said Belno. "I hate to waste your time. It may come to naught. Bezor is looking to manage immigration through the titrated release of land certificates." He patted the portfolio on his lap. "I've just come from the Bank of Lagin. They said I needed to have a passenger ship with captain and crew lined up before they would approve a development loan or issue land certificates."

"Really? What kind of rate were they offering?"

"Oh, I couldn't discuss that. They said it was confidential."

"Sure, they say that because they are afraid of a little competition. Mind if I take a look?"

Asiceles, having accepted his defeat, picked up the pieces and cleared the board so Jessup could spread out Belno's portfolio on the table.

Confident in his work, Belno stood and turned away to admire the view. From the balcony he could see more than a dozen ships and the thronging mass of humanity filling all the spaces between with frenetic activity. Far out in the harbor, many more ships moved imperceptibly in the distance. The confusion, the excitement—this was Belno's element. He knew his place in the world, and it was here in Kortholomoth, the City of Crossing Paths, land of opportunity. This city would always provide for him, and he in turn loved this city.

Behind him he heard the gentle rustle of paper as Jessup flipped back and forth from the letters and inventories and the carefully doctored map. "Asiceles, have a look at this," said Jessup.

Belno was going to be all right. He would play along with Baz's game. He would have Byan to light his cigars and bring him pickled cabbage. He would live the good life here in Kortholomoth. Not bad for a street urchin who grew up hungry on these streets. Maybe he would find an urchin of his own, some lad with potential, and take him under his wing.

Asiceles said, "If these numbers are right…"

It was a crazy world filled with talking goats and witching weather, but with a little wit and skill a man could make a place for himself. Yes, and without Elna's reckless greed unravelling his carefully laid plans, Belno could extend Belzea for months. By the time these Sartans caught on, the blame would be shifted elsewhere and Belno would move on to new markets and new investors.

"Master Gregor," said Jessup. "Have you considered a more aggressive approach? With the demand being what it is, we would be willing to put up three passenger ships instead of one."

"No, no," said Belno, turning back to the Sartans. "Lord Bezor was very clear he wants to move slowly to manage growth."

Jessup pursed his lips. "I can respect a conservative approach. I'll tell you what. We are prepared to offer you six and a quarter percent."

Belno blinked in mock confusion. "What, you mean instead of going through the bank? But who would issue the certificates?"

"We can do that," promised Andor. "We've done it before."

"I don't know," said Belno slowly. "That's not what Bezor and I discussed. Six and a quarter, you say? The bank offered an even six."

Belno came down from the Sartan apartment with a contract in hand and a song in his heart. By tomorrow the first round of land certificates and prepaid passage to Belzea would hit the market.

He waited until he was out of sight of the balcony before leaping for joy and howling. He'd done it again. *Belno, old man, you are a genius.*

A celebration was called for. What he needed was a fine brandy. It had been far too long since he'd enjoyed a fine brandy. He knew just the place: Madam Sebe's. A bit of a trek but worth it.

Once he'd left behind the port proper, Belno found himself looking over his shoulder. He had the notion, although he couldn't say why, that he was being followed.

Belno turned onto a cross street near the base of Prow-beam Rock and then cut back quickly behind a recruitment center. He flattened himself against the wall of the alley and heard steps approaching. *I am definitely being followed,* thought Belno and hurried on. The Sartans keeping tabs on him, perhaps? Or, more likely, one of Baz's associates.

Either way, he didn't intend to get himself cornered in a back alley.

He doubled back again and darted into the front door of the recruitment center, finding himself face to face with a grizzled soldier in uniform. They gaped at each other with arched eyebrows.

"Something tells me you didn't come in here to sign up," said the soldier.

Belno glanced out the window. "What? Why would you say that?"

"You want to be a soldier in the King's army?" asked the recruiter with skepticism.

"Well, maybe I do," said Belno. "Why shouldn't I?"

"A bit old for starting a new career, wouldn't you say?"

"What? You don't look so young yourself. I'll have you know I'm in the prime of my life." Through the window Belno caught sight of his tail, looking up and down the road for him. Suddenly Belno lost his breath and any further interest in continuing his banter with the soldier.

Out the door he went. "Elna?"

She turned to him and he saw that her left eye was blackened. When she made eye contact with him, her lip quivered slightly.

"Honey bear, what happened?" He went to her, took her in his arms.

"Get off me," said Elna but she did not push him away.

Pulling back a little, he looked her over. "Did Baz do this to you?" When she did not answer right away, he said, "Where is he? I'll see to this. I'll—"

"You'll what?" said Elna, rolling her eyes.

"Well, I'll—I don't know, but I'll think of something."

"You smell like cigars."

"Yes, well. You'd be proud of me, Elna. I just hooked a big fish."

One corner of her mouth tugged downward. "Belzea, again?"

"Yeah, Belzea. What else? Why mess with perfection? Hey, I'm on my way to Madam Sebe's. Remember that place? Why don't you join me?"

"Madam Sebe's closed down years ago. Don't you remember?"

"It did?" Belno was crestfallen. "Oh. Well, why don't you suggest another place? Someplace nice, my treat."

"Belno, I can't go out with you. I'm with Baz now."

"Really? Still? Even with the—?" He gestured to her eye.

She shook her head and looked away.

"Well, what were you following me for then?"

"I wasn't following you."

"I'm fair sure you were."

"I just happened to see you, that's all. I wanted to check on you."

"Naw, you were following me all right. You wanted to know where I was going. If I was going, perhaps, to meet a lady friend."

Elna snorted. "Lady friend! You ain't got no lady friend. You're still hung up on me."

"Maybe I am. Elna, you can't possibly think I was going to make off with the goat, did you?"

"It doesn't matter what I thought."

"It matters to me, Elna. I haven't slept proper since you left. It's eating me up inside. The goat escaped, that's all. He used his luck and just slipped away. I couldn't go back and face you without him, so I had to go after him. And I got him back, Elna, for you. But by the time I got back to the house, you were gone."

"I know." She looked away. "Belno, I didn't leave you on account of the goat, all right? I was gonna leave you anyhow."

He looked down at his fancy shoes. "Yeah."

They stood awkwardly, not saying anything but neither wanting to leave. "Well, how about a drink for old time's sake? Baz won't mind."

"I don't know," said Elna. But Belno could tell she wanted to.

"Let's run away together," he said quickly.

"Belno."

"I'm serious. Right now. Just walk out of the city and we'll just keep walking. We'll be long gone before anyone notices. What do you say, Elna?"

Her frown only encouraged him. "You don't love Baz. You had to find out, but now you know. Baz ain't what you built him to be. He can't make you happy. Not like me. Come on, Elna. I'm lost without you. I've eaten so much pickled cabbage my guts are all in rebellion. I get up in the morning but there is no sun without you there. Please, Elna, I am begging you."

"And what about Belzea?"

"Belzea will go on without me. Come on! If we don't go now, we'll never go."

"But we don't have any money."

"Sure we do." He rummaged in his pockets. "Look, I've got six crowns right here. That'll get us back to Dashvar in style, and from there we can pull a few jobs to get passage to Ragne. I'm telling you, Ragne is ripe for the picking. We can run Belzea from there for *years* before anyone wises up."

They took a few steps together. Elna soured her face. "But Ragne *smells* bad. Why would we want to live there?"

"Aw, it's not so bad. You get used to the smell after a few days. And we'll have so much money coming in, I'll get you some of that expensive perfume to dab under your nose and you'll smell nothing but roses for the rest of your days. I know how you love roses."

"Sure, it's all roses and perfume now, but when we get there it'll be 'aw, Elna' this and 'aw, Elna' that, and we'll be sleeping in the sty with the pigs again."

"That was one time, Elna. One time. And it was just one sow with her babes, and they couldn't have been nicer."

They walked on in silence, Elna scowling and Belno smiling. At length Elna said, "You know, money would never had been a problem for us again if you had just kept hold of that goat."

J. S. Allen, Ph.D., is a neurodivergent writer in Fort Worth, Texas. Psycholinguist, anthropologist, microbiologist, data scientist are all words that fail to describe him. Hypergraphia is a clinical term that does not adequately describe his compulsion, since early childhood, to write a hectology of interconnected tales set in an imaginary world. You just read one of them.